Transient Desires

Also by Donna Leon

Donna Leon

Transient Desires

WILLIAM HEINEMANN: LONDON

1 3 5 7 9 10 8 6 4 2

William Heinemann
20 Vauxhall Bridge Road
London SW1V 2SA

William Heinemann is part of the Penguin Random House group of companies
whose addresses can be found at global.penguinrandomhouse.com.

Penguin
Random House
UK

First published by William Heinemann in 2021

www.penguin.co.uk

A CIP catalogue record for this book is available from the British Library.

ISBN 9781785152610 (Hardback)
ISBN 9781785152627 (Trade Paperback)

Endpaper map © Martin Lubikowski, ML Design, London

Typeset in 12/16.45 pt Palatino
by Integra Software Services Pvt. Ltd, Pondicherry

Printed and bound in Great Britain by Clays Ltd, Elcograf S.p.A.

The authorised representative in the EEA is Penguin Random House Ireland,
Morrison Chambers, 32 Nassau Street, Dublin D02 YH68.

Penguin Random House is committed to a sustainable future for
our business, our readers and our planet. This book is made from
Forest Stewardship Council® certified paper.

For Romilly McAlpine

'The depths have covered them:
they sank to the bottom as a stone.'

Handel *Israel in Egypt*
Part the Second: 18

Transient Desires

1

Brunetti slept late. At about nine, he turned his head towards the right and opened one eye, saw the time, and closed his eye again. He did not move for some time, and when he next opened his eye, he saw that it was half past nine. He reached out his left arm in the hope that he would find Paola beside him, but he found only the indentation of her former presence, long since gone cold.

He levered himself on to his side and then his back, rested for a moment after achieving this, and opened his eyes. He studied the ceiling, glanced at the far corner on the right and saw the mark above the window where water had leaked in some months before, creating a brown patch that looked like an octopus, a rather small one. Like an octopus, this stain changed colour with the light, sometimes changing shape, as well, although there were always only seven legs.

He had promised Paola he would get up on the ladder and paint it over, but he was always in a hurry, or it was night-time and he didn't want to get on the ladder, or he didn't have his shoes on and didn't want to risk climbing the ladder wearing only socks. This morning the stain annoyed him, and he decided he would ask the man who did odd jobs for them to come and paint it over and have done with it.

Or his son could tear himself loose from his computer or from talking to his girlfriend on the phone and get the ladder and paint it and help his parents for a change. Detecting the distinct note of resentment and self-pity in his thoughts, Brunetti pushed them aside and considered some of the events of last night's dinner, among which were three glasses of grappa that were most likely the cause of his current condition.

As was their custom once a year, last evening he and some companions from *liceo* had met for dinner in a restaurant at the beginning of Riva del Vin, where the obliging owner always put them in the same corner by the window on to the Canal Grande.

As the years passed, their number had shrunk from more than thirty to just ten, reduced for the usual reasons: geography, employment, and sickness. Some had tired of the inconveniences of the city and had moved away; others had taken better jobs in other parts of Italy or Europe, and two had died.

This year, as well as Brunetti, the other three original organizers of the dinner had attended. The first was Luca Ippodrino, who had turned his father's trattoria into a world-famous restaurant by following three relatively simple rules: he served the same food his mother had served for thirty years to the men who unloaded the boats at Rialto; it was now served on porcelain plates and in far smaller and delicately decorated portions; the prices had been inflated almost beyond bearing. The waiting list for a table – especially during the Biennale and the Film Festival – started filling up months in advance.

The second, Franca Righi, Brunetti's first girlfriend, had gone on to study physics in Rome and now taught at the same university where she had studied. It was she who had towed Brunetti through their biology and physics classes and now delighted in telling him each time one of the laws they had studied turned out to be false and had to be replaced.

The last was a newly divorced Matteo Lunghi, a gynaecologist, whose wife had left him for a much younger man, and who had had to be encouraged through the dinner by his friends.

The remaining six were successful – or content – to varying degrees or at least behaved that way when in the company of people who had known them most of their lives. Much of that ease of communication, Brunetti believed, came of their having a common store of cultural and historical references as well as their generation's unspoken and unconsidered ethical standards.

Before allowing himself to consider what those might be, Brunetti pushed aside the covers and went down to the bathroom to have a shower.

The hot water restored his spirits, as did the length of time – his children not there to protest about the waste of water – he spent under it. He went back to the bedroom, draped the towel over the back of a chair, and started to get dressed. He pulled out the trousers of a suit he hadn't worn since the winter, dark grey cashmere and wool and bought for almost nothing when the men's clothing store in Campo San Luca had closed two years before. Strange, he thought, as he pushed the button through the buttonhole: they had seemed to fit him better when he had bought the suit. Perhaps the dry cleaning had tightened them somehow; surely they would loosen up as the day wore on and he moved around wearing them.

He sat on the chair, pulled on a pair of dark socks and black shoes he'd bought in Milano years before and that had moulded themselves to his feet as time passed and that never failed to convey a thrill of sensual delight as he slipped them on.

Before he put on his jacket, he considered wearing a vest but, remembering how warm it had been the day before, decided it was unnecessary: the good weather of late autumn could be counted on for another day. In the kitchen, he looked on the table for a note from Paola but found nothing. It was Monday, so she would not be home before late afternoon, spending the time in her office at the university, ostensibly to speak to the doctoral candidates whose dissertations she was overseeing. She delighted in the fact that they seldom came to speak to her, leaving her quite happy to sit undisturbed in her office, preparing classes or reading. Thus the life of the scholar, Brunetti reflected.

He left the house and started for the Questura, but turned immediately into Rizzardini for a coffee and a brioche, and then another coffee and a glass of mineral water. Braced by caffeine and sugar, Brunetti turned towards Rialto and the business of passing through the centre of the city at half past ten in the morning, just as the people who had done their grocery shopping at the market were beginning to be replaced by the tourists in search of their first *ombra* or prosecco, all bent on having what they had been told was a real Venetian experience.

Twenty minutes later, he turned right on to the *riva* that led to the Questura and, looking across the canal, saw the cleaned and restored façade of the church of San Lorenzo, no longer a church but a gallery of some sort, dedicated, he had been told, to the salvation of the seas. The decades-old billboard giving the year of the beginning of the ever-unconcluded restoration had been removed, as had the wooden condominium built by local residents for stray cats that had stood there for as long as Brunetti could remember.

As he arrived outside the Questura, he saw his superior, Vice-Questore Giuseppe Patta, at the bottom of the staircase at the far end of the entrance hall. Instinctively, Brunetti pulled his *telefonino* from the pocket of his jacket and bent his head over it, nodding to the officer who opened the glass door for him but not moving into the building. He stopped and poked angrily at the front of his phone, then turned to the officer and said, making no attempt to disguise his irritation, 'Do you have any connection down here, Graziano?'

The officer on guard duty, aware that Brunetti was arriving for work two hours late and that the Vice-Questore did not view the Commissario with a benevolent eye, said, 'It's been going in and out all morning, Signore. Did you manage to connect by going out there?' He nodded towards the space in front of the Questura.

Brunetti shook his head, saying, 'It's no better out there. Makes me crazy that there's ...' but stopped when he saw his superior walking towards him. 'Good morning, Vice-Questore,' he said, then added in a helpful voice, holding up his phone, 'Don't even bother going outside to try, Dottore. There's no hope. Nothing's working.'

That said, Brunetti slipped the phone back into his pocket and pointed, quite unnecessarily, towards the stairs. 'I'm going to check the phone on my desk again and see if it's working yet.'

Patta, entirely confused, asked, 'What's wrong, Brunetti?' His tone, Brunetti thought, was remarkably similar to the one he had himself used, when the kids were younger and told him they had no homework to do that evening.

Like a prosecutor holding up the plastic bag with the blood-stained knife inside to show to the press photographer, he pulled out his phone again and showed it to his superior. 'There's no connection.'

From the corner of his eye, he saw Graziano nod in agreement, quite as if he had watched Brunetti's failure to make a call.

Patta turned from Brunetti and asked the officer, 'Where's Foa?'

'He should be here in three minutes, Vice-Questore,' Graziano assured him, looking at his watch and somehow managing to seem taller when he spoke to their superior. As if summoned by the Vice-Questore's desire, the police launch turned into the canal and passed quickly in front of the church, under the bridge, and slowed to a stop at the dock just beyond where the three men stood.

Patta turned away silently from the two men and walked towards the boat, its motor reduced to a purr. Foa tossed a rope around the nearest stanchion and jumped down to the pavement, saluted the Vice-Questore, stepped back and extended his arm, as if to clear a group of pesky reporters from the space between them. Patta viewed any motion made within a metre of his person as an attempt to help him and placed a hand upon Foa's forearm to steady himself as he stepped up on to the boat.

Foa smiled to his two colleagues, flipped the rope free, leaped over the gunwale and landed in front of the wheel. The engine gave a roar, and Foa spun the launch in a tight U and headed back the way he'd come.

2

Brunetti continued up to his office, his story to the Vice-Questore about telephone problems still on his mind. What might be called the infrastructure of the Questura was, not to put too fine a point on it, a mess, and thus Brunetti's invention was completely credible. The heating system was quixotic and throughout the winter shifted its faint results from side to side of the building as it willed; there was no air conditioning save in a few select offices. The electricity functioned, more or less, although occasional surges of current had killed a few computers and one printer. By now, the staff was so inured that the occasional exploding light bulb was treated as no more than a presage of the fireworks of Redentore; the plumbing was rarely a problem; the roof leaked only in two places, and most of the windows could be closed, though some didn't open.

As he climbed the steps, Brunetti thought of the ways he resembled the building, with a bit of stiffness here, something that occasionally malfunctioned there, but he soon ran out of comparisons. The original thought, however, prompted him to drop his hand from the railing and stand a bit straighter as he climbed the stairs.

Inside his office, Brunetti tossed the newspaper he'd bought in Campo Santa Marina on to his desk. He found the room uncomfortably warm and went to open a window. The view from here had been improved, he was forced to admit, by the general sprucing-up of the church and the removal of the condominium. But still he missed the cats.

He took his phone from his pocket and punched in Paola's number. It rang a few times before she answered. '*Sì?*' she asked. Only that.

'Ah,' Brunetti exclaimed, forcing his voice into a deeper register, 'The voice of love responds, and my heart opens, brimming with the joy of . . . ?'

'What is it, Guido?' Then, before he could respond to the definite chill in her voice, she added, 'I'm here with one of my students.'

Brunetti, who had been about to ask her what she planned to cook for dinner, instead said, 'I wanted only to declare the enormity of my love, my dear.'

'Thank you so much,' she said and broke the connection without even bothering to wait for him to indulge in some romantic invention.

He glanced at the newspaper and decided it would be preferable to the reports that sat unread on his desk. It might provide information about what was happening in the world that began at the end of the Ponte della Libertà. He often chastised the children for their lack of curiosity, not only about their own country, but about the wider world, as well. How would they be able to take their place as citizens if they knew nothing about their leaders, the laws, the alliances that bound them to Europe and to places beyond?

Even before he opened the *Gazzettino*, Brunetti had outlined a speech in praise of patriotism that would have done Cicero proud. He'd had no trouble with the *Narratio*: the children were ignorant of the current state of politics in their own country. The *Refutatio* was child's play: he'd easily punched away any claim that Italy was a pawn in a geopolitical game being played by Germany and France. He was halfway through the *Peroratio*, enjoining them to assume the full responsibility of their citizenship, and approaching the end of his discourse when his eye fell on that day's headline '*Morta la moglie strangolata: Una settimana di agonia.*' So she had died, the young woman strangled by her heroin-addicted husband, but not before a week of agony, poor thing. She left one child. As was often the case, they were in the midst of getting a separation. Indeed.

He noticed a small article about two young women, identified as American, who had been found on the dock outside the Emergency Room of the Ospedale Civile in the early hours of Sunday morning. The article gave their names and reported that one had a broken arm.

Inexorably, his eye was drawn to the article below: this one dealt with the ongoing search at an abandoned pig farm near Bassano, where the remains of the two wives of the former owner – he now dead of natural causes – had been discovered. And now there were traces of a third woman, whom neighbours said had lived there for some time, and then didn't.

It was the word 'traces' that drove Brunetti to his feet and down the stairs. Outside, on the *riva*, he turned right, his body in sole command, and went down to the bar, heedless of anything save the urgent need to distract himself from the effect of that word.

When Brunetti entered, he saw that Bamba Diome, the Senegalese barman, had come on shift and replaced his employer behind the bar. Brunetti nodded in greeting but couldn't bring himself to speak. He looked to his left and saw that the three booths were occupied. Better this way, he told himself, he was here to refuel and only that. He looked into the glass case filled with *tramezzini*: they'd been made by Sergio, who still cut them into triangles, while Bamba preferred rectangles. Maybe an egg and tomato? Bamba returned and gave a brisk swipe at the counter in front of Brunetti.

'Water, Dottore?'

Brunetti nodded, 'And a tomato and egg.' He saw the *Gazzettino* on the counter and pushed it away. Seeing him reject the newspaper, Bamba said, 'Terrible, isn't it, Dottore?' and set down the glass of water and the single *tramezzino*.

'Yes. Terrible,' Brunetti said, not knowing which article the barman had read. Bamba cast his eyes towards the row of booths, saw a raised hand, and slipped out from behind the bar to answer the summons.

Brunetti picked up the egg and tomato, took a bite, and replaced it on the plate. He drank the water. He realized that, if this were to be his lunch every day, he'd give thought to killing himself. This was indeed fuel, not food: they were good *tramezzini*, but that did not alter the fact that they were *tramezzini*, not lunch. And what would follow if we slowly came to accept having a sandwich for lunch?

Brunetti, although his degree was in law, had always read history, and his reading of modern history had shown him how dictatorships often began with the small things: limiting who could do what jobs, who could marry whom, live here or there. Gradually, those small things had always expanded, and soon some people could not work at all, nor marry, nor – in the end – live. He gave himself a shake and told himself he was exaggerating: the road to hell was not paved with *tramezzini*.

He went and stood in front of the cash register. Bamba came back, rang up the bill, and gave the receipt to Brunetti. The bill was three Euros fifty. Brunetti gave Bamba a five Euro note and turned away before the barman could offer him the change.

On the way back to the Questura, Brunetti waited for the first faint stirring of returning life from somewhere inside of him.

Outside, the sun had weakened and dropped behind the buildings on his left. The weather had come to its senses, Brunetti thought, and it would soon be time for *risotto di zucca*. Leaves would begin to turn: he and Paola could wait a few weeks and then have a walk down to I Giardini and see the show the trees put on every year. They used to go and sit under the trees in the Parco Savorgnan, but three of his favourites had been blown down in recent storms, and Brunetti, at the loss of his old friends, had stopped going, even though that decision meant renouncing the pastries at Dal Mas. Until then, they had the colour show at the Giardini Reali: recently they'd been restored; besides, they had the additional attraction of a wonderful café, where the staff didn't bother people who wanted to sit and read.

Whatever nourishment had been hidden in that *tramezzino* failed to make itself felt, nor did it nudge Brunetti with a return of energy sufficient to diffuse his general unease.

He stopped at the bottom of the stairs in front of the cork board on the wall to his left. The Minister of the Interior was concerned that too many people were using their official cars for purposes that were not work-related, he read.

'Shocking,' Brunetti muttered to himself, doing his best to sound scandalized. 'Especially here.'

The memory of the peculiar lack of joy of last night's dinner brought Brunetti to a stop. He recalled speaking to two of his old friends who had taken early retirement and now found themselves, it seemed, able to talk only of the sweet antics of their grandchildren.

No one passed in the corridor, the stairs remained empty, he heard a phone ring in the distance, then it stopped. He moved away from the wall and turned, berating himself for laziness and disregard for his obligations and responsibilities. He took out his phone and, standing just metres from her office, called Signorina Elettra and told her he'd just had a call from one of his informers, who needed to see him immediately.

Luckily, when Brunetti called him, and then another informer, who had also been of use to him in the past, both men were free and said they could meet him. Although both men lived in Venice, they never met Brunetti there for fear of the possible consequences of being seen with someone known to be a policeman, and so he was to meet the first in Marghera and the second in Mogliano.

The meetings did not go particularly well. He differed over payment with both of them: the first one had no new information but wanted to be put on a monthly salary. Brunetti refused flatly and wondered if the man would next ask for an extra month's salary at Christmas.

The second was a burglar who had abandoned his calling – although not his contacts – with the birth of his first child and had taken a job delivering milk and dairy products to supermarkets. He met Brunetti between deliveries and gave him the name of the distributor who served as the redistribution point for the eyeglass frames continually stolen by employees from the factories producing them in the Veneto. Brunetti explained that, because the information was of no practical use to him and would be passed on to a friend at the Questura in Belluno, fifty Euros was more than fair. The man shrugged, smiled, and agreed, so Brunetti handed him an extra ten, which widened his smile. He thanked Brunetti and climbed back into his white delivery truck, and that was the end of it.

Brunetti spent the evening with his family, had dinner with them, attentive to what they said and what they ate. After dinner, he took a small glass of grappa out on to the terrace and sipped at it while he looked off to the bell tower of San Marco. At ten o'clock, a ringing church bell told him it was time to take his glass inside and begin to think about going to bed.

Although he had done next to nothing all day, he was tired and, to his surprise, realized that he still had not shaken off the sadness left by the evening spent with his former classmates. He went down the corridor and stopped at the door to Paola's study. Intent on her reading, she had not heard him coming, but the radar of long love made her look up and, after a moment's thought, smile. He felt his spirit warm and said, 'I'm going to bed now.'

She closed her book and got to her feet. 'What a very good idea,' she said and smiled again.

3

Brunetti arrived even later at the Questura the following morning, went to Signorina Elettra's office, and found her seated some distance from her desk, chair pushed back and to one side, computer dark and ignored. She looked up when he came in; he noticed she had some papers in one hand.

'Am I disturbing you, Signorina?'

She smiled. 'Of course not, Commissario. I was having a look at something you might find interesting.' As evidence, she held up the papers. 'It's about those young women in the *laguna*,' she said. He nodded to acknowledge that he knew about the incident, not mentioning that his source was *Il Gazzettino*.

'I've just received Claudia's full report. She was on duty that night and answered the call.' Signorina Elettra held the papers towards him. 'Would you like to have a look?' Her tone made it clear that this was a suggestion and not a question.

Brunetti reached for the papers, which she tucked into a manila folder. He thanked her and went up to his office to read them.

A little after three in the morning of Sunday, one of the guards at the Ospedale Civile stepped out on to the ambulance dock at

14

the rear of the hospital for a cigarette and found two young women, both injured, lying unconscious on the wooden dock where the ambulances arrived. He'd ducked back inside and run to Pronto Soccorso, calling ahead for two gurneys. The injured women were taken immediately to the Emergency Room.

Brunetti looked at the photos taken in the ward before he read more, and what he saw shocked him. One of them appeared to have been badly beaten. Her nose was pressed against her right cheek and there was a long bloody cut above her left eye. The left side of her face was swollen.

There was also a photo of the second victim. Her face showed no signs of an attack: the report stated that neither of them had wounds on their hands that spoke of having resisted one, although the second young woman's left arm was broken in two places.

Both wore wet jeans and sweaters and might have spent some time in the water. One had lost her left tennis shoe; neither carried identification of any kind.

The attached medical report stated that they were both given a full physical examination to assess the possibility of further injury. Both remained unconscious during this procedure. Neither showed signs of recent sexual activity.

The young woman with the broken nose, after a brain scan, was quickly transferred to the hospital in Mestre to await emergency surgery. It was at this point that the police were alerted. The officer on night duty had called, and awoken, Commissario Griffoni. She asked that a launch be sent to take her to the hospital.

Griffoni's report stated that, when she arrived, she found the young woman with the broken arm lying on a gurney in a corridor, in tears and begging in English for something to ease the pain. This catapulted Griffoni to the nurses' desk, where she showed her warrant card and demanded to speak to the doctor in charge. After Griffoni had a few words with him, things went more easily, and the young woman was quickly taken into a treatment room, given an injection, and had her arm set and put in a cast.

A room for her was found, and Griffoni, who had waited in the corridor, took it upon herself to push her there in a wheel-chair. A nurse helped her into bed, and Griffoni sat in the chair at the foot of the bed and assured the young woman that she would stay with her. Griffoni waited for her to fall asleep, which she did almost immediately. At six in the morning, the arrival of the trollies at the end of the hallway woke the young woman, who looked around, groggy.

Griffoni asked her name and the name of her companion. JoJo Peterson, she told Griffoni; the other was Lucy Watson, but then she grew agitated and asked where Lucy was and what had happened. Griffoni explained about the surgery and lied to assure her that everything was going to be all right. Soon after hearing that, the girl told her that Lucy's parents worked at the US Embassy in Rome. JoJo and Lucy were friends at university, and they were visiting from the States. She soon fell asleep again: not even the terrific sound storm of breakfast managed to keep her awake.

Griffoni wrote that Lucy Watson's parents had been contacted through the Embassy, where her father worked in Human Resources, his wife as a translator.

Brunetti's desk phone rang, and he recognized the number of Griffoni's extension.

'Yes?' he asked.

'Do you want to come up?'

'Three minutes,' Brunetti said and replaced the phone.

Upstairs, Griffoni was already standing in the corridor. This was not a sign of her eagerness to see him but a concession to the size – or lack of size – of her office: if she set her chair just inside the doorway, her back to the door, she could sit at her desk; beyond it there was a bit more than a metre for a guest's chair and then a wall.

'Tell me,' he said by way of greeting as he walked in front of her to take his place.

Pointing to the darkened screen of her computer, she said, 'The hospital has a camera at every entrance, even on the dock for the ambulances, where they were left.' She leaned over and clicked the screen into life then shifted it towards Brunetti, who saw a full-screen image that at first confused him.

He propped his elbow on the desk, rested his chin in his hand, and studied the image. He saw a pattern of rectangles, long and thin, running horizontally; beyond the rectangles, blackness. Griffoni tapped a key, and after a moment the scene brightened, almost as if a floodlight had been turned on, transforming the rectangles into a wooden floor and, beyond it, revealing the darkness as water.

'This it?' Brunetti asked.

Griffoni nodded, saying, 'They sent it half an hour ago. I've watched it only once.'

The film was, strangely, silent: the *laguna* is never quiet, docks always have the slapping of waves, however small. In the absence of motion to interest him, Brunetti looked at the information at the bottom of the screen: it told the number of the *telecamera* and the time: 2:57.

The dock suddenly shook, surprising Brunetti into grasping at the top of the table. A disembodied head appeared a bit beyond the edge, cruised on its own power across the computer screen and stopped.

A pair of hands suddenly grabbed at the handrails of the ladder to the dock, and a man appeared, moving slowly, gingerly. He kept his eyes on his feet while climbing the ladder, as though he feared falling backwards. He stepped on to the dock and looked around, then turned back towards the water and bent over to speak to someone below. A single hand appeared and passed him a rope, which he wrapped around the stanchion and tightened into place with easy, if slow, familiarity.

When the boat was moored, the top half of the other person appeared, showing the shoulders and head of a man wearing a woollen cap. He disappeared as quickly as he had appeared and was back a moment later, carrying a small woman, his arms under her shoulders and knees. He reached up and set her on the edge of the dock and then pushed her away from the edge with both hands.

He disappeared again, only to come back into sight a bit farther to the right with a second woman, held the same way. He placed her down and shoved her across the dock just as he had the first.

He called to the other man, turned and pointed off screen. The man on the dock shook his head and said something. Whatever it was, it propelled the man in the cap up the ladder and on to the dock. The other raised a hand, as if to stop him, then took a step towards him and placed his hand on his arm. The man with the cap shook free of the other and walked in the direction of the camera. He disappeared from the frame but was quickly back, passing the other and going to the top of the ladder. He turned and started down, called to the other man, and vanished. The other untied the boat and tossed the rope over the edge of the dock, then walked slowly to the ladder, turned, and disappeared very slowly after him. The camera showed only the two women lying on the dock.

The screen turned black. Griffoni's voice caused Brunetti to start, so intent had he been on the screen. 'The camera is motion sensitive and goes black when there's nothing to be filmed.'

At 3:05, a man appeared, walking away from the camera, head bent as he pulled a cigarette from an open packet and a lighter from his pocket. He turned sideways, as if protecting the flame from the wind, lit the cigarette, and, raising his head, took a deep pull at it. He froze, the cigarette fell from his hand, and he took three running steps towards the two motionless forms in front of him. He knelt, placed his fingers on the throat of the first, then the second, pushed himself to his knees and disappeared in the direction from which he had come.

Again the screen darkened. Almost immediately a number of people in white uniforms appeared. With breathtaking speed, they picked up the women, placed them on to gurneys, and hurried back inside. The screen darkened.

'How long did it take them to come to get them?' Brunetti asked.

'Two minutes and forty seconds,' Griffoni answered. 'It's at the bottom of the screen.'

'I'll never say a bad word about the hospital again,' Brunetti said. Then he asked, 'I saw the photo of her face. Who could do that to someone?'

Griffoni shrugged. 'I'd like to go back to the hospital to see what I can find out.'

Instinctively, Brunetti asked, 'Would you like me to go with you?'

'Isn't that out of your way?' Griffoni asked. It wasn't a yes, but it certainly wasn't a no.

'Not really, not if I go through Campo Santa Marina,' he answered.

She studied her palm, and it apparently decided the issue for her. 'We could go now. I'm not doing anything, and the Vice-Questore's left for the day.' Before Brunetti could ask, Griffoni said, 'Foa told me he's been invited to some sort of event by one of those foreign charities that wants to save the city.'

Brunetti was familiar with these organizations but doubtful that anyone had much of a chance of saving the city. 'Well,' he said, 'they go to expensive restaurants, and that gives people work, and that's all to the good.'

As if reading his mind, Griffoni gave one of those smiles of hers that seemed to use only the upper part of her face. Her mouth remained straight in disapproval, but her eyes registered delight in absurdity. 'It's a dinner for important Venetians, to explain to them the urgent need to save the city,' she remarked.

'From?' Brunetti asked, already making a list, starting with the pollution caused by the planes of the people who came to the charity dinner.

'I think that will be revealed this evening,' she answered.

It came to Brunetti to ask, 'How is it that Foa knows about this?'

'He has to take the Vice-Questore to the first meeting, then return later to take him home from dinner.'

Brunetti's mind fled to the notice he had been reading about the improper use of ministry cars to take officials to non-work-related events. Patta was safe: there had been no mention of boats. Cheered by that thought, he got to his feet, saying, 'Come on, Claudia, I'll walk you as far as the hospital.'

This time, both halves of her face smiled.

4

By the time they emerged from the Questura, the day had definitely abandoned any idea of warmth. Griffoni, who was Neapolitan, never left a building without carrying at least one more layer of clothing: today a caramel-coloured suede jacket hung over her arm that looked, to Brunetti, far more edible than the sandwich he'd had the day before.

'Did you get that in Naples?' he asked as she pulled it on and zipped it halfway.

'Yes.'

'It's beautiful,' Brunetti said. 'If I thought it would fit me, I'd knock you down and steal it.'

'Too much time spent with criminals, I'd say,' she answered, then added, 'My uncle has a shop.'

Brunetti threw his head back and laughed out loud.

Uncertain whether to be offended or not, Griffoni asked, 'What's that about?'

Still giving the occasional gasp of quiet laughter, Brunetti said, 'I have a Neapolitan friend – maybe he's my best friend – and if I ever admire anything, he has an uncle or an aunt or a cousin who just happens to know where to get me one. At a very friendly price.'

'Things that fell off a truck?' she asked.

That set Brunetti off laughing again. When he could control himself, he said, 'He actually told me that once. It was a pair of tennis shoes my son wanted, white, with the signature of some American tennis player, or basketball hero, on the side, and we'd had no peace in the house for a month. I told Giulio about it, when we were talking about our kids; all he did was ask what size Raffi wore. The next day UPS delivered a pair for him, with a note inside saying they'd fallen off a truck.' He broke off to laugh again.

'And you kept them? I mean, your son kept them?'

'Of course he did,' Brunetti said. 'If I'd sent them back, Giulio would have sulked for the rest of the year.'

Griffoni and he resumed walking, amiable together, she silent for a moment, considering this. Finally she said, 'Well, he is Neapolitan.'

'So?'

'How else would he respond to an insult like that?'

Brunetti stopped and turned to face her. 'Do you know him?'

'Who?'

'Giulio. Giulio D'Alessio. My friend.'

After a moment's hesitation, Griffoni asked, 'Is his father Filippo?'

Brunetti stared at her, working at keeping his mouth closed. After a moment, he said, 'Yes.'

'My father knows him. The father, that is.'

Brunetti put his hands to his ears and began to walk around in a tight circle, saying, 'My God. It's a plot. I'm surrounded by them.'

'Neapolitans?' she asked, putting her hand on his arm to stop him.

Brunetti paused, then moved to face her. 'No,' he said. 'Friends.'

Griffoni put her hand on his shoulder and pushed him away, saying, 'You really are a fool, Guido.' Brunetti was astonished by how much she sounded like Paola, who used the same word to reprove him for his worst flights of fancy. He knew enough, however, not to make this comparison to Griffoni.

He returned to his business-as-usual voice and asked, 'While we're walking, tell me what else you've found out.'

From her bag, she took a dark brown silk scarf and wrapped it around her neck. 'I don't know how you stand this weather,' she said, suggesting that Brunetti had wished it on both of them. Then, as though the sentences were related, she added, 'They were seen in Campo Santa Margherita on Saturday night. The girl who called to say she saw them remembered them because, when one of them said her name was Lucy, she remembered that her mother always sang a song with that name in it.'

'Is that all?' Brunetti asked. Surely, he thought, someone else must have seen them. They had to be in a hotel, a B&B, staying with friends: someone must have noticed their absence or found that they hadn't slept in their beds.

'This girl who called said she thought they started to talk to two men. But then she saw some classmates and went over to talk to them and forgot about the Americans until this morning, when she saw the name, "Lucy" in the headline on the *Gazzettino*.' He had seen it, too: 'Lucy and Jojo. Who are they?'

Brunetti was just about to ask if Griffoni had any news about the young woman in the hospital in Mestre, but then they turned left into Barbaria delle Tole: the Ospedale was only a few minutes away.

The lateral wall of the Basilica appeared on their right, and then they were in the *campo*. The façade of the Ospedale looked down upon them, and as they moved diagonally towards the entrance, the façade of the Basilica slid into view. Griffoni's steps slowed and her head turned from building to building, as though she'd been asked to give a prize to one of them and couldn't decide. Most days the Basilica – its majesty unmatched in the city – was Brunetti's favourite church; some days, for reasons he couldn't understand, it was San Nicolò dei Mendicoli, and for a long time, when he had known a girl who lived near it, Brunetti had most liked the Miracoli. But he'd grown bored with the girl, and then with the church.

He stopped himself from asking Griffoni if she wanted him to go in with her: it was probably better if she spoke to a woman, especially given the fact that it was two men who had abandoned them at the hospital. He wished Griffoni good luck, said goodbye, and started home.

No one was there yet, so Brunetti pulled out a glass container of olives and dumped half of them on to a plate. He took a bottle of Falanghina from the refrigerator and poured himself a glass. He went into the living room and set the plate and the glass on the table, then sat and took a sip of wine.

From the hospital's video, enlarged photos of the faces of the two men had been sent to all of the offices of the police in Venice, as well as to the Guardia Costiera, the Carabinieri, and the Guardia di Finanza. As he recalled their faces, Brunetti guessed them to be in their early twenties. Nothing else about them was visible from the photos.

Their boat, riding low in the water, had been invisible because the Ospedale's video camera was placed at the height of the superstructure of the ambulances, for how else would a person arrive there but in an ambulance? Thus, the much lower boat that had brought the human cargo could not have been seen, only the two men and the burdens, quickly delivered and just as quickly abandoned.

He took another sip of wine, ate a few olives and set the pits on the edge of the plate. He leaned back and had another small sip, then set the glass on the table in front of him. He tapped his thumbs against one another, then tried to remember some of the finger games he and his brother had known as kids. There was one where hands were turned into a church with doors that could open: that was easy to recall. Then there was another where careful manipulation would allow him to appear to detach the first digit of his thumb. He had driven the kids wild with delight with this trick when they were younger, but now, no matter how he fitted his fingers together, he couldn't remember how to do it. He folded his hands and kept them still.

Campo Santa Margherita. Saturday evening. So long as it didn't rain, there were always scores – in the summer, hundreds – of students in the *campo* at night. Chatting, drinking, moving from one group to another, meeting friends or making friends. It was the same thing he had done when he was a student. Well, minus the drugs and the quantity of alcohol.

The two young women had been seen chatting with two men, and some hours later, two men had taken them to the hospital and left them there. There was no sign of sexual activity, nor was there any evidence that either girl had attempted to defend herself from an attack.

'What's wrong with this picture?' Brunetti muttered to himself. He thought of a book Paola had told him for years he had to read, *Three Men in a Boat*. He had, and he'd hated it. These were only two men in a boat, but who were they, and why were they in a boat at three o'clock in the morning? And how was it they knew where to take the young women, or drop them off or get rid of them, depending on which opinion he wanted to convey of their behaviour? If they had a boat, they'd be familiar with the *laguna*, although not necessarily be Venetian. To know the dock of the Ospedale, they'd be Venetian. To have met the girls in Campo Santa Margherita, they might be students. If they'd succeeded in speaking to the girls, they'd have known some English, which suggested, but did not confirm, that they were indeed students.

He thought of the way the men had delivered – he decided to remain with that verb – the two Americans to the dock: one climbed gingerly up the stairs to the dock and moored the boat, then stood and watched the other lift them from the boat one after the other and put them on to the dock. Wouldn't it have been easier for him to return to the boat and help lift the unconscious young women to the dock? What had they said to one another on the dock? What's wrong with this picture?

He sipped again and ate a few more olives. Then he took his phone and called Griffoni.

'You still in the Ospedale?'

'*Sì.*'

'You with the American?'

'*Sì.*'

'Does she remember anything?'

'Wait a moment,' Griffoni said, and he thought he could hear a chair being pushed across the floor. Then she covered the mouthpiece and said something. There was a long pause; he thought he heard steps. 'They were in a *campo* with lots of students,' Griffoni began. 'The girl thinks it was called Santa Margherita. They met two guys who offered to take them for a ride.'

'Ride?'

'They had a boat, and she said they seemed like nice guys, so they agreed to go with them.' Griffoni paused but Brunetti decided to let her tell the story without his prodding.

'It was parked – as she said – near a bridge.'

There was a bridge at the end of Campo Santa Margherita, he knew, with a long *riva* on the other side.

'She said the ride was exciting at first. They went into a big canal, with big houses on both sides. And then they went past some churches and all of a sudden, she saw that they were in open water.'

'And then?'

'She said it was creepy because it was absolutely dark once they got away from the city: the only lights were far off, and they had no idea what they were. And then the boat speeded up, with its front bouncing all over the place, and the guys shouting and laughing.' Griffoni paused a moment, then added, 'She said that's when she started to be really frightened. She had to hold on to the seat because the boat was bumping so much.' Griffoni stopped.

'And then what happened?'

'And then she doesn't remember anything else. Before that, all she remembers is shouting at them to slow down and thinking she was going to be sick. And then she was in the hospital, but she doesn't have any idea of how she got there.'

'And the men?' Brunetti asked.

'They told them they were Venetian. One of them did, that is. She said he spoke English pretty well. The other one didn't say much, only spoke Italian.'

'Did she learn their names?'

'The one who spoke English said to call him Phil, and the other one had a name that began with M. Mario, Michele, she doesn't remember.'

'Anything else?'

'All she said was that one of them had some sort of tattoo on his left wrist: black and geometric, like a bracelet.'

'He and a thousand other people,' Brunetti said, then asked, 'Does she remember being in the water?'

Griffoni sighed. 'She really doesn't remember anything else, Guido.'

'What do the doctors think?'

'That maybe things will come back, but slowly. Or maybe they won't. They couldn't find any sign that she hurt her head, so they think it's just shock and cold and the pain from her broken arm and having been so frightened.'

Before Brunetti could ask anything else, Griffoni said, 'They're calling me. I've got to go back,' and then she was gone.

That left Brunetti with olive pits, an empty glass, and still no clear understanding of what had happened on Saturday night. He thought of the young woman whose face had been so distorted: how was it that a surgeon who had never seen her could reconstruct her face? Make her look like she did before?

He pulled his thoughts back from useless speculation and directed them at more practical concerns. They were Venetian, had access to a boat, perhaps even worked around or on them. Brunetti had no idea of the number of men and women in the city whose work was tied to the water in some way: it would be many hundreds, perhaps far more. As it had been from the times when La Serenissima had ruled the surrounding seas, the work often remained within certain families for generations and created among the workers a unity and loyalty common in men whose work put their lives at risk.

Brunetti picked up the dish with the olive pits and carried it back to the kitchen, placed it and his glass to the side of the sink. Then he went back to Paola's study to find something he wanted to read while he waited for the rest of the family to come home for dinner.

5

When Brunetti checked his computer the next morning, he found a mail from the Carabinieri, forwarded by Signorina Elettra, identifying the two men who had left the young women on the dock of the hospital. Marcello Vio was resident on the Giudecca, and Filiberto Duso in Dorsoduro. The name 'Duso' triggered a vague, positive response in Brunetti's memory, but he left it alone and continued reading.

They had been identified by the Carabinieri at the Ponte dei Lavraneri station on the Giudecca, who had also added that they considered Vio a 'person of interest', although they failed to explain why.

This was enough to prompt Brunetti to find the web page – and when had police stations begun to have web pages? especially on the Giudecca, he asked himself – and dial the number. He identified himself, said he'd received a message that someone there had recognized the two men whose photos the Questura had sent, and asked to speak to the person in charge.

There followed some clicking noises, and then a light contralto voice, whether male or female Brunetti could not judge, saying: 'Nieddu. How can I be of help?'

'This is Brunetti. Commissario, over at San Lorenzo.'

'Ah,' Nieddu said, 'I've heard about you.'

An involuntary burst of air escaped Brunetti's lips, which he followed by saying, 'That'll stop a conversation.' He paused, but there was no reply, so he added, 'Acceptable things, I hope.'

The laugh that came through the line was unmistakably female, the voice that followed it still low-pitched and pleasant. 'Yes, of course. Or else I wouldn't have mentioned it.'

'Probably wise, that,' Brunetti said, then added, 'As a rule, caution is.'

She let some time pass before she asked, 'You're calling about the two men in the photos, aren't you?'

'Yes,' Brunetti answered, 'I'd be grateful for anything you can tell me about them.'

'And I'd be grateful if you'd tell me why you would be,' she answered easily.

'Ah,' Brunetti said, then asked, 'Is this a stand-off?'

'No, Commissario, not at all,' she answered, managing to sound both amused and offended at the same time. Whether she was speaking seriously or jokingly, her voice remained a deep contralto that reminded him of the sound of a cello.

'I'm not sure of your rank,' Brunetti said, 'so please forgive me if I didn't use it when I first spoke.'

'Captain,' she said. Nothing more.

'Then, Captain, is this a bargaining session?'

'In a way, yes.'

'Such things are better done in person, don't you think?'

'Definitely,' she answered in a friendlier voice.

Brunetti was about to respond to her warmth with a joke and ask, 'Your place or mine?' when he was reined up short by the new rules about sexual harassment that had been imposed by the ministry in Rome and that were already ending careers and altering the rules of conversation. Thinking ahead, he saw that claiming he'd been led on by the beauty of her voice was unlikely to serve as an excuse in today's atmosphere, so he erased warmth and tried to sound like a bureaucrat.

'Since I'm the person asking for the information, I should be the one to travel.'

'If you consider it travel to come to the Giudecca.'

'Captain,' Brunetti said, 'For me, going to the Giudecca is like going on an Arctic expedition.'

In response to her laugh, he told her he could be there in an hour; she said that would be fine, then asked if he knew where the commissariato was.

'Down at the end, in Sacca Fisola, isn't it?'

'Yes. When you cross the bridge, give your name, and the man on duty will let you pass.'

'All right, thanks.'

'My rank is Captain,' she said. 'But my name is Laura.'

'Mine's Guido,' Brunetti answered, and then, '*Ciao*,' accepting the amiability of her voice and stepping across the grammatical bridge of cordiality.

Brunetti refrained from checking the police records for the two men, thinking it might be better to have no preconceptions about them when he spoke to the Captain, the better to assess the reasons why one of them was a 'person of interest' to the Carabinieri. He took the Number Two to Sacca Fisola, paying little attention to the glory on offer on both sides of the canal, and walked along the *riva* for a few minutes, then cut to the left and back towards the far corner of the island, where he remembered the Carabinieri station had been for years. The area confirmed his feelings about Giudecca: bleak cement buildings, crudely rectangular, devoid of any attempt at embellishment or adornment: cubes for living in, worsened – at least in his eyes – by the view: across the sullen waters of the *laguna* sprawled the petrochemical horror of Marghera, staggered rows of brick smokestacks from which spewed, day and night ... Brunetti's thoughts stopped there, for he had, like the other residents of Venice, little idea of what rose up in thick clouds from those stacks and even less reason to believe what he was told it was.

Night patrol police boats too often found fishermen there, boats filled with clams scraped up from the bottom of the *laguna* by nets weighted to drag along the sea bed, the better to dredge up everything, leaving desolation where they passed. The clams they caught were growing fat on what they found to eat down there, in the residue of the liquids that had, for generations, seeped out into the *laguna* from the tanks that held the petrochemicals.

Brunetti and his family did not eat clams, or mussels or, in fact, any sort of shellfish that came from local waters. Chiara could, and did, attribute this to her vegetarianism, which excluded fish of any sort. He could still remember her, when she was twelve, pushing away a plate of *spaghetti alle vongole*, saying, 'They were alive once.' She still refused to eat them, but now her reason had grown more informed, and she spurned them, saying, 'They're deadly.' Her family, accepting that she had the family trait of verbal excess, appeared to pay little heed to her opinion, but still they did not eat shellfish.

Brunetti reached the bridge of the Lavraneri, crossed it and approached the guard house. As he drew near, the carabiniere inside slid back the window and said, '*Sì, Signore?*'

'I'm here to see Captain Nieddu.'

'And your name, Signore?' he asked neutrally.

'Brunetti,' he answered.

The man shifted in his seat and turned to his left to point towards the gate in a high wire fence, beyond which began a gravel path that passed between two rows of roses trimmed almost to the ground. 'The office is at the end. I'll call and tell the Captain you're on your way.'

Brunetti thanked him and started towards the path. The gate clicked open in front of him and closed automatically after he passed through. As he walked between the roses, he wondered if it was right to cut them back so much in the autumn, and that led him to consider just how little he knew about plants and how to care for them. Behind the roses was an equally long bed of grass and, behind that, another long rectangle of dark earth that had been turned over and raked. Presumably, taller flowers would be planted there in the spring.

He had to remind himself that this was a Carabiniere station. At the end of the rows of flowers stood a two-storey brick building and behind it a brick wall. The wall had suffered more weathering and must be older than the building.

He rang the bell to the right of a metal door and stepped back two paces so that he would be clearly visible from the spy hole in the door. He pulled out his wallet and removed his warrant card. It was only then that he realized he perhaps should not have reached for anything in his pocket, but it was too late to do anything except hold up the card to whoever looked through the hole.

He heard a noise from inside, and the door was pulled open, revealing a very tall woman in her thirties with shoulder-length dark hair. She wore her uniform jacket: he saw the single bar under the three stars on her lapels. So she was a *primo capitano*, then, and probably outranked most of the men in the unit.

As he stepped forward, he put out his hand, saying, 'Good morning, Laura. I'm pleased to meet you.'

'The pleasure is mine,' the woman answered in that same deep voice. She stepped back beyond the edge of the open door, saying, 'We can go to my office and talk there.' She smiled at last, and he found that almost as attractive as her voice. Her eyes

33

were green; a number of tiny wrinkles spread out from the sides without doing her any damage. Her uniform jacket fitted her closely, making Brunetti wonder where the carabinieri of his youth – fat, moustached, wrinkled – had gone.

She led the way down a corridor, her trousers hiding her legs. Brunetti looked to the side and into the first open door they passed, and then, like a tailor in a competitor's atelier, he slowed his pace and glanced inside every open door, although he had no idea what it was he was looking for. What he got to see was pretty much what he saw at the Questura: uniformed officers sitting behind computers at desks piled with papers and file folders. The desks also held photos of women and men, children, cats and dogs, one of a man in shorts on a beach, holding up a fish almost as long as he. The walls were covered with the usual plaques and maps, photos of the President of the Republic, in one office a crucifix, and in another the lion flag of San Marco.

She stopped at the last door on the right and turned into the room. No surprises here, either, save that the desk was less littered than the ones he'd seen on the way down the corridor. Computer, keyboard, a book that looked like a volume from the standard compilation of penal law. The In box seemed to hold one thin file: the Out box was full.

She closed the door after him, went behind the desk and sat; Brunetti took the chair closer to the desk and, before he sat, pointed to the In box and said, 'You have both my compliments and my envy.'

This time she gave him a broader smile. 'Begin with flattery, Guido. It always works.'

'I didn't intend it as that,' Brunetti said, then added, 'Although the technique isn't unknown to me.'

The noise she made might have been a stifled laugh. She leaned forward, extracted a file from the Out box, and passed a few pages to him.

As he expected, they contained the photos Signorina Elettra had sent of the two men who had taken the injured young women to the hospital, enlarged almost to life size. These were clipped to some pages of standard-sized paper covered with pencilled lines of brief notes printed in a neat, clear hand. Before he began reading, Brunetti glanced at Captain Nieddu but said nothing. He found it interesting that the notes were not computer-produced and thus, being handwritten, were certainly unrecorded and unofficial. She didn't comment on this, and Brunetti turned to examining the file.

He moved the photos aside and began to read. Brunetti was expecting evidence linking the men to the victims, but the text he read sounded – he couldn't stop himself from thinking – like a bullet outline of a B-grade buddy film. Young men born in the same week, twenty-four years before, one the son of a successful lawyer, the other the son of an odd-job man who cleaned the container tanks at one of the chemical companies at Marghera. Nine years before, away from work and drunk, the odd-job man had driven his car off the road and into a cement pillar. And survived, with reduced mental and physical capacities, not described. The last note was a single, chilling, 'Institutionalized'.

Brunetti raised his head and glanced towards the Captain, but she was busy reading another file that had appeared miraculously in front of her and didn't look up. Brunetti returned to the story. Marcello Vio, who was the only son of the injured man, had two younger sisters as well as a mother. To support them, he left school at fifteen and began to work for his uncle's transport business, where he remained to this day.

Filiberto Duso, in this unlikely script, was the young princeling. He and Vio were inseparable at school, until Duso went to *liceo* to prepare himself for university and Vio went to work. They remained, however, best friends. Together, they sailed the *laguna*, always in search of adventure, and they were generally considered '*bravi ragazzi.*'

A number of recent rumours suggested that some of Vio's latest adventures were of questionable legality, perhaps the smuggling of cigarettes from Montenegro or the transport of illegally harvested clams. His uncle, not Duso, was named in conjunction with these actions, although no date nor specific action was provided. Brunetti read three short comments that spoke of, even warned of, the uncle's influence upon his nephew. On the Giudecca, it was all but impossible to escape the low murmur of Gossip, and Brunetti was wary of putting much faith in a story that was not corroborated by something more closely resembling fact.

Brunetti finished reading and raised the sheets of paper, and when Nieddu finally looked over at him, he asked, 'Is this why Vio's a "person of interest" to you?'

She nodded. 'Following in the footsteps of his uncle, Pietro Borgato.'

'Also a person of interest?'

'Even more so. And for some time. There are rumours.'

'What sort?' Brunetti asked.

She started to answer but then shrugged and stopped. 'You know how it is. People say he's mixed up in bad things, but when you ask, they don't know what sort of bad things: but they heard it from someone they trust.' She let him think about that for a short time and then added, 'A woman who lives next to one of my men said he's a smuggler, but she didn't know what he was smuggling.' She raised a hand and made a waving gesture, as if to drive these remarks away. 'It might just as easily be that she simply doesn't like him and thinks he's got to be a smuggler because he has boats.'

Because there was nothing he could say, Brunetti remained silent for a moment and then tapped at the photos and asked, 'How do you know it was these two at the hospital dock?' he finally asked.

Instead of answering, Nieddu reached to the In box and pulled out the file. She flicked through it until, finding the paper she sought, she turned it around and leaned across her desk to pass it to him.

Clipped to the top was a single photo of two young men, arm in arm, relaxed, smiling at the camera. They were dressed in shorts and T-shirts. Both were deeply tanned; one was heavily muscled. He had pushed his sunglasses back on his head, while the thinner one wore the crown of green laurel leaves that students put on to celebrate their graduation from university. Red silk streamers ran down from a large bow attached to the crown; his mouth was wide open and he seemed ready to take a bite out of the planet. Brunetti's spirit recalled the joy and wild pride he'd felt when he'd worn the same wreath for a single day: he understood Duso's expression, for this had to be Duso.

He studied both faces briefly, placed the photo on the desk, picked up the photos Signorina Elettra had sent and placed them on either side of the photo of the two young men together. He glanced back and forth: there was no confounding him, the one with the sunglasses was Marcello Vio.

'Duso's graduation party?' Brunetti asked, tapping at the photo.

'Yes. This summer.'

'Who took it?'

The Captain hesitated a moment before she answered, 'One of my men.'

Brunetti gave no indication of his surprise. 'How did you get it?'

'He saw the photos we were sent and brought that one to me this morning.'

Brunetti nodded and considered what she'd just said. To have taken the photo, the officer would have to be a friend, perhaps even a relative, of one of the men in the photo. 'Am I allowed to compliment you on this?'

She raised a hand as if to push away what he had said. 'He's the one who brought the photo.'

'That means he's probably from the Giudecca or at least from the city.'

'He is,' she said. 'He's a good man.'

'Not a boy?' Brunetti asked, surprised.

'No, he's sixty and sitting out his last years until retirement.'

'I see,' Brunetti said, doubly struck by the man's courage. He switched his legs and leaned to tap a finger on the first page of the hand-written text. 'Do you, or the officer who gave you this information, have proof of anything that's written in here?' he asked.

'Aside from information in official documents, no: there's nothing that anyone would admit having said. Only the usual gossip,' she answered, and then continued, 'It's one thing to believe that something is happening, even to know it is. But that's not the sort of evidence judges will accept.' She mirrored him by folding her arms and crossing her legs, then added, 'And you certainly don't want anyone to know you passed on the information.' She stopped speaking, seeming to want some acknowledgement from him.

Brunetti nodded; it sufficed.

'Since I came here,' she began, speaking clearly and slowly, perhaps to mask the traces of the Sardinian accent he'd heard, 'I've asked the men and the one other woman in the unit to make a note of gossip and hearsay and things that get said in the bars. It's all to be written in pencil and given to me. I copy it and destroy the original pieces of paper, so everything is clearly in my handwriting, should it ever become a problem.'

'A problem?' Brunetti inquired.

She glanced aside after he asked this and looked out of the window of her office, from which only the brick wall could be seen. She studied the wall, pulled her lips together, and turned back to face him.

'What I've heard about you, Commissario, makes me believe you'll understand if I say that the fact that I am a woman does not make my job any easier; indeed, it often leads to complications.'

When it seemed she was not going to proceed, Brunetti said, 'I have no doubt of that. Many of my colleagues don't like women on the force.'

'Or out of it, I'd venture,' she responded instantly. Then, returning to her former, and warmer, tone, said, 'I have something else for you.' She opened the drawer of her desk, pulled out an envelope, and handed it to him. She had printed his name on the flap. 'It's the factual information about them,' she said. 'Full names and addresses, phone numbers, current occupation and place of work.' She paused briefly, then added, 'Neither has a criminal record. Vio's been fined for speeding on the *laguna* three times. Nothing else.' Before Brunetti spoke, she added, 'But there's a growing … aura – an unpleasant one – in what is said about him.' She cleared her throat and returned to fact. 'There's no copy of the photo my man took.' Changing her voice and somehow managing to remove some of its beauty, she added, 'You didn't see it.'

He nodded his thanks to her and slipped the unopened envelope into the inner pocket of his jacket.

They remained silent for some time, Brunetti eager to discover where their conversation would go. The Captain, no doubt sensing this, returned to the original subject. 'I think there has to be some truth in these rumours. They've come to us from a number of people: a former girlfriend of Vio's and one distant cousin.' After saying this, she surprised Brunetti by shrugging one shoulder in dismissal.

In the report she'd written she didn't seem interested in whether Vio was smuggling cigarettes or not; Brunetti wasn't much interested, either, and believed there was no sure way to stop it. 'Do you have an opinion about him?'

She rubbed at some invisible spot on the surface of her desk while she considered how to answer. Finally she said, 'I suppose he, or they, brought in some contraband. For the money.' She looked at Brunetti, then added, 'The children of friends of mine here went to school with Vio. They say he's not particularly bright but at heart a good boy.' After a pause, she added, 'Unlike the uncle.'

'And the other one? Duso?'

She shrugged. 'His father's a lawyer,' she said. The word opened Brunetti's memory, for Duso was the lawyer of a friend, who had always praised his competence and integrity.

There was no reason to mention this to Nieddu, so he remained silent and waited for her to continue. 'He's already working in his father's office, so it's only good sense for him not to get mixed up in anything illegal his friend might be part of.' It was certainly good sense, but it didn't prove that Duso was also a good boy.

'And the cigarettes?' Brunetti asked, level-voiced.

'For the love of God, who cares?' she demanded.

Realizing they were in perfect agreement, Brunetti proposed, 'Shall we share anything we learn?'

'Gladly,' she answered. Then, although it hardly needed explanation, she added, 'As you've noticed, I haven't asked you again why you're interested in these two men. The newspaper accounts say they took them to Pronto Soccorso.'

Brunetti nodded.

'A neighbour of mine works at the hospital,' she continued, her tone grown rough. 'She told me what the young woman looked like when they left her on the dock.'

'We don't know what happened,' Brunetti said, feeling awkward at how feeble it sounded.

'But we do know who brought them,' she snapped. Then, her anger more audible, she added, 'People treat dogs better.'

Brunetti stood and shook his right leg to loosen his trousers, then brushed both hands down the sides to make the cloth fall correctly. When he was standing upright, he said, 'Thank you, Laura, for your time and your cooperation. We'll have a word with them today, if we can.' He asked if they could exchange *telefonino* numbers; she smiled and agreed and pulled out her phone.

After that was done, Brunetti turned to leave her office; she made no move to follow him to the door. When he got there, he turned around to her and said, 'One thing. When I speak to Vio, I know nothing about him or his uncle. I won't stir up waters that are yours.'

At that, she nodded. 'Good luck, then,' she said, and Brunetti left, heading back to the *riva* and the Number Two to San Zaccaria.

6

Brunetti stood on the deck of the vaporetto while he phoned Signorina Elettra to say he had a positive identification of the two suspects and wanted to bring them in for questioning. He stuffed his phone between his shoulder and his ear, pulled out the envelope, and read her their contact information. When she asked, he said he wanted the authorization of a magistrate and that Patta would surely approve, given the connection to the American Embassy. Brunetti remembered how Patta, some years ago, had ended up in the international press: *The New York Times* itself had mentioned Patta's name and said, as was its wont, that 'the arrest struck a serious blow against the Ndrangheta.' All blows against the Mafia, for the international press, were always 'serious', even 'crippling'. No major European languages were capable of using the more apposite 'futile', nor yet 'pointless'.

Brunetti specified that the two men were not to be allowed to speak to or telephone anyone once they were in police custody. He did not have to tell her that each was to be taken to a separate interrogation room and did not tell her that one of them was 'of interest' to the Carabinieri.

'Send Pucetti to get Vio and ask Vianello to take another launch and bring Duso in. All they know is that they were sent to take him to the Questura, always speaking in the singular.'

'Certainly, Commissario,' Signorina Elettra said. 'Shall I begin having a look?'

'A captain in the Carabinieri just told me they checked their records and found nothing,' Brunetti said.

Was it a clicking sound he heard, as if she'd been told something beyond belief? Or was she disappointed by what he'd said?

In either case, the noise was enough to put Brunetti back on track, and he segued effortlessly into, 'But by all means, you should take a closer look, Signorina.' His grip on his *telefonino* relaxed minimally after he said that. Then, in the way a person sends flowers after behaving badly at dinner, he said, 'One of them has an uncle who lives on the Giudecca. Pietro Borgato. Perhaps you could have a look at him, as well?'

'Do you have an idea of when you might be here, Signore?' she inquired. It took Brunetti a moment to recover from the delicacy of the question, and when he glanced at his watch, he was surprised to see that it was after one.

'I should be there before two.'

'Good. Anything else, Signore?'

In his mildest voice, Brunetti said, 'Both of them grew up in the city.'

'Indeed,' she answered, accepting his entirely informal, and equally illegal, request that she check and see what might be available in the prohibited records of juvenile offenders about the earlier behaviour of these two young men.

'Would you tell them both that I'm on my way?' he asked, knowing it was unnecessary to specify the names of Vianello and Pucetti, 'and to call me if there's any trouble.'

'Of course, Commissario,' she answered.

Brunetti thanked Signorina Elettra and ended the call. He remembered then that he had failed to phone Paola and tell her he would not be home for lunch. Hoping he had not troubled or upset her by not calling earlier, he put in their home number. Perhaps he could speak to her before she started cooking.

The phone was picked up after four rings and, a moment later, a voice he did not recognize said, 'Ristorante Falier. I'm sorry to tell you that the restaurant is not open for business today. Please call another time. Thank you for your understanding.' The phone was replaced.

As a form of penance, Brunetti chose to have two *tramezzini* in one of the bars lined up on the Riva degli Schiavoni; he could bring himself to eat only a bite of each, and could not drink the wine. Telling himself not to grumble, he turned off the Riva and continued until he reached the bar at the Ponte dei Greci, said hello to Sergio, the owner, and asked for an asparagus and egg and a tuna and tomato. He stood while he ate them, drinking a glass of Pinot Grigio, then had a coffee. Thus lunch for the working man, he told himself as he walked down to the Questura. Next he'd be stopping to eat a slice of pizza or buying a paper box filled with spaghetti to eat while walking. 'Or while sitting on the Rialto' he muttered to himself, surprising an elderly woman whom he passed on his way back.

He entered the building, raised a hand in response to the salute of the man at the door, and went up to Signorina Elettra's office. He had not seen her before he left to go to the Carabinieri station and, when he reached her office, found her at her desk, partially dressed for autumn or dressed for part of autumn. Brown sweater, beige trousers, brown shoes. There was no reference to the red and yellow of autumn leaves, no sign of the glorious orange of ripe persimmons. Nor were there traces of pomegranates dressed in their imperial scarlet. The sight of those three sober colours left Brunetti feeling somehow cheated.

Not even the vase of red chrysanthemums sufficed to appease his colour-deprived eyes.

He smiled and asked, 'Any news?'

When she swivelled on her chair as he approached her desk, Brunetti caught a glimpse of the arm of the jacket hanging from the back: theatre red velvet, the sort of colour one of the wildly mad emperors would have liked: Heliogabalus, perhaps. It cheered him and restored his faith in he wasn't quite sure what.

'Foa called to say he'd be back in,' – she paused and looked at her watch – '... in about ten minutes.'

'What rooms are free?' Brunetti asked.

'Two and Four,' she said, naming the least comfortable of the interrogation rooms, both painted an unfriendly green, each with a cheap plastic table and four plastic chairs. Although there were 'No Smoking' signs on the outside and inside of the doors, both rooms stank of cigarettes, the floors covered with flicked-away ash that was no sooner removed than again flicked to the floor by the next person to be questioned. People had complained about the smell for years, both among those questioned and those asking the questions, but the fact that granting a suspect the right to smoke sometimes led to a loosening of their resolve not to speak legitimized the custom, and so suspects were some-times permitted to smoke, and sometimes it soothed them into the truth. And sometimes it did not.

Brunetti took out his *telefonino* and called Griffoni. When she picked up, he asked, 'You've heard we've found them?'

'Yes.'

'One of them will be here in ten minutes. Would you like to ...'

'*Sì*,' she said, so loud as to force him to hold his phone away from his ear. There was noise, then a loud slam, followed by a metallic rattle, after which he heard what must have been footsteps.

He stepped out into the hallway and went down towards the stairwell. Just as he arrived, Griffoni, left hand on the railing, swung herself around into the stairs leading down to the next floor. When she saw him, she raised her hand from the bannister and slowed her pace.

'They aren't here yet,' Brunetti called up to her. Griffoni reached the bottom step and walked towards him. 'Tell me,' she said. The flush of colour on her face, left tanned by the summer sun, made the contrast with her blonde hair and green eyes even more startling. It also made it more difficult to believe she was from the South.

'The Carabinieri on the Giudecca recognized them,' Brunetti said. 'Neither of them has a record.'

'You aren't bringing the two of them in together, are you?' she asked.

'Claudia,' Brunetti said slowly, nothing more.

'Sorry, sorry, sorry,' she said. 'Of course.' She backed up a step, saying, her voice suddenly tight and nervous, 'I saw the girl today.'

'The one in Mestre?'

'Yes,' she said, looking at the floor.

Brunetti waited and, in the face of her continued silence, finally asked, 'And?'

Griffoni raised a hand and brushed at the side of her mouth, something she did when she was nervous. She looked down at her feet again and shook her head. 'Guido,' she said, 'she's nineteen years old.' She looked back at him and went on, 'She hasn't regained consciousness, and they can't operate until she does.'

Before she could say anything else, they heard voices from below. There was a man's voice, loud with fear, and the lower, calm voice of Pucetti. 'If you'd come with ...' Pucetti began, but his voice became inaudible, no doubt as he turned towards the back of the building and the interrogation rooms. The louder voice said, 'I don't know what you're ...' but then it too softened and disappeared as the person who must be Vio followed Pucetti.

Knowing he had only moments to explain things to Griffoni, Brunetti said, nodding his chin in the direction of the disappearing footsteps on the floor below, 'This one works as a boatman, and his friend who was with him is the son of a lawyer and works in his father's office. All I learned is that the boatman is a "person of interest" to the Carabinieri on the Giudecca. There are rumours that he's been smuggling cigarettes and clams.'

She made a puffing noise to comment on the irrelevance of this.

'And perhaps other things,' Brunetti said.

'Only rumours?' she interrupted to ask.

Suddenly Pucetti appeared at the bottom of the steps and called up, 'Commissari, I put him in Room Four.'

'Thanks, Pucetti,' Brunetti said, starting down the stairs towards the young officer. It had been some time since Pucetti had worked with him, so he suggested, 'Would you like to stand in with us?'

'Oh, yes, sir,' Pucetti said, perhaps too enthusiastically.

'Claudia?' Brunetti asked.

'By all means,' she said. 'Come along, Pucetti. We'll see what he knows about boats.'

Inside the room, the young man wearing the sunglasses in the photo Brunetti had seen stood behind a chair, hands gripped on its back, as if poised there for a moment, sure that he was soon to be on his way. He wore faded jeans and a dark blue sweatshirt, sleeves turned back to show thick forearms, one encircled by a tattooed band. He had a round face, a turned-up nose, and wore his hair in the current fashion, shaved close on the sides long on top, but even with these signs of youth, he looked older than in the photo Captain Nieddu had shown Brunetti, with dark circles under his eyes and a face drawn tight as though with pain. His skin was dry and pale beneath the remnants of his summer tan, and Brunetti thought he could hear his breathing.

'Have a seat, Signor Vio,' Brunetti said as he approached the table. He waited for Vio to pull back the chair and sit. When he did not, Brunetti sat and reached towards a switch on the top of the table, flipped it to the right, and said, 'Our conversation will be recorded, Signor Vio. This way there will be no doubt about what we discussed. I hope that's all right with you.' Brunetti added this last in a way that made it clear he neither hoped nor cared whether it was all right with Signor Vio.

Vio pulled out the chair and lowered himself into it gingerly, one hand on the back of the chair, a motion which Brunetti translated into the visual equivalent of *Argumentum ad Misericordiam*, the appeal to pity. Brunetti pulled himself back from the thought of the young woman in the hospital, still unconscious, warning himself not to fall into the same error by assuming this man's guilt because of what the girl had suffered. Vio sat, upright as a Victorian maiden, back not touching that of the chair, and made no attempt to hide his nervousness as his eyes shifted around the room. He had a two-day-old beard behind which Brunetti could see the perfect teeth of his generation. His breathing was shallow and quick.

Brunetti had brought no papers with him. Sometimes people were disconcerted when he seemed to remember details about them, facts, without having to consult a document. He sat opposite Vio; Griffoni had taken the chair to Brunetti's left; Pucetti stood to the right, leaning against the wall, arms at his sides, playing the role of the uniformed officer ready to leap across the table and restrain the person being questioned at the first sight of misconduct.

'Could you tell me where you work, Signor Vio?' Brunetti started in a neutral tone.

'Work?' Vio repeated, as if asking the meaning of the word. He coughed a few times and put his right hand to his mouth.

'Your job, Signor Vio. You have a job, don't you?'

Vio sought a more comfortable position, seemed to wince at the motion, and returned to his stiff, upright position. 'Yes. I do. Work, that is. For my uncle.' Any Venetian hearing him speak would know he came from Giudecca and from a family of workers, probably generations of workers; further, they would not be surprised to learn he had left school early.

'And what do you do for your uncle?' Griffoni asked.

Vio's eyes snapped towards the sound of her voice, as if women were not meant to have one. He gave her question some thought and answered, speaking to Brunetti, not to her, 'I load and unload what my uncle has to transport in the city. Sometimes I'm in charge of the boat; sometimes not.' He breathed, Brunetti thought, like an old person: how could he make a living hauling heavy objects? How indulgent must his uncle be?

'Do you mean that sometimes you drive the boat?' Brunetti asked.

'Yes.'

'Do you have a licence, Signor Vio?'

'Yes, I do,' he said and swivelled to the left. As he reached for his pocket, he winced and froze, then moved cautiously back to his position looking across at Brunetti.

'That's all right, Signor Vio,' Brunetti said. 'We can easily check.'

Vio's eyes opened in surprise, but he said nothing.

'What sort of boat do you drive for your uncle?' Griffoni asked.

'Sort? It's a transport boat. He has three different sizes,' Vio started to explain, but he was cut short by a cough. When it stopped, Vio continued. 'I can handle them all.'

'I see,' Griffoni said, 'And is your licence good for all three sizes of boat?'

Vio nodded and she said, not unkindly, 'You have to say some-thing, Signor Vio.'

The young man cleared his throat before he asked, 'What do I have to say?' To Brunetti, it looked as though Vio tried to take a deep breath to calm himself but failed at that and settled for a few quick breaths.

Brunetti smiled across at him and explained, making himself sound almost avuncular, 'We're recording the conversation, so you have to answer the question with words.'

'Oh, I see,' Vio muttered and stared across at the switch. 'Thank you. Yes, the licence. Mine is valid for all of the boats.'

'Do you have a boat of your own?' Brunetti asked.

'I have a pupparin,' Vio answered, 'but I don't need a licence for that.'

'I had one when I was your age,' Brunetti offered with every semblance of truth. 'But I never wanted a motor for it.'

'Me neither, Signore.'

'Then what do you do for Redentore?' Brunetti asked, sound-ing both curious and concerned. Didn't he have his own boat, big enough for a group of friends to go out into the *bacino* to see the fireworks? What sort of Venetian would miss the chance to do that?

The young man's face relaxed a bit. 'My uncle lets me take one of his boats.'

'Oh, that's very kind of him,' Griffoni broke in to say. 'It must be nice for you that he trusts you so much.'

'Well, he knows I'm a good pilot,' Vio said, obviously proud to be able to say it. He coughed again. This time he pulled out a not very clean white handkerchief and wiped at his mouth when the coughing stopped.

Behind him, Brunetti heard Pucetti shift his feet. He consid-ered the differences between these two young men, so similar in age, yet one so bright and one so naive.

'It must be nice to be able to take your friends out into the *laguna*,' Griffoni said admiringly, quite as though it was her dream in life to go out on the water in a boat with friends.

'Yes, it is, Signora,' Vio answered.

This was too easy, Brunetti thought, reluctant to drop the net over the boy's empty head. And why, he asked himself, did he think of Vio as a boy?

'Do you do that?' Brunetti asked.

'Do what, Signore?' Vio asked.

Brunetti smiled before he answered. 'Take friends out into the *laguna*.'

Because he was opposite Vio, Brunetti could see on his face the moment the question registered. The young man had apparently thought that the slight warming of tone on the part of his two interlocutors was a sign of their goodwill, that he had managed to impress them as a good employee and thus a good person who, obviously, was there by mistake. Brunetti's question put an end to that dream and brought Vio back to the cruel reality that he was in the Questura, and the police were interrogating him.

'Oh,' Vio said, his hands grasping at one another, 'that doesn't happen very often. Redentore.' He looked at his hands, stopped their embrace, and placed them palms down in front of him, where he could keep a close eye on them.

'Redentore was months ago,' Brunetti reminded him. 'Have you been out with friends since then?'

'No!' Vio's answer came too fast and too loud. 'I work on the weekends. I don't have time.' Any other defence was cut off by a short bark of a cough and then another series of quick breaths.

'Really?' Griffoni asked when he stopped, quite as though she were in possession of different information. She twisted her mouth and raised her eyebrows, glanced aside at Brunetti and asked, 'That's not what you heard, is it, Commissario?'

'Well,' Brunetti answered, stretching the word for as long as possible. 'Maybe there's been some mistake.'

'Perhaps,' Griffoni said, sounding unpersuaded.

Vio's head moved back and forth, as if he thought he might understand what was going on if he managed to keep his eyes on Brunetti and Griffoni all the time they spoke.

Brunetti returned his attention to Vio, saying, 'We'd like to ask you some questions about Saturday night, Signor Vio.'

Vio's mouth fell open and he stared, speechless, at Brunetti, then at Griffoni. He sat still – prey – waiting, too frightened to move.

Brunetti smiled again, amiability itself. 'Could you give us an idea of what you did on Saturday night, Signor Vio?'

'I ...' he began, and they could see him trying to remember what Saturday was, and when he had that figured out, when Saturday was. 'I went for a walk.'

'Were you at home when you decided to go for your walk?' Griffoni asked. Then she smiled to suggest that she was merely trying to pass the time.

'Yes.'

'And where is home, if I might ask?'

'Near Sant'Eufemia.'

She allowed her smile to soften and said, 'You have to be patient with me, Signor Vio: I'm not Venetian, so I don't know where that is.'

For a moment, it seemed that Signor Vio didn't know, either, but then he burst into speech, saying, 'It's down at the end of the canal before you get to Harry's Dolci. Number 630.' He raised an arm, as if to point towards his home, but the gesture was cut off by a deep wince of pain and a single, barked cough. Out came the handkerchief, and he wiped at his mouth again.

'Thank you, Signor Vio,' Griffoni said.

Brunetti interrupted to add, 'There's not much to do there on a Saturday night, I'd say.' Then, thinking he should make it clear to Vio that he knew the place he was talking about, he added, 'Even Palanca closes at ten.'

'No, not there,' Vio said.

'Oh, where did you go?' Griffoni chirped, suggesting that he had but to name the beautiful Venetian location where he'd decided to go and she'd be out of the room and on her way to see it the instant he stopped speaking.

Brunetti and Griffoni had developed a symbiotic ability to delude and deceive suspects or, indeed, any people they interviewed together. They took turns being the good cop or the bad cop; sometimes they even switched roles during an interrogation. They had never discussed this, did not plan before speaking to someone: they simply looked for weakness and dived towards it, no more thoughtful than sharks.

'On the other side,' Vio said, grudgingly.

'Of the Giudecca Canal?' Griffoni asked, as if she believed there could be some other canal to cross from the Giudecca.

'Yes.'

'And where did you go?'

Vio opened his mouth to answer, but before he could, Brunetti interrupted to ask, 'Did you see anyone you know?'

Vio's mouth slammed shut, almost involuntarily, and they both watched him retracing his steps through the city on Saturday night. And they saw him meet someone, at least open his eyes with surprise and look about him, as if in search of that person. His breathing became more agitated, and his nervousness seemed to prevent him from taking in enough oxygen.

Vio nodded and waved a hand, unable to speak.

After waiting some time for him to get his breath back, Brunetti asked, with a complete absence of friendliness, 'Who did you meet?'

'Someone from work.'

'Who?' Brunetti continued.

Vio remained silent for a while and then said, 'My uncle's secretary,' and Brunetti disguised his pleasure at this answer: a
woman was more likely to tell the truth when asked if, and
where, she had seen him. No, he told his ever-constant eaves-
dropper: not because women were more honest – though he
believed they were – but because they were more afraid of having trouble with authority.

'And where did you go?' Brunetti asked.

'Campo Santa Margherita,' Vio answered. 'That's where I
saw her.'

'Oh, did you walk all that way?' Griffoni asked, with great
display of sympathy, as if she suspected that the walk to anywhere in the city from any of the stops the Number Two vaporetto
made on its arrival from the Giudecca was the same distance as
Venice to Rome.

'No,' Vio said, almost inaudibly.

'Oh,' she all but chirped, 'Did you take a boat?'

'Yes.'

Proudly, the foreigner showing off her familiarity with the
vaporetto, she asked, *'Numero Due?'* Brunetti hoped she would
not overdo this fey demonstration of familiarity with the routes
of the vaporetti and ask if he'd gone all the way to Santa Marta
before getting off.

Vio sat alone on his side of the long table. The chair on his left
was empty, and Pucetti, still silent, stood almost two metres from
him. Yet Vio looked uncomfortable, as if people were crowding
in at him from every side. He looked, in a word, trapped.

He lowered his head and spoke to the top of the table.

'Excuse me,' Griffoni said pleasantly. 'I'm afraid I didn't hear
you.'

The young man mumbled something.

She gave a small laugh and said, 'Sorry, I still didn't hear what
you said.'

He looked up and across the table at her, there beside the stolid Brunetti. He pulled his lips inside his mouth and made a soft humming sound. His fingers tightened until they became two fists resting on the table.

He closed his eyes, opened them, closed them again and kept them closed while the humming noise grew louder.

Vio opened his eyes again and turned to Brunetti. He opened his hands and pressed them against the table, as if to give himself strength. 'I took . . .' he began, then pushed himself suddenly to his feet and turned as if to flee the room. His foot blundered into the leg of the chair and, trying to free himself, he twisted his body sharply; once, twice, unaware of what trapped him and wanting only to escape it. When his foot finally pulled free, his entire upper body twisted again to the right.

He moaned, then moaned again as though the other people in the room had suddenly pressed sharp objects against his skin. He collapsed against the table, tried to find something to cling to, failed, and started to sink to the floor, his moaning louder.

Suddenly, as though there had not been shock enough, he was racked by coughing and a tiny thread of blood-mottled saliva came from his mouth, paralysing the others until his body fell to the floor.

7

The first to react was Pucetti, who braced his hands on the surface of the table and leaped over to land beside Vio, who was reduced to whimpers and savage coughing. The young officer tore Vio's shirt partly open and reached to put his palms on his chest, but one of his fingers caught on the shirt and pulled it entirely open. His hands, one palm above the other, rose above Vio's chest, ready to press down to re-start the beating of his heart, when Griffoni, who had come around the table, pushed Pucetti so hard that he fell away from Vio and crashed into the wall.

Brunetti knelt on the other side of Vio and saw what she had seen.

'Look at him, look at him,' Griffoni said in a rough voice, pointing down at Vio's chest.

He was a man who worked all day, heaving and hauling and shifting heavy weights from one place to another, and he had the torso of every body-builder's dreams. The ribs on his left side could be counted, as clearly defined as the slats in a wall. But the ribs on the right side had relaxed into the body and could not be discerned. The entire right side was bruised almost black in a streak as wide as an iPad that ran from collarbone to waist.

Vio moved, moaned, moved again, and then his entire body was shaken as he gasped in air, fish-like, and then again and then again. He expelled it all at once, along with another trickle of blood-threaded saliva. There followed a racking cough that shook his entire body and brought forth more saliva.

Brunetti pulled out his phone and dialled 118, gave his name and rank and told them to send an ambulance to the Questura immediately and to send a doctor with the ambulance. He cut off the call, knowing he was unable to explain the situation but wanting to leave the line open should the hospital try to contact him.

Brunetti looked back at Vio and saw that the coughing had slowed and grown weaker. Griffoni had somehow managed to find a blanket and was stretching it over the young man's body: Pucetti had disappeared. Brunetti dared not touch the young man for fear of adding to the damage so clearly etched on his body. He got to his feet, helpless in the face of damage he could not estimate, suffering he could not relieve.

He stood there, surrounded by the latest products of technology, promising to help him call up aid from the entire country – from the entire world – if he chose. A man lay at his feet, twisted in pain, bleeding, barely able to breathe, and Brunetti had no idea what to do. Except to wait for the arrival of those who knew more about saving lives or resolving the mysteries of the human body.

Brunetti had been present at the birth of both of his children, if to be standing in the hall outside the delivery room – there by virtue of his brother's connections at the hospital – was to be present. There, too, he had heard the laboured gasps of pain, with no specific idea of what was causing them, although he knew full well what would stop them. And did.

The sound of the approaching siren pulled him back to this room, these groans, this suffering man. The siren stopped. He put his hand on Griffoni's shoulder and lifted his chin towards the other side of the room. Together they moved there. A moment later, a white-jacketed woman came quickly into the room, followed closely by one of the emergency crew carrying a canister of oxygen and a mask.

The woman looked at the man on the floor and then glanced around the room. Seeing Griffoni and Brunetti, she said, sounding inappropriately calm, 'Tell me what happened.'

Brunetti chose to speak. 'We're police officers and were questioning him. He coughed a lot and seemed to have trouble breathing. With no warning, he stood, twisted his body to one side, and collapsed.'

'When did this happen?'

Brunetti looked at his watch. 'Sixteen minutes ago,' he said.

She nodded and turned to the man behind her, reaching for the oxygen mask. She knelt and slipped it over Vio's nose and mouth, felt his pulse, looking at the bruise.

The doctor took a stethoscope from the pocket of her jacket and placed it on Vio's chest. She studied his face while she listened, moving the stethoscope to the compass points of his chest. Then she put the stethoscope in her pocket and leaned down over Vio.

Two more men came into the room: one carried a rolled-up stretcher.

'Signore,' the doctor said, bending down over Vio, 'can you hear me?'

Vio made a noise.

'We have to move you,' she said. As she spoke, both men moved closer, and the one with the stretcher unrolled it.

'It's going to hurt, Signore,' the doctor said, shifting closer to Vio and taking his hand. 'But I want you to try not to move. I think your rib has punctured your lung, and it should – if you can stand it – remain where it is for as long as it can while we take you to the hospital. If it moves, it might do you more damage.'

Vio made no sound, and she asked, 'Do you understand?'

This time a grunt.

She ran her hands across the sides of her trousers to warm them and leaned towards him again. 'I'm going to touch you now. Don't be afraid.'

Vio did not acknowledge what she said. After a moment she placed first one hand, and then the other, on the sides of his chest and moved them around, her fingers pressing lightly. Vio groaned but did not move. The doctor shifted her fingers on to the bruised flesh, and the groan became a bit louder.

She removed her hands and pulled a small bag towards her, opened it, and turned back to Vio. 'I'm going to give you something for the pain, Signore. It will help, but you will still feel pain. Please, please try not to move while my colleagues put you on the stretcher.' Silence. 'Do you understand?'

In response, Vio coughed but managed to say, '*Sì*,' nothing more. She removed a small phial of clear liquid and a plastic-wrapped syringe. Quickly, efficiently, she injected the liquid and patted his hand a few times, as if hoping to comfort him or prepare him for what was coming.

The doctor got to her feet and stood beside the doorway; the attendants drew closer to Vio. Brunetti and Griffoni passed into the hallway, moving a metre down the hall. They heard scuffling, a click of metal on tile, a sigh, a muffled groan, and then one of the men came into the corridor, then the other, a white-faced Vio lying on the stretcher they held. The third man followed, holding the oxygen and staying close to the stretcher.

Brunetti and Griffoni pressed back against the wall and watched as the attendants disappeared down the corridor. After a moment, the doctor emerged, holding her bag. She nodded to them and said only, 'We'll take him to the Ospedale Civile.'

Brunetti and Griffoni trailed them across the entrance hall and out the main entrance. An ambulance was moored at the dock, motor running. The attendants started towards it, and at that moment, Brunetti heard the approach of another boat. He turned in the direction of the entrance to the canal and saw the police launch, Foa at the wheel, Vianello beside him, to his left a young man with dark hair tousled by the wind.

Foa pulled up nose to nose with the ambulance; Vianello pushed past the young man and jumped to the *riva*, his face blank with shock. 'What's wrong?' he called to Brunetti.

Before Brunetti could answer, the young man leaped from the deck and ran to the stretcher, which the attendants had set down while waiting for the confusion of boats to be sorted out. Blind to the people standing near the stretcher, he knelt and bent over Vio. 'Marcello, Marcello,' he said, panic searing his voice.

Brunetti took a step towards them, but Griffoni grabbed his arm and locked her fingers around it, pulling him so hard as to set him back on his heels.

Vio opened his eyes and said something, then moved his hand towards the other man. Duso – who else could it be? – covered it with both of his but said no more.

The doctor drew up beside Duso and tapped him on the shoulder. 'All right, stop that now. We're taking him to the hospital.' She turned to the three attendants and said, 'Put him on the boat.'

They did as they were told and lifted the stretcher, pulling Vio's hand free from Duso's. They climbed aboard and slipped the stretcher through the doors, and then the doctor climbed in after them. Duso raised a hand towards the ambulance as the doors slammed shut and the motor roared. The third man went to stand by the pilot. Duso remained kneeling on the pavement, too surprised to react, capable only of watching the ambulance disappear, first from sight, then from sound.

Brunetti pulled his arm free from Griffoni's grip and walked over to Duso. He reached down to the young man, who took his hand and pulled himself to his feet.

Brunetti saw the tears on the young man's cheeks before he succeeded in wiping them away. Voice choked, Duso asked, 'What happened?'

'He fainted when we were talking to him,' Brunetti explained. 'The doctor who came thinks he broke a rib, and it's punctured his lung.'

Before Duso could speak, Brunetti went on, making up the story he thought the young man needed to hear. 'She didn't seem very worried about him, but they need to take X-rays to be sure.' He saw that Duso was responding as much to his calm tone as to the story he was telling.

Brunetti gestured to the door of the Questura and said, 'Would you come this way? It won't take long.' Once inside, he stayed close to Duso's side as Griffoni led them both towards the back of the building, to the interrogation room next to the one where Vio had collapsed.

There, everything was orderly: two desk lamps on the long table, chairs on both sides, even a carafe of water and four glasses.

Brunetti waved to a seat on the opposite side of the table, farther from the door, and waited while Duso pulled out the chair and sat: the chair was directly opposite a double electrical socket, half of which was in fact the lens of a camera that projected the top half of the person being questioned on to a television screen in the next room. The larger desk lamp took care of the audio.

Brunetti and Griffoni sat on the other side of the table, Brunetti directly opposite Duso. Brunetti found comfort in the certainty that Vianello was observing Duso: his friend's bat-like sensitivity to voices doubled his ability to understand what was meant, not only what was said: where some heard defiance, Vianello sensed fear. Where others heard submission Vianello sensed deceit.

Brunetti turned his attention to the young lawyer.

Questioning a lawyer was never easy, both Brunetti and Griffoni knew. Believing themselves the only true interpreters of the law, lawyers often further assume that the police have little knowledge of the law's many twists and turns, its seeming contradictions, nor of the multiplicity of interpretation it offered to its followers. This lawyer at the start of his career, and thus less experienced than his older colleagues, might not pause to consider that the two people with whom he was soon to speak had studied law and could have been, had they chosen to be, lawyers. It might also have surprised him to learn that their joint years of experience of the law probably exceeded that of his father or any of the lawyers in his office.

Youth often thinks in images, rather than words, so it was also possible that Avvocato Duso sometimes saw himself as a slayer of dragons, capable of charging through the defences of any who stood in his way. He worked but a moment's walk from the Gallerie dell' Accademia, where, had he visited the collection with any regularity, surely he would have seen Mantegna's small wooden panel of San Giorgio in full armour, the saint glancing to his left and thus drawing the viewer's gaze away from what lay behind his feet. There lay the dragon, head thrust in front of the frame in a triumph of *trompe-l'oeil*, just as the sliver of spear protruding from its jaw was proof of the saint's triumph.

Griffoni's touch on his arm interrupted Brunetti's reverie; he turned his attention to the young lawyer. 'Avvocato Duso,' he said formally, 'let me introduce myself: Brunetti, Commissario di Polizia.' He turned towards Griffoni, who nodded. 'This is my colleague, Commissario Claudia Griffoni.'

That done, Brunetti continued with the legal formalities. 'We've asked you to come to speak to us about certain matters. I inform you that this conversation is being recorded.' He glanced across at Duso, and asked, 'Is that clear?'

Filiberto Duso was a handsome young man in a country where this is the norm; thus, he seemed not at all aware of it. His cheekbones were high and well defined, his nose thin and straight. His summer tan lingered, setting in contrast his blue eyes. He was clean-shaven and had two dimples on either side of his mouth: they creased when he smiled. His hair was in need of cutting.

'Filiberto Duso,' he finally said, making no attempt to extend his hand across the table.

'Signor Duso, thank you for coming to speak to us,' Brunetti began by saying, curious how Duso would deal with a remark that cried out for a sarcastic response.

The young man had obviously had time to recover at least a bit from the shock of seeing his friend being carried to an ambulance. His smile was easy and assured, but not warm, when he said, 'Because I'm a lawyer, it is my obligation, as well as my pleasure, to be of help to the police.'

'Thank you,' Brunetti said simply and turned aside to Griffoni. Perhaps she could succeed in provoking him?

'It's about the events of Saturday night that we'd like to speak to you, Signor Duso,' she said.

'Which events?' Duso asked.

As if he'd not spoken, Griffoni went on. 'We're curious about your movements that night. We'd like to learn if your memory is similar to that of Signor Vio.'

If either Brunetti or Griffoni had thought the mention of Vio's name would affect Duso, they were mistaken, for he answered calmly, 'I had dinner with my parents at eight, and I was with them until at least ten.'

'And then?' she asked mildly.

'Then I went back to my own apartment.'

63

'Could you tell us where that is?'

'Dorsoduro,' he answered, then added, before she could ask, '950. Along the canal, just around the corner from Nico's.'

She nodded, as if she knew exactly where that was.

'Ah, near the boat stop,' Brunetti interrupted. 'It's very convenient for going to the Giudecca.'

'And to the station,' Duso added, as if he were finishing Brunetti's sentence. 'Especially if I can catch the Number 5.2. Then I'm at the station in eighteen minutes.' He offered the time to Brunetti, as if he hoped it would be helpful to him in the future. Brunetti nodded his thanks.

Well, isn't he clever? Brunetti thought. He'd happily sit here all morning and talk about vaporetto schedules and the fastest way to get to the station.

'Let's stay closer to your apartment, Signor Duso, shall we?' Brunetti asked in a friendly voice. 'Your home is also very close to Campo Santa Margherita, is it not?'

Duso leaned back in his chair and smiled easily. 'I'm afraid I'm too old to be interested in Campo Santa Margherita any longer, Commissario.' Before Brunetti could question that, Duso went on. 'I spent a lot of time there when I was at university. Perhaps too much time.' He sighed, as would an old man remarking that, when he was a child, he understood as a child, but now he was a man and had put away childish things.

Duso moved forward in his chair and folded his hands in front of him. 'Besides,' he continued, 'it's not the place it was when I was younger.' Duso restrained himself from shaking his head sadly, Brunetti saw, and went on. 'There was alcohol, then, plenty of it.' That remark was followed by a rueful smile. 'But far fewer drugs.'

Brunetti waited to see what gesture Duso would use to show his disapproval, but he did not move. Instead, he resumed speaking. 'Today, it's a drug bazaar: people in the office tell me you can get anything there.'

'You're not interested?' Griffoni asked.

Duso smiled at her question, shrugged, and said, 'Not any more, I'm not.' The broad smile returned and he said, 'I don't think there's such a thing as retroactive arrest, so I can tell you I tried drugs once or twice: hashish, marijuana, I even took some pills once that someone gave me when I had to stay up to study for an exam.' He shook his head in wonder at the things he'd got up to while still a student.

'But now I'm not,' he reaffirmed, giving them both a serious look.

'That's certainly very interesting, Signor Duso,' Brunetti said. 'But could we return to the subject of Campo Santa Margherita?'

'And the events of Saturday night,' Griffoni added.

Duso tilted his head and allowed himself to look surprised. 'I'm afraid this is very confusing, Signori,' he said. 'I don't know why you keep taking things back to Campo Santa Margherita.'

'Were you there on Saturday night?' Brunetti asked directly.

Duso looked back at him, then at Griffoni, then at the top of the table, and Brunetti could almost hear him playing the odds. Marcello would never have said anything, so who could have seen him there? Who, in the many groups, the ever-shifting and re-forming groups of young people, could have seen him and recognized or remembered him? Who could have seen them getting into the boat with the two Americans?

Duso looked up. 'Why do you want to know?'

'Because we're police officers,' Brunetti answered, 'and because we are interested in a crime that began in Campo Santa Margherita.'

It was an indication of how busy Duso's mind must be that it took him some time to ask, '"Began in"?'

'Yes,' Brunetti answered. 'That's why we want to confirm that you were there.'

'What crime?'

'Leaving the scene of an accident,' Brunetti began. 'Violation of the rules of navigation. Refusing aid to an injured person.'

At that, Duso said, speaking sharply, 'But we ...' and stopped himself.

'You what, Signor Duso? Took them to the hospital and left them on the dock? Without calling anyone? At three in the morning?'

Duso looked across at Brunetti and asked, voice less steady than it had been, 'I have the right to make a phone call, don't I?'

'Yes, you do,' Brunetti said. 'You're free to do it here, any time you wish.'

Saying nothing further, Duso took his *telefonino* from the inside pocket of his jacket and pushed in a number. It rang three times, and a man's voice answered.

'*Papi*, it's Berto,' Duso said, sounding a decade younger. 'I'm in trouble.'

8

How he wished he had not heard him say that, Brunetti thought.
How much like his own son Duso had sounded: contrite, frightened, uncertain what damage his behaviour would do to his
father's career. That fear was not expressed in Duso's words, of
course, but hid in the struggle among fear, respect, and shame
that began when he first addressed his father and was not finished even by the time he said goodbye and sat, eyes closed,
hand lying palm up on the table, like a modern Christ trying to
prepare himself for the first nail.

Brunetti realized he had enjoyed dealing with the young lawyer, had taken pleasure sparring with him and seeing how good
the younger man would some day be at it. He had appreciated
his manners, even as the two of them took their first jabs at one
another. The young man thought quickly, did not descend into
sarcasm, was relentlessly polite.

They are so fragile, young people, Brunetti reflected, their
self-assurance such a thin layer. They'd grown up more than a
generation after Brunetti and his contemporaries, and many of
them had had feathered nests to live in, constructed and padded

67

by their successful parents, themselves the heirs of the people who created the great financial Boom of the Sixties.

Brunetti had gone to university with their parents. He still remembered the envy he had felt for some of them, with their jackets from Duca D'Aosta, the store long since disappeared from Frezzeria and moved out to Mestre, of all places. And their Fratelli Rossetti shoes, new with every changing season, and how he'd longed for a pair of tasselled brown loafers, which he'd wear without socks when he'd saved up enough money to buy them. And now he had a pair and didn't much like them any more and wore them with socks.

He leaned forward in his chair and said, 'Signor Duso?'

There was no response.

'Signor Duso?' Brunetti repeated in a normal voice.

Duso opened his eyes, saw his open hand, and snatched it back before sitting up. He pulled the sleeves of his jacket down and straightened his tie. 'Sì, *Commissario*?' he inquired, almost managing to keep his voice steady.

'I wonder if we could continue?' Brunetti asked. 'You were telling us about Saturday night,' he added, knowing this was not the case. But phrasing it this way might make it easier for Duso to continue with the story.

Duso put both hands on the table, fingers threaded together, and stared down at them. 'Marcello and I went to Campo Santa Margherita to see if we could meet some girls.'

'Marcello Vio?' Brunetti asked.

Duso nodded and said, 'Yes. We do it every couple of weeks, and Saturday was probably going to be the last time it would be warm enough for us to stay outside.'

'Are you usually successful?'

'Most of the time,' he said, head still lowered and attention given to his hands. 'Some of them were in class with me or are still studying, so I know them, or we meet girls that Marcello knows and then we go out; or we meet tourists; sometimes we go swimming.'

'And the girls you met on Saturday night, were they girls you knew?'

He shook his head. 'No. We started talking to them. I speak English; Marcello does, although only a little, but it didn't matter to the girls.'

He paused and Brunetti wondered if this was the moment when Duso was going to begin building a case against the two young women and explain how they had insisted that they go out into the *laguna* at night, how romantic it would be; no, go faster, please go faster. And maybe the girls had suggested that they find a beach somewhere?

'Why was that?' Griffoni asked, perhaps because she didn't want to listen to what she thought Brunetti was expecting.

'Well, they'd just got here and they'd been walking around the city all day, and from the way they talked, I knew they were interested in the city, and then one of them said she'd love to see the canals at night.' He thought about this and added, 'It was after midnight by then.'

'But you went out into the *laguna*, didn't you?' Griffoni asked.

'That was after,' he said simply.

'After what?' she asked.

'We spent about an hour riding around in the city, but after that Marcello told me he was bored and hungry and wanted to go to that bar over at the Tolentini that's open until two. I explained this to the girls, and they laughed and said they had lots of food with them.'

'At one in the morning?' Griffoni asked.

As if she hadn't spoken, Duso went on. 'We went out to the Punta della Dogana and sat on the steps.' He relaxed a bit as he talked about this. 'They had everything with them: salami, and ham and cheese, and two loaves of bread, and olives, and toma-toes. Enough food for all of us, and a bottle of wine.

'I asked them why, and they said they were going to take it back to their room that night if they didn't find a nice place in the city where they could eat.' He looked across at Brunetti and said, 'So we had a picnic.'

Duso's smile broadened and he said, 'When we were done, they made us collect everything: all the papers and scraps and napkins and bags. We had to collect it all in one of the plastic bags, and the one called JoJo put it under the seat at the back and told us we had to throw it in the garbage the next morning.' He pulled his bottom lip into his mouth and closed his eyes. When he opened them, he said, 'She made us promise.'

'And then what did you do?' Griffoni asked.

'We went out ... into the *laguna*.'

'Where in the *laguna*?' Brunetti asked, not that it made much difference.

'We were heading towards Sant'Erasmo.'

'That's quite a distance,' Brunetti remarked. 'At night.'

'I know, I know. That's what I told Marcello, but he said we were already on the way, and he was going to swing around the island and go back that way.' Duso shrugged, saying, 'I don't know why.

'I told him to hurry up. It was cold and it was after two, but Marcello's really happy only when he's on a boat, like he's got salt water in his blood: there's nothing he likes more. So we went along, and the girls were cold and I was, too, but he was Captain Marcello, and he wouldn't turn back.' He stopped speaking.

'What happened then?' Brunetti asked.

Duso looked across at Brunetti, nodded, understanding that it was time, and continued. 'They were both standing, jumping up and down to keep warm. They already had our sweaters over their shoulders, but both were cold.'

It seemed to Brunetti that Duso wanted to keep talking so as to delay telling them what had happened, but then it came. 'There was a sound, almost like an explosion, and the boat stopped. Water came over the prow and the sides and soaked us. The boat just stopped, the way you can walk into a wall when there's *caigo*.' He was Venetian, after all, so he'd use the Venetian word for the densest fog.

'The girls fell forward. I was right next to them, but I fell off my seat into the boat, so there was no way I could stop them. One of them fell against the side of the boat and hit her head, and the other one fell down into the bottom, half on me, but she still banged against the side. I think she broke something: her wrist or her arm.'

'What did you do?'

'For a while I just lay there. I hit my head enough to make me stupid for a minute. Then they both started screaming, and I heard Marcello going "Uh, uh. Uh," like someone had hit him.'

He looked across at the two of them and said, 'I didn't know what to do. I didn't know where we were or if the boat was going to sink.' He closed his eyes. 'I keep remembering how dark it was. I could see lights, far away, maybe on Sant'Erasmo.' His breathing had quickened, and he said, 'It's so dark out there. And everything's so far away.'

Neither Griffoni nor Brunetti spoke: they sat and waited for Duso to calm himself.

'I asked the girls if they were all right.' He gave a small laugh entirely absent of humour and added, 'I guess what I really wanted to know was if they were still alive.' He tried to laugh, but it came out more choke than laugh.

'They were moaning. I got them to lie down beside one another, and I put the sweaters over them. And then I went back and asked Marcello what was wrong. He said he'd fallen against the side of the seat in front of him, and it hurt. I told him we had to get to the hospital: for him and for the girls.' Hearing his voice begin to slip from his control, Duso took deep breaths and closed his eyes until he seemed to quieten down again.

'But what did you hit?' Griffoni asked.

'A *briccola*. Lots of them have come loose because the tides are stronger, and they're floating around in the *laguna*. They're *big*, and people keep running into them.'

Before Duso lost himself in explaining the dangers to navigation in the *laguna*, Brunetti asked, 'Then what happened?'

'Marcello said we had to go back, no matter how. I didn't know where we were or how to navigate, but he did.'

'And then?' Brunetti asked.

'The girls were lying in the bottom of the boat, just sort of whimpering, and I was sitting next to Marcello with my arm around him, trying to keep him warm. The motor was still working, and he said we'd take the girls back, and that I had to help.'

'What did that mean?'

'He said we had to take the girls to Pronto Soccorso.'

'How long did it take you to get to the hospital?' Brunetti asked.

'I don't know, maybe half an hour. I wasn't thinking clearly any more, but it seemed it took us a lot longer than it took us to get out to Sant'Erasmo.'

'And when you got there?'

'Marcello said he could get up on the dock and hold the mooring line, but I had to lift the girls up and put them there. He said it hurt too much for him to do it.'

'Is that what you did?'

Duso nodded a few times. 'He pulled the boat up to the dock and stopped, then he climbed up – I had to give him a push from behind so he could get up the ladder. Then I gave him the mooring rope.'

'Did you manage to move them?' Griffoni asked.

'Yes. I picked them up one by one – they were small, both of them – and put them on the dock. They didn't say anything. I thought maybe they'd – you know – fainted or something.' Brunetti recalled the video: Duso had been visible, and it seemed that he'd had little trouble lifting the girls to the height of the dock and pushing them across the wooden boards. In the video, they hadn't moved; Brunetti remembered seeing no sweaters.

'And Marcello?'

'He stayed up there while I moved them. I told him to push the alarm by the door, but he stood there like he was paralysed; couldn't even talk. So I went up on to the dock and pushed the alarm by the door, to let them know inside that there was trouble.' He paused here and looked at Brunetti and then at Griffoni. 'He stood there with a hand in the air, like he didn't want me to do it, but he didn't say anything.' He paused for a moment, as if he expected a question, but when neither of them asked, Duso said, 'So I went down the ladder, and after a minute, Marcello came down, too. And we left.'

'I see,' Brunetti said.

When he looked over at Duso, the young man was wide-eyed, staring at the wall behind Brunetti's head. He opened his mouth to speak, stopped, opened it again, and finally said, 'I saw her face when I set her down.'

9

'Where did you go after that?' Griffoni broke the silence to ask.

Duso turned his head and glanced at her before looking down at the table in front of him. He said nothing.

Brunetti watched the young man's face, saw his lips contract and relax and his eyes blink. He appeared distracted, his attention pulled away from the room where they sat.

Brunetti and Griffoni exchanged a glance but remained silent for some time, until Griffoni asked, 'Could you tell us where you went next, Signor Duso?'

'Oh, sorry,' Duso said. 'Could you repeat the question, Dottoressa?'

'Where did you go then? After you put the young women on the dock of the hospital.' She gave him a small encouraging nod but did not smile.

Duso blinked again a few times, as though he'd had to come back from reverie and needed a moment to clear his head. Finally he said, 'Marcello started down towards the Arsenale, going fast. He kept saying he had to get the boat back.' Hearing this,

Brunetti wondered what damage the boat had suffered but did not think this the time to ask Duso.

The young man continued. 'We put our sweaters back on. They were soaked, but they kept out the wind. I sat next to him: I still wanted to try to keep him warm. But I kept falling asleep.'

'Where did you go?'

'Towards the Arsenale, but then he turned in somewhere, and we went past the Church of the Greci and were in the Bacino, and then he really speeded up. The next thing I remember is pulling up in front of his uncle's boathouse.'

'On the Giudecca?' Brunetti asked.

'Yes.'

Brunetti didn't ask any more about that; he could find out later where it was. 'What did you do?'

'Marcello said we had to moor the boat and cover it after we cleaned it,' Duso explained, then added, 'Marcello had stiffened up all over, so I had to clean it.'

Hearing the mounting irritation in his voice, there for the first time, Griffoni asked, 'What time would it have been, Signor Duso, when he asked you to cover the boat?'

'Around four, I guess,' Duso said after a pause to consider.

'Thank you,' Brunetti answered, then asked, 'Could you tell me what you did then?'

'I went to Palanca and waited for the vaporetto, only I fell asleep in the *embarcadero*. The *marinaio* had to wake me up when the boat came.'

Brunetti imagined this was hardly the first time that a crew working the night shift had had to wake someone sleeping on the benches inside an *embarcadero*. He nodded and asked, 'Did you go home?'

'Yes. Of course,' Duso said, then added, with a touch of self-pity, 'There was nowhere else to go.'

'And the next day?' Griffoni asked.

'I slept until noon and went down to Nico's for a coffee and a brioche.'

Brunetti resisted the impulse to observe that this explanation managed to leave a good deal of the day unexplained. 'And what else?'

'I went home again and back to bed.'

'Until?' Brunetti asked.

'Until about eight that night.'

'What did you do then?' Griffoni asked.

'I went out into the kitchen and ate the leftovers my mother had sent back with me on Saturday.'

'And then?' she inquired.

'I went back to bed.'

Knowing that the records of his phone calls could be easily found, Brunetti inquired, 'Did you speak to Signor Vio?'

Duso's face registered the sound of his friend's name. 'No.'

'He didn't call?'

Duso placed his hands palms up on the table and read the runes in them. The message must have told him that there was no danger in revealing the truth here. 'He called three or four times, but I didn't answer.' He closed his eyes and sat silent.

Brunetti recalled a remark attributed to Stalin: 'No man, no problem.' Said like that, it sounded bleak and merciless, but daily life allowed for many substitutions: 'no contact', 'no email', 'no phone call'. Fading memory, our ever-willing helper, would take care of all of the details, and the problem would dissolve.

'Why is that, Signor Duso?' Griffoni asked.

Duso opened his eyes and looked at her. 'I didn't want to know anything.'

'Did you call the hospital?' she asked.

He went silent on them again, but neither Griffoni nor Brunetti extended the possibility of a different question: they sat equally silent, determined to wait him out for an answer. Finally he said, 'No, I didn't.'

He stopped speaking, but, again, they waited him out.

'On Monday, I went to work,' Duso finally said. 'Someone had the *Gazzettino*, and I read the story. All it said was that the girls had been left at the hospital in the night and were being treated there, and that one of them was being sent to Mestre for surgery.'

'Was that enough for you?' Griffoni asked blandly.

'Yes. If they were in the hospital, then they were safe.'

Brunetti quelled the impulse to question Duso's certainty that the young women would be safe in the hospital. Instead, he asked, 'Has Vio tried to call you again?'

'Yes. He called to say he saw the article.'

'That's all?' Brunetti asked.

'No. We talked about it, and then he said he thought he hurt himself when he fell in the boat.'

Brunetti decided to return to the reality in this room and said, 'Avvocato Duso, I'm afraid you've forgotten that there are legal consequences to be considered.' He gave the young man time to answer, but Duso chose to remain silent.

'As I said before,' Brunetti continued. 'There is the failure to report an accident at sea in which passengers were injured,' he began, 'but more importantly, there is the failure to provide assistance to those persons. That is a crime both on land and at sea.'

'But we did provide assistance,' Duso said. 'We took them to Pronto Soccorso.'

'Another way to describe what you did would be to say you abandoned them on the dock, Signor Duso,' Griffoni remarked.

The young man's face flushed with anger, or fear, that he failed to suppress. 'That's not true. Not true at all. I rang the alarm bell beside the door.'

'Did your friend see you do it?' Griffoni asked.

After a moment's hesitation, Duso said, 'I don't know. He should have, but I don't know for sure.' Then, seeing how hard her face remained, he asked, 'You don't think I'd leave them there without ringing the alarm bell, do you?'

Griffoni sat back in her seat and folded her hands in her lap. She looked at her upright thumbs and tapped them together a few times before finally saying, 'I'm afraid I have no choice but to believe exactly that, Signore.'

'What?'

'That you'd leave them there without ringing the alarm bell.'

'I don't understand,' he said, voice rising towards the end of the sentence.

'There is no alarm bell at that entrance, Signor Duso. There was, once, until about six months ago, when it was removed.'

All Duso could do was repeat, 'I don't understand.'

'They had too many false alarms, Signor Duso. Especially during the summer. Boats pulled up, usually late at night, someone jumped on the dock and punched the alarm, then got back in the boat, and off they went, and by the time someone got to the door, they were long gone.'

She waited to watch Duso grasp the meaning, and then the consequences, of what she had said, and before he could ask, she went on. 'I was there yesterday. There is no alarm button. They were found by chance, by someone going out to have a cigarette.'

Both of them could see that Duso was stunned by this. Griffoni continued, 'They took me out on the dock to show me where it used to be.'

Duso looked confused more than frightened. 'But I pushed it.'

Brunetti turned to look at Griffoni and saw her thumbs separate as she pulled her hands apart and placed them on the desk. He'd seen the video and tried to summon up the image it had shown. It was taken from above the doors, and thus it looked away from the building and from the alarm.

Griffoni pressed her hands on the table and turned towards Brunetti. He anticipated her movement and said, speaking more loudly than was his wont, 'Claudia, could I have a moment with you?'

He got to his feet, making sure his chair made a lot of noise scraping on the floor and being banged into place.

Griffoni stood, as quietly as he had been loud, and walked to the door. Duso was caught up in his own thoughts.

In the corridor, Brunetti said, 'Tell me.'

She looked across at him, shaking her head in obvious confusion. 'I was in a hurry, Guido. I'm sure there was a sign, but I don't remember seeing a button.'

He considered this for some time and asked her, 'Do you have the number for Pronto Soccorso?'

She pulled out her phone and found the number. After she punched it in, he said, 'Ask whoever answers to go out on the dock and take a photo and send it to you.'

She smiled and nodded. When the phone was answered, she announced her rank and name and said she had a request in relation to the two young women who had been left on the dock during the weekend. All obstacles fell at the mention of the victims, and the photo arrived on Griffoni's phone within three minutes.

'Pronto Soccorso' was printed in red on a white plastic plaque attached to the wall to the right of the automatic doors: a red circle below the words had been X'd out by two pieces of black electrical tape; traces of the red could be seen in the interstices where the two pieces of tape crossed.

She showed the photo to Brunetti, who tilted his head and narrowed his eyes. 'It could be,' he said. 'Night time, confusion, fear.'

Griffoni looked more closely at the photo. 'It's anyone's guess.' She let some seconds pass and then admitted, 'If I saw it, I'd probably try to push it.'

'There's still not reporting an accident,' Brunetti said, but he said it lamely, knowing how hard it would be to bring this to court. How long would it have taken an ambulance to get to them and take the young women to the hospital?

'Shall we go back?' Griffoni asked.

A thought came floating by, and Brunetti ignored Griffoni's question. He stood in front of the door to the interrogation room, trying to remember something one of the two men had said or suggested. Or perhaps it was more a sense of their reaction to the accident. Vio did not speed to the hospital, although the girl had said he'd been eager to speed before the accident, and the police had fined him countless times for speeding.

What had changed with the accident? The boat must have been damaged to some degree, but if Vio managed to get it back to the Giudecca, it could not have been serious. He would surely be accountable to his uncle for that, but he had not hesitated to take the boat back to his uncle's mooring place and tie it up there.

'Guido?' he heard Griffoni say.

'Yes?' he asked.

'Let's get back in.'

He opened the door and stood back to let her enter. They found Duso where and pretty much as they'd left him. He still looked stunned, as though he'd been hit by something heavy he had not noticed coming at him.

'You can go now, Signor Duso,' Brunetti said, not explaining their absence nor what might have happened to allow him to make this decision.

Griffoni took over here and said, 'Abandoning an injured person, as you are certainly aware, is a serious crime, Signor Duso. Therefore, you are obliged to inform us if you have any intention of leaving the city.' She let that sink in and then added, 'For whatever reason.'

As if drugged, the young man got to his feet, nodded vaguely to them both, and left the room.

'What did you think?' Brunetti asked when they were back in his office.

'I think he was honestly surprised when I told him the alarm wasn't there any more.' Griffoni was sitting in one of the chairs in front of his desk, legs stretched in front of her. She pushed the chair back on its legs and latched her hands behind her head. She closed her eyes and after a moment said, 'The light was dim. They were both still shocked by what had happened. Perhaps by what they were doing. So, yes, he could have mistaken it for the alarm.'

'You believe him, then?' Brunetti asked.

She released her hands and let the chair settle to the floor very softly. 'I think it's possible,' was all she was willing to say.

They sat in easy silence for some time until Griffoni said, 'I suspect Duso's spent the last few days looking at the statutes regarding failure to offer help to victims of an accident.' She smiled and added, 'He's probably also taken a look at nautical law.'

She let Brunetti consider this and then continued. 'They didn't intend any harm and they got them to the hospital as fast as they could. That certainly ...'

After a moment, she continued in a louder voice, 'But did Vio actually think he could get away with this? Just drop them off at the hospital and go home, and no one would wonder who took them there or what had happened to them?' She looked over at Brunetti and asked, 'Do you think he could be that stupid?'

Rather than spend time in a discussion of Vio's intelligence, Brunetti and Griffoni remained in his office to mull over the young man's behaviour. 'Why didn't he go to Pronto Soccorso himself?' Brunetti asked. 'He knew he'd been hurt.'

'Adrenaline,' she said aloud, then, 'They were both pumped full of it.'

'In which case,' Brunetti said in an explanatory voice, 'he would have gone back to the hospital when it wore off. But he didn't.' Then, speculating, he added, 'He was afraid of something, I'd say.'

They must have given up at the same time. Griffoni asked, 'Now what?' just as Brunetti said, 'I don't understand it.' Both lapsed into silence.

Finally Brunetti said, 'I think I'll go over to the Giudecca tomorrow and see what I can find out about the transport business.'

'Would you like me to come along?' she asked.

For a moment, Brunetti was tempted, but then he thought of what it would be like for him to show up to ask questions of Giudecchini in the company of an attractive, tall, blonde whose every statement was a declaration that she was not Venetian. 'I'd rather go over there by myself,' he finally answered.

'So you can question them more easily in that sneaky, underhand way you sly Venetians use against one another?' she asked.

'Something like that,' he answered with a bland smile. 'I'd like them not to be distracted.' He left it to Griffoni to believe he was talking about her inability to speak Veneziano and not her appearance.

This time, she stood and kicked her feet out in front of her to free them after sitting for so long.

As though to show there were no hurt feelings on her part, Griffoni said, 'Besides, if I were to go, I'd have to take my passport.'

'I think people on the Giudecca are more accustomed to looking at police warrant cards, Claudia,' Brunetti said and, since the day had been long enough, added that it was time for her to go home.

She did not protest.

When she was gone, Brunetti checked into his computer and sure enough, there it was, Borgato Trasporti, Giudecca 255, offering water transport and shipping for the entire *laguna*, to the islands, the mainland, to Jesolo and Cavallino. Free estimates. In business since 2010, Pietro Borgato, owner. He checked the address and found that it was along Rio del Ponte Longo, put his phone in his pocket, and started for home.

On the way, Brunetti made a list, a short one, of people who might be able to give him information about the business or the man who ran it. The first person he called was a lieutenant at the police station near Sant'Eufemia, who told him he knew Pietro Borgato and didn't much like him. No, he'd never given the police any trouble, had never done anything that would get him arrested, but years ago he'd called the police to say that a neighbour's dog had bit him, and he wanted the dog put down. It was, he explained to Brunetti, one of those cases that left an impression, though he didn't specify which kind. Brunetti thanked him and restrained his curiosity about the fate of the dog.

Next he called an old classmate of his who worked in the Human Resources section of Veritas, the company responsible for the garbage collection in the city and, after an exchange of information about their children, said he wanted to ask a favour of the *spazzini*.

'*Gli spazzini?*' repeated his friend. 'Why in God's name do you want to talk to the garbage men?'

'Not to all of them, Vittore, just to whoever's in charge of Giudecca 255.'

'All right,' his friend answered after only a moment's hesitation and told Brunetti to hold the line while he took a look. A minute later he was back: 'Valerio Cesco, 378 446 3967,' he said. 'That enough?'

'Perfect,' Brunetti answered, wrote down the number, and gave profuse thanks.

As soon as the call ended, he dialled the number. The phone was answered on the second ring: 'Cesco.'

'Signor Cesco,' Brunetti said, almost choking on the thickness of the Veneziano he forced himself to speak. 'This is Commissario Guido Brunetti.'

'Police Commissario?' Cesco asked.

'Sì,' Brunetti answered. He waited for Cesco to say something, and when he did not, went on. 'I'd like to ask you about one of the people on your route.'

'Who?'

'Pietro Borgato.'

Brunetti listened to silence for what seemed to him a long time before Cesco asked, 'Why do you want to know about him?'

'He's come to our attention,' Brunetti answered.

'Ah,' Cesco said quietly. 'He has a transport business.'

'Yes. I know that.'

'Lots of boats and lots of coming and going.'

'Well, I'm happy to learn he has enough work,' Brunetti answered in a friendly voice.

'Yes. He does,' Cesco said flatly.

'Can you tell me anything about his transport business?' Brunetti asked.

Cesco made a noise; half sigh, half snort. Then he said, 'Not on the phone, I won't.'

'Sensible man,' Brunetti answered. 'Could we meet somewhere?'

'I usually take the 6:52 from Zattere to Palanca, but if you like, I can meet you at the *embarcadero* at 6:40 and take the earlier boat.'

Making his voice as friendly as he could manage, Brunetti said, 'I suppose you're talking about tomorrow morning?'

'*Sì*, Signore.' When Brunetti was slow in answering, Cesco said, 'Just be glad it's not January.'

Brunetti could not stop himself from laughing and agreed he'd see him there. He hung up the phone and said aloud, 'What have I done?'

10

That evening's dinner did a great deal to relieve Brunetti of the thought of next morning's ordeal, even allowed him to laugh at himself for asking that question for nothing more arduous than getting up early.

Paola had decided to roast a chicken after filling it with a combination of quinoa, rosemary, and thyme. She explained to them that she'd stolen the herbs from the garden of a colleague who had invited her to pick up a book after class.

'Stolen'?' Chiara inquired.

Paola glanced across at her daughter. 'The plants were sitting there, overgrown, neglected, dry – one might even say abandoned – so all I did was trim them. It was an act of liberation.'

'You didn't ask her?' Chiara insisted.

'I didn't notice them until I was leaving,' Paola said in a less patient voice.

Chiara, who took a dim view of the eating of meat, took an even dimmer view, it seemed, of the justification of crime.

'If she'd stopped wearing a bracelet, and you liked it, would you feel the same about "liberating" that?'

Raffi, who had been following the conversation, smiled, then returned his attention to his chicken leg before his mother could see his expression.

Instead of answering her daughter, Paola turned to Brunetti and said, 'You're the one familiar with logic and the rules for making a syllogism, aren't you?'

'I suppose so,' Brunetti admitted, forking up another piece of chicken.

'So what would you call what Chiara's just said?'

Brunetti finished his chicken and took a sip of wine. He set the glass down and, in a very serious way, declared, looking at his daughter, 'I'm afraid you've fallen into your old habit of using the *argumentum ad absurdum*. The two actions are somewhat similar, but they are not the same, however mind-catching the comparison might be at first hearing.'

He emptied his glass and poured it half-full again, adding, 'So it's just a rhetorical trick.' Before she could say anything in her own defence, Brunetti smiled at her and added, 'Very clever, I must say, and likely to be effective.'

'That's what I thought,' Paola said. 'But I also thought it would be more forceful if it came from you.'

'Because I'm the king of logic?'

'Something like that,' Paola conceded.

Chiara, whose fork was poised over the round zucchini her mother had filled for her with the same stuffing she'd used for the chicken, said, 'Lots of people use it, making it sound like two things are alike, when they really aren't.'

Raffi chimed in here to say, 'Politicians do it all the time.'

'I don't know why people even bother to talk about politics,' Chiara observed.

'Excuse me?' This from Paola.

'You heard me, Mamma. Why bother? People talk about politics, the government changes, people talk some more, there's another election, and after it, the people and the politicians are still repeating the same things, and nothing changes.'

'That, my angel,' Paola broke in to observe, 'is much the same thing I thought when I was your age.' Before Chiara could protest, Paola added, 'And still think now.'

Brunetti suddenly realized how much he longed for them to stop or the subject to change. If he could just tabulate all the hours he'd spent talking about politics and politicians during his life and could pack them together like a snowball and somehow add them to his life, how much longer would he live? Even more interesting, how else might he have used that time? He could have learned another language; to knit and have made sweaters or long, uneven scarves for everyone. What colour Judo belt would he be entitled to wear by now?

'Guido? Guido?'

He looked across the table at Paola and asked, smiling at her, 'Yes, my love?'

She cast up her eyes, though not her hands, which held a large bowl. 'I asked if you'd like some persimmons and cream.' She set the bowl on the table next to another one that rippled with a sea of cream. She put two large spoonfuls of whipped persimmons into a smaller bowl and slid the cream in front of Brunetti.

'You trust me with this?' he asked in exaggerated concern.

'No, I don't, but I've never known you to let the children go hungry.' She spooned more of the slippery mush of persimmons into two of the remaining bowls and passed one to each of the children.

Brunetti had flattened the surface of his persimmons with the back of his spoon and dropped four or five spoonfuls of whipped cream on top of it. To him, it looked like an orange sea with thick clouds floating on the surface.

He scooped up more persimmons, held the spoon above his bowl and let some of the orange mush dribble on the clouds.

'Guido,' Paola said in her schoolmistress voice, 'if you insist on playing with your food, you can go to your room.'

'May I take the bowl with me, m'am?'

Paola closed her eyes, shifted her bowl forward on the table, and laid her forehead down where it had been. 'He's going to drive me mad, and then, when I'm locked in the attic, he will have to take care of the children.'

Much as he would have enjoyed hearing the rest of her scenario, Brunetti – who thought it would appear heartless to continue eating while she described her tragic future – said in an entirely normal voice, 'This is really wonderful, Paola. I like it that you always put a little bit of sugar in the cream.'

Paola sat up, thanked him for the compliment, and continued eating her dessert. The children had long since finished and were sitting, as quiet as baby chicks, their empty bowls held in their outstretched hands, making soft plaintive noises.

Brunetti woke in the middle of the night, pulling himself free from a dream in which he was behind the wheel of a car, driving at high speed. Just as the car approached a curve in the tree-lined road, he reached to the seat beside him and pulled up a bottle of gin, a drink he loathed. As he put the bottle to his lips, he gave himself a great shake and opened his eyes: the car, the road, the gin were gone, leaving behind an explanation of why Vio had gone so slowly on the way to the hospital.

If he had been stopped by the police, with the injured young women in the boat and the damage of the accident still to be seen, the police would have tested him and Duso for alcohol and drugs and if he tested positive, he'd lose his licence and perhaps be convicted of a crime. Once the girls were in the hospital, however, there was no longer any evidence that he had been involved in an accident, and so he risked far less.

With that realization, he returned to sleep until the alarm woke him at 6:15.

When Brunetti arrived at the *embarcadero* at the Zattere, there were seven people already inside. He excluded the three women and the priest and was left to choose among a man wearing well-ironed jeans, white leather tennis shoes and a brown suede bomber jacket, a white-haired man in a business suit, and a man in his thirties wearing fashionably torn jeans, similar white tennis shoes, and a short blue double-breasted jacket with a decidedly nautical look.

Approaching the man in the bomber jacket, he inquired, 'Signor Cesco?'

The man looked at him, surprised, while the man in the blue jacket said, 'That's me, Signor Brunetti.' He stepped closer to Brunetti, shook hands, and pulled a packet of cigarettes from his pocket. 'Let's go outside while I smoke this,' he said quite amiably. His skin was weathered, as was often the case with men who work outdoors, and his dark hair was cut short, a flash of white just above both ears. His face was lightly scarred by the acne of his adolescence, his eyes attentive, his mouth broad and turned up in a grin.

'I suppose that means I don't look like a *spazzino*,' he said. Once they were back on the wooden platform in front of the covered landing, he lit his cigarette and breathed in welcome smoke. 'Should I take that as a compliment?' he asked.

Brunetti shrugged. 'My father worked loading and unloading boats at the port,' he said with an easy grin although in a less exaggerated Veneziano. 'So it doesn't occur to me that there's any need to disguise being a *spazzino*.'

'Tell that to my classmates,' Cesco said, this time without a smile.

'Classmates where?' Brunetti asked, his curiosity real.

'Ca' Foscari. I graduated six years ago with a degree in architecture.'

Brunetti nodded but said nothing.

'Like you, I didn't have a father who could give me a job in his office or even ask a friend to do it.' He puffed on his cigarette for some time, looking in the direction of San Basilio, whence the boat would come. He took a final deep pull on his cigarette and walked to the garbage cans at the entrance to the landing, rubbed it out, and dropped it in.

When he was again next to Brunetti, he said, tilting his head back towards the garbage can, 'Less work for my colleagues on this side.'

Brunetti nodded, then asked, 'What about Pietro Borgato?'

Cesco braced his hands on the railing and said, 'Are you allowed to tell me why you're interested in him?' His attention was suddenly distracted by the arrival of a boat from the right. It touched the landing gently and stopped.

Brunetti moved towards it and got on board; Cesco and most of the people waiting at the *embarcadero* followed. The sailor slid the railing into place. Most people remained on deck during the swift crossing, but the two men did not speak. They got out on the other side and walked out to the *riva* in front of the *embarcadero*. Finally, Brunetti answered Cesco's question, 'No, I can't tell you.'

'I didn't think you could,' Cesco said, 'but it's nice to know you guys are interested in him.'

Brunetti made an inquisitive noise.

Cesco pushed himself away from the railing and turned around to lean against it, hands propped on the iron bars.

'Because he's gone up in the world.' He grinned, then added, 'And because I don't like him.'

'Why's that?' Brunetti asked.

Cesco considered this for a moment, then answered, 'Because he gives me orders. Tells me how to do my job.'

Smiling, Brunetti asked, 'Could you perhaps be more specific?'

Cesco laughed and turned around to do a few semi-push-ups against the bar while considering his answer. Finally he said, 'Once he came out with his bag of garbage in his hand while I was sweeping something up – dog shit, I think – and he told me I should wash it with water and dropped the bag on the ground. He could just as easily have put it in my cart, but he dropped it on the pavement.'

'What did you do?'

'I swept up the dog shit and dumped it in my cart, picked up his bag, and walked away.'

'Did he say anything?'

'He called me a shit,' Cesco said. *'Sei uno stronzo.'*

'And you?'

I kept on walking and picked up the bags in front of the next houses.'

'And he?'

'I don't know. I was busy.'

Brunetti decided not to pursue this and asked, 'How do you know he's gone up in the world?' He paused and added, 'If I might ask.'

'Because I'm the garbage man,' Cesco said, his smile back in place. 'My route takes me into a courtyard on the opposite side of the canal from where he has his boats moored. It's where I usually stop to have a cigarette in the morning. Sometimes I leave my cart there and go and have a coffee, then come back and have another cigarette.' Brunetti began to wonder if he'd fallen into the hands of a fantasist, who was going to report that Pietro Borgato was one of the people who dumped garbage into the canal and tell Brunetti to go and arrest him. Giving no sign of this, he nodded to Cesco to continue.

'A couple of months ago, when I went into Campiello Ferrando opposite his place, I noticed two boats, Cabinati, with closed cabins, moored at the entrance to his place. Big things, they looked new but not brand new, if you know what I mean.'

Brunetti nodded.

'They were different from the boats he already had, more like taxis, but bigger,' Cesco said. 'Then two guys came out of the warehouse with an engine: at least 250 horsepower, maybe even more.' Because they were speaking in Veneziano, the garbage man took it for granted that Brunetti would understand the power – one might even say the majesty – of an engine this size, far bigger than necessary to transport even the heaviest cargo.

Brunetti did and exclaimed, '*Madonna Santissima*' as an expression of his surprise. Then he asked, 'What did you do?'

'I parked my cart in the usual place, made some noise putting my broom inside, lit a cigarette, and stepped behind the cart. It's what I've done there six times a week for the last four years.'

'So you were invisible?' Brunetti interrupted to show that he was following the story and had an idea of where it was heading.

Cesco smiled and said, 'Exactly. I stood there, smoking my cigarette, and watched them. They went back into his warehouse and brought out another motor. Same size.' He paused and, as if programmed by the script, Brunetti knew the surprise was coming, just now. He decided to give a prompt and asked, 'What did they do then?'

Cesco could not help smiling. 'They started installing the first motor. Borgato was there and drove them like they were mules.

Swearing at them, correcting them, cursing their mothers, telling them they had to get them installed fast.'

He looked at Brunetti, who said nothing, but nodded, leaving it to Cesco to move on to the climax.

'I looked at my watch, and I'd been there ten minutes, so I stepped around the cart, tossed my cigarette into the bottom, and grabbed my broom. I swept a little in the courtyard: it's what I do every day. Then I stuck my broom back in the cart and left.'

'Did they notice you?'

'As you mentioned,' Cesco said with a broad smile, 'I'm invisible. I finished my route: it took about three hours, and I took my cart back to the *magazzino* where we leave them and parked it there.'

'And then?' Brunetti asked, as he suspected Cesco wanted him to.

'I went back to the courtyard.'

'And?' Brunetti asked.

'Both boats were gone.' He paused, reached towards the pocket where he kept his cigarettes, but pulled his hand back and said, 'Since then, I've seen the boats a number of times, so he's using them. But they come in early in the morning.'

Brunetti watched Cesco trying to decide whether to say something else, so he made himself look as much like an oak tree as possible: patient, motionless, secure.

Cesco gave in to temptation, pulled out his cigarettes and lit one, then turned to Brunetti and said, 'Once, when I pulled the cart in there – it was raining – one of the big boats was on the other side. He and his nephew – what's his name? Marcello? – were scrambling around in it, with a hose, washing it down. The nephew was kneeling, using rags to wipe up the water and wringing it out over the side. Borgato kept telling him to hurry up.'

94

He paused for some time, occasionally puffing at his cigarette. Brunetti did not stir.

'Borgato went back into the warehouse and came out with one of those black plastic garbage bags and started picking up stuff from the bottom of the boat and shoving it into the bag.'

'Could you see what it was?' Brunetti asked.

'A jacket, a couple of shoes, a scarf. I remember that because, even in the rain, I could see how happy looking it was: lots of bright colours.

'Did you see anything else?'

Cesco shook his head, then started to speak again. 'Finally, they got on the boat, and the nephew started the motor, and they backed down the canal, turned around, and left.'

'Do you have any idea where they went?'

'No.' Cesco walked back to the entrance to the *embarcadero* and rubbed out his cigarette before tossing it into the garbage container. As he walked back towards Brunetti, his smile broke out again, and he said, 'Professional habit.' He paused a step from Brunetti and said, 'I've never seen either of the boats there again.' He pushed up the sleeve of his jacket and checked the time. 'I've got to go,' he said.

Cesco stepped back from the railing and turned away from the water. He offered his hand to Brunetti, who shook it gladly.

'Thanks for your help,' Brunetti said.

Cesco stuck his hand into his pocket. 'Glad to do it,' he said. He turned from Brunetti and started down the *riva*, a man on his way to work.

When Cesco had been gone a few minutes, Brunetti went into Palanca and had a coffee, a brioche, and another coffee. Leaving the bar, he walked down to Ponte Piccolo and crossed it, right at the first *calle* and down to Campiello Ferrando, which ended in a canal. He turned right, and in three steps was in a courtyard, a garden on his right. A warehouse stood on the other side of the canal, two large boats moored in front of it: he assumed it to be Borgato's warehouse.

He went back to the *riva* and stood for some time, watching the sunlight bring the day back to life. He glanced at his watch, surprised that it was not yet eight. He went down to the Redentore stop to wait for the Number Two.

11

Brunetti was in no hurry to get to work and decided to walk from Valaresso and observe, at this time of the morning, the absence of people in the Piazza. So it proved to be, with so few people he could have counted them had he chosen to. He ambled, delighting in the sight of the flags swirling about in the breeze, and the horses poised, front legs lifted delicately, gazing down the Piazza, as if pausing to decide which way to go. How wonderful they were, even if only copies, how bold and excessive, like so much within his line of sight.

He looked around the Piazza again, still only spotted with people, and thought of his mother's often-repeated warning that he should never make a wish, for fear it would be granted. For years we Venetians had wished the tourists to disappear and give us back our city. Well, we'd had our wish, and look at us now.

He cast off this thought, paused after passing the bell tower, and turned to sweep a panoramic look from left to right. Could a normal person see this and not be affected? Finding no answer, and not much liking rhetorical questions, anyway, Brunetti shrugged and continued on his way to work.

He stopped in Signorina Elettra's office first, but she wasn't there. He turned to leave but saw Vice-Questore Giuseppe Patta standing in the doorway of his office, watching him. Brunetti's first reaction was relief that he was standing well over a metre from her desk and facing it, not close to it and appearing to examine the papers on it.

'Good morning, Vice-Questore,' he said. 'I was hoping to see Signorina Elettra.'

'Why?' Patta surprised him by asking: it was not usual for the Vice-Questore to demonstrate interest in police matters unless they somehow called his authority into question or necessitated his making a decision.

'I asked Signorina Elettra to get some information for me, Dottore,' Brunetti answered, making light of the matter by being as vague as possible.

'About what?' Patta inquired quietly enough for Brunetti to suspect a trap of some kind.

'She said her father knows a very good watchmaker on the Giudecca. I've got an old Omega my great-uncle …'

'Giudecca?' Patta interrupted, then asked, 'Don't they have a bad reputation?'

Brunetti smiled and did his best to give an easy little laugh. 'I think that's a bit of folklore, Dottore. Left over from my parents' generation.'

'You're not trying to protect them, are you, Brunetti?'

Instead of asking – as one would when speaking to someone who knew nothing about Venice – what the Giudecchini needed to be protected from, Brunetti repeated his mini-laugh and said, 'Of course not, Vice-Questore.' That seemed to satisfy Patta, who turned back into his office and closed the door.

Next he tried Vianello. He went down the hall on the first floor and into the office where the Ispettore worked and saw him in the far corner, speaking with two other officers, all three of them in uniform. When he noticed Brunetti, Vianello held up a hand to signal that he would be with him quickly. Seeing a copy of that day's *Gazzettino* on Vianello's desk, Brunetti went over to Vianello's chair and began to page through the newspaper. Attention was paid to the arrest of two politicians in Lombardy for the buying of votes; while another article reported the arrest of 138 people in a maxi-round-up of Mafia collaborators: politicians, businessmen, and lawyers, as well as one banker, all involved in a ring of loan-sharking and the sale of government contracts for road-building and maintenance. The article used two of the by-now-familiar photos of the latest autostrada bridge to collapse as well as close-ups of flaking cement pylons that, with steel support rods poking out on all sides, did not encourage a sense of security in anyone who chose to drive on an autostrada with bridges suspended on these pylons.

He slid the paper aside as useless and found, under it, *La Repubblica*, which he opened to the Culture section, having read more than enough about the state of the country. And what did his wondering eyes behold but a review of a new translation of the *Annals* of Tacitus? He had read them as a student, seeking help from what he'd thought even then a very unexciting translation, and had sensed that genius lurked behind the Latin he struggled through and the translation he plodded through.

Aware of motion beside him, Brunetti turned away from the paper and saw Vianello.

'*Il Gazzettino* not good enough for you?' Vianello asked, nodding with his chin at the newspaper Brunetti had moved aside.

'It's not good enough for anybody, I suspect,' Brunetti answered.

'Then why do you read it every day?'

'*Vox pop,*' Brunetti countered. 'I think it really is the voice of the people here: their concerns, their preferences, their crimes.'

He looked at Vianello, who seemed unpersuaded by his defence of the newspaper.

'Besides, they list the names of the pharmacies that are open on Sunday,' Brunetti concluded and covered one newspaper with the other.

Vianello pulled out the chair in front of the desk and sat. 'What is it?'

'I'd like you to listen to something,' Brunetti said.

Vianello, sensitive to the change in Brunetti's voice, shifted his chair closer.

'I was out on the Giudecca this morning,' Brunetti began. 'I had a look at the place where Vio's uncle has his transport business.' Vianello nodded. 'But before that I spoke to the garbage man who's in charge of the streets around it.'

'The garbage man?' Vianello repeated, not without a certain surprise.

'He told me that Borgato's got new boats but doesn't moor them there.' Before Vianello could ask for clarification, Brunetti explained his conversation with Cesco about the motors and their size, excessive for ordinary transport.

It took Vianello only an instant to say, 'If he's not a fisherman with a very big boat, then there's no reason he'd have engines that powerful.' Interested now, Vianello asked, 'Is that all he said?'

Brunetti hesitated before answering. 'That he said directly, yes, but it didn't sound like he had any great fondness for Borgato.'

'Doesn't make him sound like a reliable witness.'

Brunetti shrugged this aside, knowing how few witnesses were reliable. 'He's intelligent and observant, and he saw men fitting the motors – he was certain they were at least 250 horsepower – on to the boats. His feelings for Borgato are irrelevant to what he saw.'

Vianello shifted back in his chair and folded his arms, saying nothing.

'All right, all right, Lorenzo,' Brunetti conceded. 'Big motors on boats that belong to someone who transports cargo in the *laguna*,' he continued, then added, 'and who is rumoured to be involved in some sort of smuggling.'

'It might be that they're simply transporting larger quantities,' Vianello said, then, after a long pause, added in a milder tone, 'All right. I'll ask some people to have a look around.'

'It could also mean that he's going out into the Adriatic to get these larger quantities,' Brunetti conceded.

'Of?' Vianello asked.

'I'm afraid we have to ask the Guardia Costiera for help with this.' A sudden smile flashed across Brunetti's face as he recalled a friend who might be of some use to him in this matter.

Over the years, Brunetti had made many friends: some had remained friends over decades, some had moved through life with him for a time and then diverted on their separate ways, or, truth be told, he had ceased to find them interesting and had allowed attrition to do the work of separation for him. Among his friends were those Paola called, 'Guido's strays,' men and women who, at first consideration, might seem out of place in the lives they had chosen or that they had stumbled into. They were not misfits, for most of them had found the place where they could fit and lived there comfortably and happily: but the world often strived unsuccessfully to understand why they were there.

Brunetti knew from experience how people could be trapped in the wrong place in life from having attended three years of Latin class with Giovanni Borioni, son of the Marchese of some place in Piemonte the name of which Brunetti could never remember. 'Rocca Something', Giovanni had called it to Brunetti some months after they met: this name had replaced the real one. Giovanni had lived in Venice with his mother; she legally separated from il Marchese, who remained in Torino. He had decided that a classical education would be best for his eldest son, and thus the *liceo classico*, and thus the Latin classes, for which Giovanni was perhaps not best suited.

Brunetti had tutored his friend Giovanni for three years, not only in Latin. After this, like il Marchese, Giovanni's absent father, Brunetti had taken great pride in Giovanni's graduation from *liceo*, had stood beside him and embraced him when his name was read out. It hardly mattered that, by the time of the happy event, Giovanni had lost all memory of *'amo, amas, amat'*. After graduation, Giovanni not only left behind his knowledge of Latin grammar but had renounced his father's plans for him and had enrolled in the faculty of agriculture at the University of Modena. Today he was not only the Marchese but a farmer, having turned the family's vast land holdings in Rocca Something into an experiment in biological farming. Brunetti's children had spent weeks in the summer working for Giovanni, returning to Venice tanned and fit and even more respectful of Nature and its boundless worth than they had been before going there.

But this is to digress, for the importance of Brunetti's friendship lay not with Giovanni himself but with his younger brother, Timoteo, a lawyer specializing in nautical law and thus a consultant to the Navy as well as to the Guardia Costiera, those forces charged with the defence of Italy's sea borders and the waters surrounding the country.

Over the years, Brunetti had met Timoteo with some frequency; the lawyer had always been honestly curious about Brunetti's work, insisting that his own was, 'a boredom made of files, folders, and reports'. Brunetti, widely read in Venetian history, was equally curious about nautical law. Because it is but weak human nature to like the people who show interest in one's work, these two men, who met rarely but communicated with some regularity, thought of the other as a good friend.

Thus it was automatic that Brunetti should call Timoteo and ask for an introduction to the person in charge of the Guardia Costiera in Venice, just as it was automatic that Capitano Ignazio Alaimo, the officer in charge of the Capitaneria di Porto, would accept a call from Commissario Guido Brunetti, after being asked to do so by his friend, Timoteo Borioni.

The mills of the gods grind exceeding slow: those of the Italian bureaucracy, however, are capable of great speed, depending upon the impulse to which they respond. In the case of a nautical lawyer who was the brother of a Marchese and himself the good friend of an admiral or two – one of whom was responsible for the added gold bar on the insignia of rank worn by Capitano Alaimo – to ask a favour of that same captain was – not to put too fine a point on it – to give an order. And thus the phone call of Commissario Guido Brunetti was passed to the Captain, who said the Commissario was certainly welcome to visit that very afternoon, if he chose. Tomorrow morning? Nothing easier. Eleven? Perfect.

Paola had once been asked by the department of Italian at Oxford, the university where she had taken her degree, to return as a guest lecturer, free to choose any English text she wanted, so long as parallels could be drawn to Italy. She had agonized over which of Henry James' texts to use, until destiny had caused her to take Maria Edgeworth's novel, *Patronage*, on vacation. Brunetti recalled lying on the beach in Sardinia, trying to read Livy, while Paola insisted upon reading out entire passages dealing with the advancement up the ladder of success made by idiots, villains, and the indolent because of the power and patronage of their parents' friends.

At first Brunetti had feared the book would drive her into a crisis of moral and political denunciation, as vicious sons, idiot cousins, a panoply of breathtakingly incompetent men, were pushed forward by their relatives' positions in the government, the connections of a wife's family, or simple blackmail.

Instead, Paola had spent days reading, forced to pause only by the energy and time it took to exclaim, 'Oh, it's my Uncle Luca.' 'That's just how Luigino got the job.' Or, 'He's like the one who lost his job as ambassador because he had an affair with the wife of the Minister of Agriculture.'

12

These thoughts did not encumber Brunetti the next morning when, accompanied by Griffoni, he was taken to the Capitaneria on a police launch, piloted by Foa, both he and the launch gleaming in the sun.

A uniformed sailor saluted their boat as it arrived and helped Griffoni and Brunetti step up to the dock in front of the bright orange Capitaneria building, which stood on the Zattere, that long, straight promenade that looked across to the Giudecca and was graced by having very few private enterprises in evidence: even the supermarket at the bottom end near San Basilio, large as it was, had only one inconspicuous door and was thus difficult to find. Brunetti told Foa he could go back to the Questura: they would take the vaporetto back.

The sailor in the white jacket slipped around them and hurried across the broad *riva* to the front door and pulled it open then waited for them to enter. He joined them, saying, 'I'll take you to Capitano Alaimo.'

Neither of them had ever been inside and so they were busy looking about them, if only to see how the other half lived. There was no question that the view from the front door was far better: the Questura had a canal and a church, but those things were to be seen from almost every street corner in Venice. Here, instead, anyone leaving the building was treated to a panorama of the entire Giudecca, from the Molino Stucky down to the other end, where some of the more menacing combat and pursuit boats of the Guardia Costiera were moored.

They continued into the *palazzo*, drawn by the glimmering white jacket of the sailor. They ascended a broad marble staircase; the wall they approached as they climbed the first ramp held a vast painting of what must be the battle of Lepanto. Galleons and galeasses, flying either the crescent moon of the Turks or the cross of the Europeans, filled the entire Gulf of Patras, sailing at one another in straight lines, their cannons puffing out tiny white clouds while the Madonna looked on approvingly from above at what was to ensue.

'And we have a black and white photo of the President of the Republic,' Griffoni said.

Brunetti thought it wiser not to comment.

At the top of the stairs, the sailor led them to the second door on the right. He knocked, waited, entered, and stood to attention just inside the door while they both entered the room. Two men in uniform sat at facing desks, busy with their computers. Behind the man on the right a map of the Laguna Nord covered most of the wall. On the left was the Southern part, showing the *laguna* all the way down to Chioggia.

When Brunetti withdrew his attention from the maps, he saw the sailor now standing in front of a door at the far end of the office, Griffoni beside him. He walked over to join them. The sailor looked at Griffoni, then at Brunetti, as if his gaze would suffice to keep them immobile, and leaned forward to knock.

'*Avanti*,' a male voice called from inside.

The sailor opened the door, let them pass in front of him, slapped his heels together and saluted, then closed the door behind him as he left.

A small man, almost a statue of a man in miniature, got to his feet and came around the desk. He walked quickly towards them, took Griffoni's hand and bent to kiss it, then shook Brunetti's, saying, 'Please, please, come over here where we can talk.' Because he was perfectly proportioned and had such self-assurance, Alaimo seemed no less notable than other men. He had very thick, curly dark hair clinging closely to his head. His skin showed how many years he had spent on the decks of ships: lines fanned out from the corners of both eyes, and two vertical lines cut down either side of his mouth. His eyes were pale grey and seemed out of place on his face.

Looking away from the Captain, Brunetti realized how large the office was, big enough for the Captain's desk and, to its right, a four-person divan and three matching chairs separated from it by a low table. In answer to Alaimo's wave, Griffoni chose a seat on the divan, which gave her a view out of the windows; Brunetti took the chair facing her but slightly to her left. Captain Alaimo ignored the other chair facing her and sat on the one at the end of the table, thus placing himself equidistant from the two police officers in a kind of human isosceles triangle. Brunetti noticed that the chair Alaimo chose was lower than his and thus allowed the Captain's feet to touch the floor.

Brunetti glanced around the room and saw a line of gouaches showing scenes from the various eruptions of Vesuvio. One was painted from the perspective of the sea, another from a distant point that must have been to the north. Two showed giant plumes of white smoke and flame rising high above the dome of the volcano, one with a flood of magma burning its way down the slope; another showed three cane-carrying gentlemen standing on a high slope, backs to the viewer, staring off at the flames of the eruption in the distance; the last looked across a calm sea on which white-sailed vessels went about their quiet business while, in the background, a tunnel of white smoke rose up, ten times higher than the volcano itself.

Seeing that his guest was interested in the paintings, Alaimo said, 'An ancestor of mine painted the one in the middle.'

Brunetti got immediately to his feet and, sure enough, found the name, 'Giuseppe Alaimo' painted at the bottom.

'Was he a painter by profession?' Brunetti asked. 'It's very fine work.'

'No,' Alaimo said and laughed a bit. 'He was a doctor.'

'Which eruption was this?' Brunetti asked, still looking closely at the painting. 'Do you know?'

'There's no year on it,' Alaimo said. 'But family legend says it was 1779.'

'One of the bad ones,' Griffoni interrupted, allowing Brunetti to hear, for the first time, her Neapolitan accent, a faint trace of which he had detected in Alaimo's voice.

Alaimo whipped around to look at her. 'What?'

'Not as bad as some of the others in the eighteenth century, and nothing special if you include the entire known history, but still bad.'

'But you're working here,' Alaimo said, as if that fact ruled out what he was hearing.

'But I come from there,' she said, waving her hand at the paintings.

His embarrassment audible, Alaimo said, 'I'm sorry, but I didn't hear your surname.'

'Griffoni,' she offered, 'Claudia Griffoni.'

'*Oddio*,' Alaimo exclaimed, putting his hands to his head, as if he were trying to keep it from exploding or he was going to pull his hair out. 'I should have known. A woman as beautiful as you, Signora, could only be from Napoli.'

108

'The same is true of a man as gallant as you, Capitano,' she gave back, leaving Brunetti to wonder when a boat of the Capitaneria di Porto would be placed at Griffoni's private disposal. He remained calm, apparently rapt in his continued study of the paintings, quite as if the melodrama were not being played out behind him.

There followed a predictable list of subjects: where in Venice can one get decent coffee? Mozzarella? The Captain had it delivered once a week, and if she'd like ... How will they survive another winter here? Did he/she know him/her? His aunt the abbess of the Chiostro di San Gregorio Armeno. Common friends, a favourite pizzeria deep in the heart of the Spagnoli quarter, the fastest way to get to the airport.

After the briefest change of gears, they proceeded, perhaps in deference to Brunetti's presence, to list some pleasant aspects of life in Venice.

Brunetti, because he could not see them as they spoke, was particularly sensitive to their voices, to Griffoni's Neapolitan accent, which grew stronger with every passing sentence. He was surprised to realize that, when she gave in to the linguistic influence of Napolitano, she sounded less bright and, surprisingly, almost shockingly, more vulgar, whining her way through all she missed and culminating in the lack of a good *discoteca*.

In the years that she had worked with him, Brunetti had heard none of this, just as he had never heard that voice. Was this what people meant when they spoke badly of '*I terroni*'? Did people from the South appear cultured and intelligent only when they adapted to Northern standards? But put them back in the soup of Napolitano, and they reverted to type? Or had the presence of a Neapolitan man so affected her hormones as to turn her into little more than a simple-minded flirt?

He decided he'd heard her prattle on enough, turned away from the paintings, and asked, 'Would it be possible for me to interrupt you, *signori*, and return our attention to Venice?'

Alaimo turned, his face failing to disguise a flash of relief, and said, 'Of course, Commissario.'

And Griffoni chimed in with, 'It's so easy to forget when you start talking about home.' She graced Alaimo with a many-toothed smiled and then asked, in a voice that sounded at least a decade younger than the one she had been using, 'Could I trouble you for a glass of water, Capitano?'

Alaimo jumped to his feet, saying, 'How rude of me not to have offered you something to drink.' Turning to Brunetti, he asked, 'What may I offer you, Commissario?'

'A coffee, perhaps,' Brunetti answered, eager for anything that would release him from the stupor induced by the last minutes of conversation.

Alaimo hurried to the door. As he opened it and stuck his head outside to speak to his staff, Griffoni reached out her foot and kicked Brunetti's knee. Stunned, he leaned forward without thinking and rubbed at the spot she'd kicked.

'Leave this to me, Guido,' she said in a low, insistent voice.

Brunetti was about to protest when he saw the coldness in her eyes. 'Do it,' she said, leaned back, and smiled at the returning Alaimo.

The Captain sat, said their drinks would be there in a moment, and, ignoring Brunetti, asked Griffoni what it was that had brought them to speak to him.

Griffoni returned to her Neapolitan voice and said, again giving a small laugh that succeeded – even that, poor little thing – in sounding vulgar to Brunetti's newly alerted ears, 'I'm sure you've seen the photos we've sent of those two boys who took the American tourists to Pronto Soccorso the other night.' Her pronunciation reminded him of the girls from Forcella he'd known during the time he had been stationed in Naples, years ago.

Alaimo nodded. 'From the Giudecca, aren't they?'

The door opened just then and another white-jacketed cadet came in, carrying a tray on which stood three glasses of water and three coffees. As the cadet set them silently in front of Alaimo and his guests, the Captain said, 'I thought you might like a coffee, as well, Dottoressa.'

'Ah, how kind,' Griffoni said, not commenting on how bad the coffee was 'up here'. Apparently the Rhapsody of Napoli was over, though she kept the Neapolitan accent in place. My God, Brunetti thought, is this the same woman I've trusted with my life?

When all of them had drunk the coffees and sipped at the water, Griffoni continued. 'Yes, from the Giudecca; at least one of them: Marcello Vio. The other, Filiberto Duso, lives in Dorsoduro.'

Griffoni paused and took another sip of water. Into her silence, Alaimo asked, 'What is it you'd like to know about them, Dottoressa?'

Griffoni replaced her glass on the table and said, 'Neither of them has ever been reported or arrested. Well, Vio for speeding in his boat, but he's young and he's Venetian, so I think we can dismiss that.'

Alaimo smiled again and raised his hands, as if to suggest that boys would be boys.

'In our files at the Questura, we have nothing on them,' she said, then added, as though it made some sort of difference, 'And they did take the young women to the hospital.' Then, casually, she added, 'So, before we leap to conclusions about them, I'd like to know ...' here, she turned to Alaimo and gave a warm smile, 'if you've ever had any trouble with either one of them,' and then she added, 'or with the uncle.'

Alaimo sat back, folded his hands, and after a moment said, 'I certainly know the name Vio.' He paused in thought for a moment and then said, 'But the other one – Duso – I've never heard the name.'

Griffoni smiled and nodded; Brunetti did the same.

'What I can do,' Alaimo said amiably, 'is see what I can find out here, if any of the men have had dealings …' here Alaimo paused and added, '… or trouble.'

He looked from one to the other and said, 'Can this wait a few days? That will give me a chance to see what the people here in the office know, if anything. Would that be all right?'

Brunetti nodded; Griffoni smiled.

The three of them got to their feet simultaneously. Alaimo accompanied them to the door of his office and shook hands, formally with Brunetti, in a more friendly manner with Griffoni, and bade them farewell.

'Orsato,' the Captain called, and the man sitting in front of the Laguna Nord got quickly to his feet. 'Sì, Capitano,' he said, although he did not salute.

'Would you take the Commissari downstairs?'

'Of course, Capitano,' the man answered with a bow.

The cadet accompanied them downstairs to the door to the *riva*, then opened it for them. Outside, the panorama of the Giudecca had been waiting.

Brunetti turned to the left and started towards the *embarcadero*, where they could get the Number Two.

After only a few steps, he slowed to a stop and turned towards Griffoni to ask, 'What was all that about?'

'He's a liar and not to be trusted,' she snapped, again speaking like an Italian and not a Neapolitan.

'What?' Brunetti asked, having judged Griffoni's behaviour, as, at the least, strange.

'For the last twelve years, the Abbess of the Chiostro di San Gregorio Armeno has been a Filippina, Suora Crocifissa Ocampo, and thus is unlikely to be his aunt, as he claims.'

It took Brunetti a moment to react. 'I'm not sure that's enough to mean he's not to be trusted,' he said. 'He could simply have been boasting.'

'Then why did he calm down when I revealed my full stupid, vulgar self to him?' Before Brunetti could comment, she added, 'And calm down even more when I made it clear we had no real interest in Vio?'

Brunetti continued walking, replaying the scene in his memory. Indeed, Alaimo had seemed far more comfortable with the Griffoni who had slipped free from her professional restraint and had revealed the triviality of her own concerns. Anyone exposed to the woman who acted and spoke as she had would hardly consider her a person serious in the pursuit of justice. Or a threat.

The pleasantries about Naples, the folklore of the volcano, the diversion of their conversation into banalities: all had seemed to please the Captain. But it made no sense.

13

On the way back to the Zattere stop, Brunetti, walking beside a now-silent Griffoni, thought about Capitano Alaimo. Brunetti conceded to him the charm common to most Neapolitans, whose society and culture, having suffered invasion from countless sources for more than two millennia, had learned the art of the friendly manner and welcoming smile. They'd smiled at the Greeks, the Romans, even the Ostrogoths, which is to make no mention of the Byzantines and the Normans, the Angevins and the Spaniards, all the way up to the Germans and the Allies. They'd tried to fight them off, bargained, bribed, surrendered, and finally admitted the victors through their gates. Centuries of this created the strategy of survival: amiability, flattery, joviality, deceit. Where are to be found the Greeks, the Ostrogoths? The towering walls of Byzantium? But the Neapolitans? Are they not still at home, and are they not still charming?

Brunetti pulled his mind away from these reflections. It was too easy to read history as you pleased, see what you chose to see in the actions of people and cultures long gone.

'Excuse me?' he said when Griffoni stopped walking and put her hand on his arm.

'I don't know where your thoughts are, Guido, but they're not here.'

'No,' he admitted. 'I was thinking about Naples.'

She failed to conceal her surprise. 'What, specifically?'

'How you've survived invasion, occupation, war, destruction: things like that,' he answered, managing to make it sound normal.

She grinned. 'You've forgotten sitting beside an active volcano that can go off any time it wants. And that when that happens, there will be more than three million people trying to escape.'

'Including your family?'

She shrugged. 'They live a ten-minute walk from the Bay, so they could try to swim, I suppose.'

'You sound very calm about it,' Brunetti said, surprised.

'Either you worry or you don't,' she said, sounding resigned. 'I used to, but I can't any more.'

'Just like that?' Brunetti asked. 'You can just switch it off?

She turned away from him and walked towards the ticket machines. She tapped her boat pass on the sensor, and the twin metal bars swung back and let her enter. Just as they were beginning to close, a well-dressed man hurried in right behind Griffoni without bothering with a boat pass.

'Not my business,' thought Brunetti, tapped his card on the sensor, and moved to stand next to Griffoni. 'Tell me more about why you think he's lying and why, of all things, about an abbess.'

'I think he wanted me to believe he came from a good family, so important that one of them can become an abbess.'

'An abbess is that important?' asked Brunetti, making no attempt to hide his astonishment.

'Religion's different for us.'

'Does that mean you're ...' he began, then flailed round to find the right phrase, '... a believer?'

She let out a snort of laughter. 'Of course not. But it's important to look as though you are, and that you respect it.'

When Brunetti made no response, she continued. 'It's one of the codes of behaviour. We have to be polite to women, and we have to be solemn about religion.' Before he could question this, she said, 'If you don't trust me, come to the Duomo some day when the Bishop's showing the blood of San Gennaro,' she suggested, then added, 'The liquefaction of the blood, that is.'

'And Alaimo believes that?' Brunetti asked.

'It doesn't matter,' she answered without a second's hesitation. 'But he thinks someone with my background would believe it. And would be impressed by him if he had an aunt who's an abbess.' She raised her hands and shook them in the air, fingers spread, as a sign of confusion. 'What people believe makes no sense.'

Brunetti started to say something but she held up a hand and said, 'Trust me, Guido.' Then, as if this would explain things, she added, 'We have deceit in our marrow.'

The vaporetto arrived. When they were aboard, she said, speaking directly to Brunetti but speaking softly, 'It's simple. He doesn't want to tell us what he knows about what's going on.'

As Brunetti watched the Palanca stop approach, he considered what Griffoni said. The vaporetto pulled up, moored, waited for the passengers to leave and more to come on board, cast off and backed away a bit, and then continued on its sober way towards the Redentore. 'But why?' Brunetti asked. Both of them understood from his tone that it was not a question; no more than a request for speculation.

Griffoni said nothing, perhaps because she had become familiar with this habit of Brunetti's in responding to confusing information: open the drawer and start pulling things out to see what's there.

Into her silence, he suggested, 'Whatever might cause the officer in charge of the Capitaneria di Porto to lure us away from a possible suspect is important.'

'It's not our job to patrol the waters, Guido. You're not Andrea Doria.'

Ignoring her, Brunetti insisted, 'If he doesn't want us to know about Vio, there's a reason.' When Griffoni did not respond, he asked, 'Right?'

'Maybe Alaimo knows they're up to something and wants to be the one to arrest him,' Griffoni suggested.

'He's not a policeman, Claudia. That's us. We do the arresting. Alaimo can catch them out on the water, but we're the ones who do the arresting.'

Brunetti put his hands in his pockets and rolled back and forth on his feet a few times. The boat banged into the *embarcadero* at San Zaccaria but he didn't register the shock and continued rocking back and forth. The sound of the railing being pulled back broke into his reverie, and he stepped to the opening, standing to one side for a moment to let Griffoni pass in front of him.

They turned right and started in the direction of the Questura. He was about to speak but saw that there was something else she wanted to say so remained silent. He saw her attempt to speak, then stop herself. They continued walking and still she didn't speak.

'Just say it, Claudia,' Brunetti told her.

Giving no sign that she'd heard him, Griffoni kept walking. Just as they came down the Ponte della Pietà, she swerved towards the water, stopped at the edge of the *riva*, and looked across at San Giorgio. 'May I say a few words about Veneziano?' she surprised him by asking. She wasn't looking at him but at the church.

'If you'd like to, I'd be interested,' he said.

'I've become accustomed to it. When you and Vianello and the others speak it, I listen to what you say and understand a lot of it. Not all, but most.'

'I'm happy to learn that,' Brunetti said, utterly confused as to why they were having this conversation – if it was a conversation – now.

'I don't …' she began, turning to face him. 'I don't hear it and immediately assume that you all have to be stevedores or bargemen, barely literate and that reluctantly so.'

'I'm happy to learn that, too,' Brunetti said, even more confused and deciding to accept her whimsy.

'But,' Griffoni went on as though he had not spoken, 'the instant I start to speak with a Neapolitan accent – and I wasn't speaking Napolitano with Alaimo, or …' she paused here and took a breath – 'you might have fainted at the sound.' A depth charge exploded in Brunetti's conscience, and he felt his face redden.

'At the mere sound of my accent, you began to assume that everything I've done in the last years is open to question, and at heart I might remain the ignorant *terrona* that many of our colleagues still suspect me of being.'

It was by force of will that Brunetti kept her gaze and allowed her to see the flush of shame he could not control and could not stop. For a horrible moment, Brunetti feared that he would begin to cry.

He opened his mouth to speak but could find no words. He was her closest colleague here, he knew things about her that no one else here did, and yet she still saw this in him. The shame of it was that she was right. Was this what Blacks and Jews and gays lived with – the possibility that the crack would open in the ice beneath their feet at any step, sucking down all hope of friendship, all hope of love, all hope of common humanity?

He put his palms to his eyes and rubbed at them until he could look at her again.

'I apologize, Claudia,' he said, his voice hoarse and uncontrollable. 'From the deepest place in me. Please forgive me.'

'We're friends, Guido. And there's more than enough good in you to make up for this.' She reached over and touched the side of his face. 'It's gone, Guido. Gone.' She turned away and started walking again. When he drew up beside her, she said, 'So shall we work on the premise that Alaimo bears further examination?'

He wanted to say that she was the expert on Naples but thought it might be wise to remain distant from the city until the risk of volcanic activity was eliminated, then had an attack of guilt at still being able to think so lightly of Naples. He wondered when they would be able to talk naturally to one another again. It might help if someone took a shot at one of them, who was then saved only by the valiant heroism of the other. Immediately, he regretted no longer being able to make jokes like this with her. She had said that it was gone, but Brunetti thought it might take a bit more time before that could be true.

'Yes,' he finally answered. He glanced at his watch, and saw that it was almost 12:30. In need of time to get away from the justice of Griffoni's observations and admitting his cowardice to himself, he said, 'Let's have a closer look after lunch.'

She smiled and nodded, then after a long pause, said, 'Good idea. I'll see you this afternoon.'

The children were there for lunch, so Brunetti did not mention the – he didn't even know what to call it: scene, interchange, confrontation, conversation – with Griffoni. Paola had prepared a risotto with cauliflower and quick-fried veal cutlets, two of his favourites, but he barely finished the risotto and refused her offer of a second cutlet. Nor did he drink a glass of wine, as was his habit at lunch.

Conversation thus fell to the children, who vied with one another in their enthusiasm for the various foreign television series they watched on their computers. Brunetti feared these programmes were hacked – he preferred the verb 'pirated' – and wondered if Raffi was capable of doing that. He avoided the question because he didn't know how he should respond if his son admitted to a crime. Or his daughter.

He was certain that neither of them was capable of theft: Chiara had once found a briefcase on the vaporetto and, uncertain that it would be properly reported by the crew, had chosen to give it to her father at lunch, leaving him to open it, find the name of the owner, and call him to report its being found.

But streaming services, it seemed, were fair game to both of them. He had inquired about this some time before and been told that, because the programmes and films did not belong to a specific person, no one would be hurt if they were not paid for. Brunetti presented the argument of copyright, only to be told that there was no single author in this case, but an enormous multinational company that, it turned out, owned huge palm oil plantations in Indonesia and thus, it seemed from what they told him, had renounced all moral right to profit of any sort. The most tangential facts could be put together in justification of almost anything. How was it that he had missed the coronation of the non sequitur?

After the kids had disappeared, Paola asked him what was wrong; Brunetti kissed her cheek and said he'd tell her later, then left and grumbled his way back to the Questura.

14

The first thing Brunetti did when he got back to his office was phone Griffoni and ask her to come down, saying he was reluctant to risk his life again by encountering the obstacles presented by her chair and desk. Her laughter was a presage, he hoped, of a return to their easy collaboration.

A few minutes later, she came in without bothering to knock and took her usual seat facing him. She leaned forward and placed a manila cover on his desk, opened it, removed a single sheet of paper, and placed it on his desk too. Then she took out a set of papers held by a paperclip and set that beside the single sheet. In response to his question, Griffoni covered the single sheet and said, 'From Elettra. About Vio and Duso.' Finally, Brunetti thought, they've come to a first-name basis.

'What about them?' Brunetti asked.

'The juvenile file of Marcello Vio. There's none for Duso.'

'She's not here?' Brunetti asked.

'Not today, but her spirit is ever here with us,' Griffoni said with mock solemnity. Then, more briskly, she continued, 'She doesn't trust us to go into some places by ourselves without leaving traces that we've been there, so she found Vio's record and sent it to me,' she said, then continued, reminding Brunetti of the no-go areas Signorina Elettra kept for herself. 'She won't show me how to get information about the military, anything that has to do with crimes against children, or anything that might require access to the Vatican.'

He realized this was not the time to question Signorina Elettra's decision and so pointed to the paper under Griffoni's hand and asked, 'What's in it?' She shrugged. 'Nothing surprising. Vio and boats, Vio and boats, Vio and boats. Driving big ones without a licence for them. Speeding. Driving at night without lights. He's lucky he still has a licence.'

'Lucky?' Brunetti asked.

'I figure some of the people who stopped him knew him or knew his uncle and let the small things pass. Boat people: they stick together. And there's no record he ever broke anything but maritime rules.'

'Maritime *laws*,' Brunetti corrected her.

She smiled and repeated, 'Laws.'

She held up the paper and waved it in the air. 'His problem – at least as I see it – is *testosterone*.'

'Then,' Brunetti began, pointing to the other papers she had placed on his desk, 'what are those?'

'Some family history, about Vio's uncle, Pietro Borgato,' she said, smiling.

Failing to hide his surprise, Brunetti asked, 'Did she send them to you?'

'No. She's hasn't had time to start on him,' Griffoni answered. 'So I had a look myself. Instead of lunch.'

She pushed the papers towards him with a single finger, leaving it there, and said, 'It'll be easier if I simply tell you the things that caught my attention.'

Brunetti nodded, so she continued. 'Water's in the family blood. Borgato's father started with the ACTV as a crew member when he was in his early twenties. By thirty, he was the pilot of a vaporetto. His son Pietro followed him into the company as a simple sailor. I'm told it's always helped if someone in your family puts in a good word for you; even better if someone in the family already works on the boats.'

'Just like anywhere,' Brunetti commented.

She nodded and went on. 'But Pietro was a different sort of man. His work record is bad: he complained, argued with passengers, asked people to show him their tickets – which was none of his business – and was finally disciplined for getting into a fight with a colleague and then fired when he got into a fight with a passenger.' Before Brunetti could ask, she said, 'There's no explanation of the fight in the ACTV records, only that he hit a passenger and was fired.'

Looking down at them, she tapped at the papers, as if to summon something from them. 'The passenger was a woman,' she said, surprising Brunetti. 'It sounds like the whole thing was hushed up and he was let go.'

'No charges against him?'

'No, my guess is that ACTV decided they'd buy the woman's silence if she didn't press charges.'

'That makes sense,' Brunetti said, meaning it. 'Never offend the tourists.'

'She was Venetian,' said Griffoni, then glanced at him, and, seeing his surprise, reached for the papers. She paged through them and finally read out, 'Anna Bruzin, 35, housewife, Canareggio 4565.'

'What else?' Brunetti asked.

'The usual,' Griffoni answered, turning a page. 'A few scuffles in bars that we responded to. Only one charge, for having thrown a man into the water. But two days later, the man came in and said he was drunk, and that he fell in while Borgato was trying to pull him away from the water. And the charge was dropped.'

Brunetti couldn't stop himself from letting out a puff of air. He looked across at her, but she was looking at the page. 'You ever known a … ?' he broke off for a moment and then asked, 'Did this happen on the Giudecca?'

Griffoni checked the report and said, 'Yes.'

'I've never known a Giudecchino, drunk or sober, to fall into the water,' he said, then shook his head a few times.

Griffoni waited a moment or two and then continued. 'After he was fired, he disappeared from the city until about ten years ago, when he came back and bought the warehouse he has now and two boats, hired two men, and went into the transport business. Since then, he's bought two more big boats and a smaller one and become a successful businessman.'

'More testosterone?' Brunetti inquired.

Griffoni shook her head. 'Either his has decreased with age, or he's learned how to control it. There's no further mention of violence.' She glanced at the pages, flipped to the last, and said, 'He's come to the attention of the police – the water police – only for illegal mooring.' When Brunetti did not respond, she added, 'I found that in the records of the city police – aside from that, there's nothing.'

Silence settled on the room and remained in control until Brunetti asked, 'Do you know where he went when he left the city?'

'No,' Griffoni answered. 'I haven't looked for any change of residence, but if he wanted to rent a place to live, he'd have to do that.'

'If he worked, there'd be records,' Brunetti said. 'He'd pay taxes.' Then, before she could point it out, he added, 'Unless he worked in black.'

Griffoni suggested, 'If he worked anywhere, it would probably be on a boat: fishing, transport.'

'So that means Trieste,' Brunetti continued, running his mind along the coastline of Italy, 'or Ancona, Bari, Brindisi, the ports in Sicily, Naples, Civitavecchia, and Genova.'

'I'll check for residence first,' Griffoni said. 'That'll be easier than trying to find where he might have worked.' She started to speak, paused, then said, 'Guido, I'm not sure I understand why we're going to all of this trouble about him.'

'Borgato?'

'Yes.

'I'm not sure I understand it myself,' Brunetti confessed. 'But the whole thing puzzles me, and I suppose that means it interests me.'

Again, she paused, and again she went ahead. 'You sound like you're tired of watching crime shows on television and want to change the channel so you can look at a different series, with bigger thrills.'

'For the love of God, don't wish that on me,' Brunetti said, laughing. She looked up at him directly then – eager, smiling – the familiar Claudia, back at work. 'When Borgato returned to Venice,' Brunetti continued, speaking normally again, 'he had enough money to buy a warehouse and two boats, so he must have earned it wherever he was during those years. So check his finances: bank records, loans, anything.'

Griffoni slid the manila cover towards her, pulled a pen from Brunetti's side of the desk, and wrote down a few things, paused a moment, and added something else. Suddenly she got to her feet, leaving the papers and keeping the folder in her hand. 'I'll see what I can do,' she said and left.

Because Paola was meeting with colleagues for dinner, the family was on its own, cast off by the mother to go out and hunt and gather for themselves. The children had cadged an invitation from their grandparents, and Brunetti had resigned himself to making himself a pasta with the sauce Paola had left in the refrigerator for him. He was prepared to grate the parmigiano fresh.

No one was there when he arrived, and he went immediately to Paola's study, which over the years had come to serve as his reading room. Paola had sent him a message that afternoon to tell him the new translation of Tacitus had arrived and was on her desk, as indeed it proved to be. He grabbed it up and had a quick look at the blurbs on the back cover, all enthusiastic. Book still in his hands, he kicked off his shoes, lay down on the sofa, and started to read.

Brunetti had always preferred to read while horizontal. His habit was probably the result of the poverty of his family: a child who loved reading and who was raised in a house that was heated minimally, if at all, during the winter would perforce develop the habit of reading in bed. Even now, in a far grander house – and a far warmer one – he still concentrated better on books that were propped on his chest.

He ignored the introduction as well as the notes from the translator and decided to open the book at random to get a taste of what awaited him. Thus he found himself reading the story of Sejanus, chief of the Praetorian Guard, the man the Emperor Tiberius referred to as 'the partner of my labours,' little realizing that his partner was busy – as many subsequent historians asserted – with the labour of clearing his own way to the throne of the Caesars, first by murdering Tiberius' only son while keeping in his sights his two grandsons.

A phrase caught Brunetti's attention, and he went back and read it again, and then again. 'I give only one example of the falsity of gossip and hearsay, and I urge my readers to beware of incredible tales, however widely they might be believed and instead to believe the unvarnished truth.'

Brunetti let the open book fall on to his stomach and stared out the window at rooftops and windows that reflected the setting sun. Two thousand years ago, the bulk of the population illiterate, most news was transmitted by word of mouth, and Tacitus was warning his readers to be careful about believing what they heard and to trust only unvarnished truth. 'Whatever that is,' a voice whispered to Brunetti's inner ear. Had Tacitus been a prophet as well as an historian, Brunetti wondered, by so well anticipating the consequences of television and social media?

Brunetti returned to the world of two thousand years before and read on. Unfortunately, the following few years were missing from the original text, although Sejanus must certainly have continued to plot and perfect his flattery of Tiberius. When the text resumed after that gap, Sejanus had fallen, and his memory, and family, were in the process of being destroyed.

But why, Brunetti wondered, should he believe the story as Tacitus tells it? Did his sources tell him the truth? Did they even know the truth? Almost a century had passed between these events and the time Tacitus wrote of them. Much could have been lost from the common memory, or distorted, or deliberately obscured.

Brunetti's thoughts moved to the newspapers he read and those others that were available at the news-stands. Each day, they reported the news and made their readers aware of the events the editors judged to be of political, economic, medical or social importance. And how different those explanations were, how conflicting their interpretations. Only the sports pages were reliable: the scores given could be checked and authenticated, as could the rankings in the various leagues. But wait a minute. If the news gave the sum written on a player's contract, it did not report accurately how much the player would actually receive. Endorsements, interviews, marketing, even his appearance at a dinner or a party, the cars he was given, the shoes, the clothing: how to calculate this? Where was the 'unvarnished truth'?

A key turning in the lock of the front door pulled him back from the wanderings that often resulted from his reading. At first he thought it was Paola, because she could always fit the key into the lock without repeated trying. But he waited for the way the door closed. Too loud for her. And then the first heavy footstep.

'*Ciao*, Raffi,' he called out in welcome.

His son appeared at the door, almost as tall as Brunetti, with a mass of dark hair he said he was too busy to get cut, now so long that the top of his backpack pushed at it. Suddenly, Brunetti saw him with new eyes, and saw that his son was handsome. No sooner had he thought this than he searched for a way to alter the thought and judge him as no more than not bad looking, anything that would avert whichever jealous spirits might be waiting to hear words of praise.

They sat at opposite ends of the sofa, talking about the business of their day. Raffi explained that he had decided to come home to write an essay for his Italian History class instead of having dinner with his grandparents. He talked about the teacher of this class, a vocal member of the Lega that had once wanted a separate Northern Italy, to be called Padania, but had now taken the other compass points under its all-encompassing wings.

The teacher and Raffi had already differed on a number of points, including the Italian presence in Abyssinia before the Second World War, which the professor presented as a golden age for Abyssinia. When Raffi mentioned the use of poison gas, dropped from planes, during what he chose to call an 'invasion', the teacher denied it. 'The people threw flowers at the feet of our soldiers,' he insisted.

'Why does he dismiss everything I say? Even if I tell him where I found the information?'

Brunetti felt the desire to lean over and ruffle Raffi's hair and tell him to calm down. Instead, he stretched out his legs and put his feet on the table in front of them. 'There's no use in trying to reason with him, Raffi,' Brunetti said in a soft voice. 'He's decided what's true and what isn't, so anything you say in argument against him will only provoke him.'

'But he's a teacher, Papà. He's supposed to tell us what happened in the past and where to find the evidence.'

That was true enough, Brunetti thought.

'Your grandfather was there,' he said suddenly.

Raffi turned towards his father, mouth open in surprise. 'What?'

'My father. Your grandfather. He was there during the occupation.'

'I never knew that,' Raffi said.

'Well, he was.'

'How do you know?' Raffi asked urgently.

'My grandmother had his service record,' Brunetti explained. 'She needed it to claim her widow's pension.'

'Didn't he have a pension already?' Raffi asked, confused. 'From the army?'

'He was awarded one,' Brunetti said, then quickly added, 'but family legend always said he refused to take it.'

'But your family was poor, wasn't it?' Raffi asked, as though he'd heard something about such a situation and thought he knew what it meant.

'He told them he wouldn't take it,' Brunetti said.

'That's crazy,' Raffi objected, but seeing Brunetti's sudden glance, added, 'If they were poor, I mean.'

Brunetti shrugged and smiled, as he so often did when talking about his father's side of the family. 'He said it wasn't right to take money for doing what he did there.'

'So he didn't have a pension?'

'No, not for going to Abyssinia, but he did accept one for being wounded and held as a prisoner of war. He thought it was right that the state paid him for that.'

Raffi rubbed his hands across his face and back through his hair. 'I don't understand,' he said. 'He was a soldier just the same, wasn't he? Both times.'

'Yes, he was,' Brunetti answered, suddenly uncomfortable at the fact that his son hadn't instantly perceived the difference.

'So why wouldn't he take the pension?' Raffi asked.

'Did you ever read about what our soldiers did in Addis Ababa? After the attack on Graziano?'

'He was our general, wasn't he?' Raffi asked.

'Yes,' Brunetti answered and left it at that, not eager to enter into a discussion of the General or his behaviour.

'What happened?'

'Bombs were thrown at Graziano. At a meeting. And he allowed the troops to ... well, to punish the people of the city.'

'How?'

Brunetti thought about how best to answer this and finally said, 'Any way they chose.'

Raffi's face went blank and grew minimally paler, so much so that Brunetti saw clearly where the moustache and beard were growing.

Raffi leaned against the back of the sofa and folded his arms. 'I don't know what that means,' he said after a long time.

How strange this scene was, Brunetti thought: usually it was the sons and daughters who came to their parents with the revelation that their nation's history had not been made by saints and angels, that it too had done the dirty jobs that are part of history, and it was the parents who tried to explain that times had been different then, people had thought in different ways, valued other beliefs, other lives.

Indignant youth, discovering the viper hiding under the flag, perhaps wrapped in it. Brunetti remembered the shock of it, the impulse towards shame, the false comfort of the irrelevant fact that just about every nation had done the same, and probably would do so again.

His son's face was blank, his cheeks red, and Brunetti could think of nothing to say to him.

They sat like that for some time until Raffi leaned forward, elbows on his knees. He turned his head and looked at his father. 'Where did you learn all this, *Papà*? About history and people, and the way they are?'

Brunetti had never thought about this and so had no answer to give his son. 'I don't know, Raffi. Part of it is that I listen to what people say and try not to make a decision until I've heard everything.' That was badly stated, he knew. 'And I read a lot.'

'That's all?' Raffi asked as if fearing some sort of trick or evasion on his father's part.

Brunetti slapped his palms on to his knees and pushed himself to his feet. 'I'm also more than three decades older than you are, so I've had more experience.'

Raffi nodded. 'That helps.'

Smiling, Brunetti leaned across and roughed up his son's hair, saying, 'I wish I could get your mother to think that.'

15

The next morning, Brunetti went first to Signorina Elettra's office to see if she had arrived. Indeed she had, today wearing a dark blue velvet suit with red piping around the lapels and down the outside of each trouser leg. It glowed with the reflected light of new velvet and gave her the look of an exceedingly modest commander of vast armies with a part-time job as the doorman at an exclusive London club. 'I like your suit,' he said after he'd entered the office and seen her standing near the copier.

'Oh, how very kind, Commissario,' she answered graciously. 'I suppose I shouldn't say this, but it is good to be back.'

'Rome too busy?'

'Too crowded,' she said and gave a dramatic shudder, quite as if she were accustomed to living on a moor in Yorkshire and did not see another person for weeks at a time.

This proved too much for Brunetti and he asked, 'In comparison with?'

'Oh, I'm sorry, Commissario. I didn't mean the city itself, but the Questura. There are hundreds of people there.'

'There must be more crime in Rome,' Brunetti ventured.

'Well,' she said and gave a long, obviously thoughtful, pause, 'the government and the Vatican *are* there.'

Brunetti considered how best to respond to this. 'I had more in mind the larger population,' he said.

'Of course, of course,' she agreed. 'That certainly must be taken into account, as well.' Then, detaching her attention from numbers, she said, 'They have deliciously secret files there. No matter where you put your hand ...' she began, paused, considered, and corrected herself ...' speaking metaphorically, that is ...'

'Of course,' Brunetti interjected, and, deciding not to express interest in anything she considered 'deliciously secret', asked if there was any news about Marcello Vio's condition; she shook her head.

'And the two Americans?'

'The one with the broken arm was released yesterday and is in a hotel. The father of the other one arrived from the United States yesterday afternoon.' Seeing Brunetti's response, she explained, 'He was at a meeting in Washington and had to come back directly. He's in a hotel in Mestre.'

'And his daughter?

'The hospital said there was no information available about her.'

'Did you say it was a police matter?'

'Yes, but it didn't make any difference.'

Brunetti thanked her and left the office but hesitated before going up the stairs to his own. It might be opportune to talk to Marcello Vio again while he was still in the hospital: people are not necessarily weaker while they are there, but they are often dispirited and thus more likely to respond to the chance of conversation.

Intentionally, Brunetti took a longer way to the hospital and turned into Barbaria delle Tole, intent on passing by the window of the shop that had for years sold Japanese furniture and prints. He'd bought a squat ceramic vase there, years ago, that still stood in the kitchen, holding a bouquet of wooden cooking implements. His haste must have made him walk past it, he thought, and turned back, eager to delight, as he always did, in the pieces exposed in the window, especially a long calligraphy he'd been looking at for years, never sure where he could put it but always glad to see it again and renew the temptation to have it.

It was gone. That is, the windows that had once held the calligraphy were papered over on the inside. A sign in the window read, '*Cessata attività.*' He hardly needed the sign: the paper was enough to tell him the shop had gone out of business. There was no explanation. He went into the caffè next door and approached the bar. A white-haired man looked up.

'What happened to the Japanese store?' Brunetti asked, pointing his thumb to the left.

The man shrugged and said, 'Usual story. The owner of the building died, and his son doubled the rent when the lease expired.' He picked up a glass and began to dry it with a not particularly clean towel.

'Where'd they go?' Brunetti asked.

'I think they sell everything online now, but I'm not sure.'

'You know what's coming?' Brunetti asked. Because they were speaking Veneziano, he felt he had the right to ask.

'Murano glass,' the man answered, emphasizing the first word.

'Murano, China?' Brunetti asked.

The man snorted in response and picked up another glass.

Brunetti thanked him, went back outside, and continued towards the hospital.

Inside, he was directed to the ear, nose, and throat ward and didn't bother to ask questions, familiar with the odd places patients ended up as a result of crowding.

He followed the signs, passed through the columned garden on the ground floor, and, after asking his way a few times, found the ward. He stopped at the nurses' desk, was recognized by one of them, and explained that he wanted to see Marcello Vio. He was directed to the third door on the right and found Vio in a two-bed room, near the window, his attention given to his phone, ear pods in place. He was sitting up, braced against a number of pillows. The other patient, an old man who had not shaved for days, slept in the nearer bed, one eye protected by a plastic cup bandaged over it.

Brunetti stood at the door and watched Vio. He looked thinner than he had when Brunetti last saw him, thinner and paler, his face now clean-shaven, drawn with stress or tiredness. His expression suddenly changed in response to whatever was happening on the screen. Tension, fear, concentration led him to push one of the pods deeper into his ear; soon came sagging relief. He looked up, turned to the window and then to the door. The sight of Brunetti washed all expression from his face, but then a trickle of some unpleasant emotion caused his eyes to narrow and his hand to lower the phone on to the bed cover.

He raised both hands and removed the pods but said nothing.

Brunetti approached the bed and extended his hand; Vio shook it and quickly returned his hand to his phone, as if to save it from Brunetti's interest.

'Good morning, Signor Vio. I thought I'd come along to see how you are. I thought they'd let you go sooner.'

Vio shook his head. 'No, they decided not to take the risk and to keep me here.'

'Risk?' Brunetti inquired mildly.

'I broke a rib and cracked two others, and they're afraid that the broken one could still hurt my lung.' As he spoke, his hand sought out the ribs under discussion and covered them protectively.

Brunetti nodded enough times to give evidence of concern.

Vio looked down at his hands.

Uninvited, Brunetti moved around the bed and pulled the chair standing against the wall up close to Vio and sat down, only an arm's length from him. He watched Vio move minimally away from him, then stop with an involuntary groan when he moved too quickly.

'When we were interrupted, Signor Vio, you were just telling me that you took one of your uncle's boats and went across the canal to Campo Santa Margherita.' Brunetti's lie emerged seamlessly.

He waited until Vio nodded, and then went on. 'I live not far from the *Campo,*' Brunetti said untruthfully, 'so I know what it's like late at night, how crowded it is with students and young people meeting and talking together over a drink.'

He gave a small laugh to introduce another lie. 'My son often goes there with his friends.' Vio remained silent.

'He meets girls there, of course.' Again Brunetti gave a small laugh, then asked, 'Is that why you went there that night, Signor Vio?' Then, before Vio could answer, Brunetti added, 'I'd like you to think very carefully before you answer that question, Signor Vio.'

Vio's eyes grew wider, perhaps with surprise. They were sitting so close that Brunetti could see the sweat in front of Vio's ears. 'Why do you say that, Signore?' Vio asked, speaking very softly. He pushed air from his chest, then took a deep breath, only to push it out again. He placed his palms beside him on the mattress and pushed himself higher against the pillow, moving with the caution of an old man.

'Is this like being in the Questura?' Vio asked, sounding suddenly very young. He raised his hand and pointed at Brunetti and then at himself. 'You and me, I mean,' turning this last phrase into a question.

'In a way it is, yes,' Brunetti answered. 'Only there's no recording being made.' To show his good faith, Brunetti took his phone out and turned it off, then showed the unresponsive screen to Vio.

'So it's more like a conversation?' Vio asked.

'Something like that,' Brunetti confirmed. 'There's no recording and no witness, so it can never be used as evidence.'

'About what?' Vio asked.

'About what happened last weekend, out in the *laguna*.'

'With the girls?' Vio asked.

'Yes.'

'It was an accident,' Vio said with whatever force he could muster.

'What happened?'

Brunetti saw him bite his lower lip and close his eyes. He opened them after a moment and said, 'I hit a *bricola*. I was in the right canal: I know the *laguna* like I know ...' he began but proved incapable of finding a comparison. In Brunetti's silence, he amended it to, 'I know it very well.'

'But still you hit the *bricola*,' Brunetti said and waved his hand towards Vio's chest, 'very hard.' He waited for Vio to respond, but he chose not to.

'You were knocked against something,' Brunetti went on, 'hard enough to break your rib; one of the girls broke her arm in two places, and the other one's still in intensive care.' He waited three long beats and added, 'She's very badly injured.'

Vio said something, but with his head bent down and speaking to his hands; it was impossible to understand what it was. 'Excuse me?' Brunetti asked.

'I didn't want to do that,' Vio said.

'No one wants those things, Marcello. That's why they're accidents. It was dark, you were going too fast, and you ran into something you had every reason to know might be in the water.' Then, making his voice sound cool and dispassionate, he went on. 'As the person in charge, you were responsible for the security of everyone on the boat.'

Vio remained silent, shaking his head a few times, as if this would somehow counter Brunetti's remarks and erase the collision with the thick wooden pole floating loose in the water.

'I took them to the hospital,' Vio said petulantly.

Suddenly fed up with Vio's justifications, Brunetti said, 'She hit her face, the other one broke her arm, but you took a long time to get them to the Pronto Soccorso.'

'I ... I ... didn't want ... to ...' Vio began.

'You didn't want to be stopped by the police and tested for alcohol, Marcello. Let's be honest about this, all right? So you took a long time, the girl bleeding all over the boat.' Brunetti allowed himself to exaggerate to worsen Vio's position.

Vio looked up, suddenly angry. 'Did Berto tell you that?'

'It doesn't matter who told me, Marcello. What matters is that you did it.'

Brunetti stopped, and was surprised to feel himself shaking with emotion. Strangely, he found it impossible to define what emotion it was: some mix of rage and pity and profound sadness that youth could be so rash and so vulnerable and so easily damaged. He waited for the tremors to stop, keeping his eyes on the floor and then the wall: anything but the face of the man in the bed.

Vio made a sudden move, and Brunetti looked up to see him drag the elbow of his pyjama sleeve across his face. Brunetti forced himself to relax the muscles of his stomach and unlocked his jaw.

Forgetting he was a father, remembering only that he was a policeman, Brunetti returned his attention to Vio and said, 'You've broken a number of laws, Signor Vio; the most serious one is that you failed to offer help to an injured person.' When Vio remained silent, Brunetti added, but in a calmer voice, 'You're a boatman: you know that's your duty.'

Vio's voice was very soft when he said, 'But we did. Berto rang the alarm. He hit it a couple of times.' Vio looked at Brunetti, his eyes eager that he should be believed. When Brunetti did not respond, he said, 'Berto did it. I saw him. He'll tell you.' His voice had risen as he spoke. 'Then we got back in the boat. We didn't want them to see us when they came to get them.' He reached his hand towards Brunetti, winced at the sudden pain, and pulled it back.

'I see,' Brunetti said. He had no doubt that Vio believed Duso had activated the alarm and that help was coming. But it wasn't coming, and it didn't arrive until fate or chance sent a smoker out into the night to have a cigarette.

16

Both men remained silent for some time. Vio kept his head bent and shifted his phone from side to side on his lap. Brunetti tried to sort through the tangle of his own thoughts and feelings. He had no idea of what judges – should it ever come to a trial – would decide. How measure, how prove, a person's intent? Only actions mattered, and surely they had taken them to the hospital with the clear purpose of getting them medical help.

'Had you been drinking?' Brunetti asked.

Vio's surprise could not be masked. 'No, Signore. I don't drink if I'm going to be in the boat.'

'Unlike most of your colleagues,' Brunetti said neutrally.

Vio actually smiled, as though he'd not thought of this.

'Drugs?' Brunetti asked in the same dispassionate tone.

'I don't like them.'

As if talking to a friend about some trivial matter, Brunetti asked, 'Did you ever try them?'

'Once. When I was about fourteen. I don't know what it was, but it made me sick, really sick. So I never did it again.'

'Were you in charge of the boat when the accident happened?'

'Of course,' Vio answered, unable to hide his surprise at such a question. He must have read Brunetti's expression, for he said, 'Aside from two other men who work for my uncle, I'm the only one who can pilot that boat.' Vio could have been reciting the Pythagorean Theorem, although Brunetti doubted he was familiar with it.

'I see,' Brunetti responded. And then, curious, he asked, 'Doesn't Duso know how?'

'Yes, sir. I taught him, so he's good.'

'But not good enough for your uncle's boat?'

Vio was a long time in answering the question. 'It's against the rules. He doesn't have a licence, so he can't drive anything over 40 horsepower.' After a moment's reflections, Vio added, 'Besides, he could never handle that boat.'

If Brunetti were to say the same thing to Vianello, he realized, or indeed to any of the men who were familiar with boats, proposing that someone would not be allowed to drive a boat bigger than permitted by his licence, they would fall about laughing. A licence was a suggestion, not a limitation; it was a kind of non-restrictive formality, and some people piloted any boat they chose to, regardless of the power of its engine. Not the really big transport boats, Brunetti admitted to himself, but certainly the smaller ones.

'At the Questura,' Brunetti began, 'you said your licence was good for all of your uncle's boats.

Vio's face still registered pride in his own capacities when he continued, 'Yes. My uncle made me get them all: he said he didn't want any trouble with the water police.' He paused, as if uncertain whether to say what he was thinking, and then added, 'I got them all with no trouble. First try.' Vio's smiled broadened as he said this, it made him look younger.

'Good for you,' Brunetti congratulated him. 'How long have you worked for your uncle?'

'Oh, I started when I was a kid. Just loading and unloading the boats.'

'How old were you?' Brunetti asked.

'Fifteen. He wouldn't take me until then.'

'Because of school?'

Vio laughed at this, then gasped in a low breath as though the act had hurt him. 'Oh, no. To work as an apprentice, I had to be at least fifteen. He didn't care about the school.' Vio's mouth fell open after he said that. 'I shouldn't tell you something like that, should I?'

This time it was Brunetti who laughed. 'I was helping my father unload boats when I was fifteen, so don't think about it.'

'He paid me,' Vio said earnestly, as though this private honesty would make up for taking his nephew out of school.

Brunetti laughed again, even longer this time. 'That's more than my father's boss did for me.'

'Where did you work?' Vio asked, his curiosity real.

'Anywhere. Everywhere. My father got hired by the day, or maybe by the week. Usually at Marghera, but sometimes at Rialto. I guess I went along to make up for what he couldn't do.'

'I don't understand,' Vio said.

'My father's lungs were no good, so he really couldn't do a day's work, but he had a good reputation: everyone knew he wouldn't steal anything. So the boat owners called him, and he brought me along to make sure a full day's work got done.' Vio seemed fascinated by what Brunetti was telling him, perhaps surprised that a policeman could also be a real person.

'I guess my father was a bit like your uncle,' Brunetti said, smiling.

Vio looked puzzled. After a long time and with something approaching melancholy in his voice, he said, 'Oh, no, not at all.' A few seconds passed and Vio raised his hand, as if to cover his mouth or push back what he'd said.

Before Brunetti could ask anything else, they were interrupted by the arrival of a nurse, who entered after knocking only once. She was old enough to be Vio's mother, heavy-bodied and round-faced. She nodded towards Brunetti but did not speak to him.

'I've brought it, Marcello, I had to look for the right size for you.' Smiling, she held up what looked like a bulletproof vest, dark brown and apparently stiff. 'Wear this during the day, and I guarantee you can go back to work.' She smiled again, obviously proud of having found the vest for him. She opened it as she approached the motionless Vio and said, 'Here it is. Why don't you try it on and see if it helps?' She turned to Brunetti to explain: 'It's stiff, Signore, so it'll hold him straight and keep his ribs away from his lungs.' Turning back to Vio, she held the vest up higher and shook it, as if some surprise were going to jump out.

Vio made no move to do what she said and barely glanced at the vest.

'Come on, Marcello; try it on. I'm sure the fit is perfect: I had to keep asking to see different ones in the rehab, and I'd almost given up when they found this one.' She waved it again, smiling at Vio encouragingly.

The young man sat up straighter and slid his legs to the side of the bed. Gingerly, he lowered one foot to the floor, then the other until finally, hands braced on the bed behind him, he stood upright.

'Turn around and put out your right arm.' Vio obeyed, and she slipped the vest over it. Lured by the momentum of getting dressed, he turned slightly and slipped his other arm into the vest, then turned back to show her the result. Seeing this, Brunetti found himself thinking of a similar scene, the arming of Achilles with a 'breastplate brighter than the flame of fire'.

The nurse stepped around Vio and checked the fit at the back. 'As I said: perfect.' She helped Vio seal the Velcro tabs that ran up the front of the vest and could be adjusted to the body of the wearer.

She made a sudden move and pulled a handkerchief from her pocket, waving it in the air.

'Try to take this from me,' she said.

Brunetti winced when he saw how low she suddenly held it and what that would require Vio to do, but the young man bent obediently forward and down. As he reached out, she bent with him and lowered the handkerchief even more. Vio continued towards it and grabbed it from her hand, laughing. He held it above his head and then passed it back to her, saying, 'It's magic, this thing. Nothing hurts.'

The nurse looked at Brunetti, a man closer to her in age and experience, and said, 'They never listen.'

Brunetti smiled at her and said, *'Brava, Signora.'*

Vio leaned back against the bed and asked the nurse, 'Can I keep it on?'

'Yes. Wear it to sleep in tonight and wear it to the X-rays tomorrow morning. And then wear it all day for the first few days you're home.'

'Does this mean I'll be able to go home sooner?' Vio asked.

'Of course you'll get home soon,' she said, smiling.

'Good,' Vio said. 'I have to get back to work.'

The nurse reached over and touched his arm, saying, 'Don't rush things, Marcello.' She waited until he was back under the covers again, then said goodbye to both of them.

'Does it hurt less?' Brunetti asked.

Vio tilted his head to one side and gave a minimal nod: he was a real man and pain didn't matter to real men. 'Yes, and I'll try to be careful,' he said. When he saw a look of real concern on Brunetti's face, he added, 'It's not bad at all. I broke my foot once, and that was bad.'

'Yes, feet are awful,' Brunetti answered, thinking that Vio needed a bit of sympathy. Even if it was for a previous injury, it might help. He thrust around for a topic they might have in common. 'I guess you're lucky to have steady work to go back to.'

Vio's face went blank. 'Why?' he asked, then added, 'I don't understand.'

'My friends are always telling me their kids can't find work, no matter what they do.'

Vio's surprise was painted on his face. 'I didn't know that,' he finally said.

'Some of them have been out of school for years and haven't even managed to get an interview.'

'That's too bad,' Vio said with real sympathy. 'A man needs to work.'

'I think so, too,' Brunetti answered, happy to speak to Vio with no ulterior motive. He decided not to suggest that a woman needed work, as well, and asked, instead, 'Your friends are luckier?'

'There's always work if you're willing to take it,' Vio began. 'The boats need men to fix them or load them, and you see the guys delivering freight all over the city: carrying it from the boats, stacking it up outside the supermarkets. There's lots of jobs doing restoration, but Bosnians and Albanians have taken over the heavy work. If you know someone who has a company, or maybe someone in your family does, you can still get a job, even if it's just hauling rubble to the boats or bringing the cement to the construction site.' Vio rested his head against his pillow and closed his eyes. 'And places like Ratti, and Caputo, they always need men to deliver the stoves and washing machines and connect them.' He shifted in the bed and looked as though he were going to name more jobs available to young men not locked in chains by their university degrees and incapable of even so much as imagining that these jobs existed. But before he could continue, his eyes closed and his breath began its even, long rasp as he sank into sleep.

Brunetti watched Vio, thinking how much he looked like a large boy, face washed smooth by sleep and the relative absence of pain. Brunetti felt a sudden chill rise up from his past and remind him that, without the secure widow's pension his mother had begun to receive when he was still a teenager, he would surely have thought himself lucky to find one of those jobs or to be recommended for one by some old friend of his father. Just last week, he'd read that Veritas had advertised three jobs as garbage men and had received almost two thousand applications, most of them from university graduates.

The country of Dante, Michelangelo, Leonardo, Galileo and Columbus, and two thousand men competed for jobs as garbage men. '*O tempora, o mores,*' he whispered under his breath and left the room silently.

Outside the hospital, Brunetti called Vianello to see what his friends on the Giudecca might have said about Pietro Borgato. As it turned out, not much. From what Vianello had managed to discover without giving any sign he was trying to learn anything, Borgato was considered a hard man and an equally hard worker. His ex-wife, who was from a small town in Campania, still lived there with one of their two daughters. The other lived with her husband in Venice. His nephew worked for him, but there was general agreement that Marcello would not take over the business, for no better reason than that his uncle judged him incapable of running it. No one Vianello had spoken to dissented from this judgement. There was a general belief that Marcello was a good boy, alas, in a world where good boys were not suited to running a business like his uncle's, or like his uncle ran his business. When it was clear that this was all Vianello had to report, Brunetti thanked him and ended the call.

The officer at the reception window of the Questura saluted when he saw Brunetti but left his hand in the air, extended to stop him. 'There's someone waiting to talk to you, Commissario. He's Venetian, so I told him to wait over there.' He pointed to the other side of the large entrance hall.

Brunetti turned in time to see Filiberto Duso getting to his feet from one of the four chairs that stood in front of a faded photo of a previous Questore no one in the Questura had ever bothered to look at carefully.

The young man took a few steps towards Brunetti, stopped, then moved towards him again.

'Ah, Signor Duso,' Brunetti said. 'Is there some way I can help you?' He continued towards Duso with an extended hand.

Duso gave a weak smile, let go of Brunetti's hand, cleared his throat a few times, and finally said, 'I'd like to speak to you, Commissario.' He looked at Brunetti, then around the room, and said, 'I have to.'

'Of course. What about?'

'Marcello,' he said, speaking in a hoarse voice, almost as if the name frightened him.

Responding to the urgent tone, Brunetti said, 'What's wrong?'

'He's afraid someone's going to hurt him.'

17

Brunetti put his hand on the young man's arm and left it there. Duso stood immobile, frightened at the sound of what he had just said.

'Come back here with me,' Brunetti told him, walking towards the guard. The man saw them coming and, responding to a gesture from Brunetti, unlocked the door to the small office next to his, where the translators listened to and transcribed the recordings of the interrogations where they had assisted the police in questioning suspects who did not speak Italian. As he had hoped, the room was empty. Table, four chairs, a locked cabinet with the tape recorders, and rows of files containing the transcripts.

Brunetti pulled out a chair for Duso and waited until he sat, head bowed, then moved around the table to sit opposite him. The young man had not shaved that morning and looked as though he had slept badly. Long experience had taught Brunetti to wait out the time that would ensue before the other person found the energy or courage to speak. He sat, folded his hands on the table in front of him, and looked down at them, not ignoring Duso but certainly not paying him over-much attention.

Footsteps passed beyond the door. The larger door to the *riva*, and to freedom, opened with a double squeak and closed with three. Brunetti, hearing it only a few times, realized that the sound would drive him mad if he sat near it all day. He looked at his wedding ring, twirled it around once or twice with his thumb. What pleasure it gave him to touch it, as though it were some sort of cult object, invested with magic powers, always near at hand, like a friendly spirit.

'I went to see him yesterday,' Duso said with no introductory noises or hesitation.

Brunetti nodded but made no mention of having been to the hospital himself that morning.

'He looked awful and couldn't stop moving around,' Duso said. 'He shifted from side to side, like he was trying to make the pain go away.'

Again Brunetti nodded.

'I asked him if I could call a nurse or help him get up. I even asked if he needed to go to the bathroom,' Duso said in a small voice, as though he were confessing some breach of the rules concerning intimacy between male friends.

'He said no, that he was all right, but then he said he was frightened and didn't know what to do.'

After some time had passed, Brunetti asked, 'Did he say what he was frightened of?'

'No, not at first. He changed the subject and asked me what I was doing, but it was obvious he wasn't interested, not really.' Duso threw his hands in the air, then clasped them together and allowed them to drop on his lap.

'We've been best friends since we were kids,' he said in a pleading voice, as though he wanted Brunetti to judge that Vio thus had the obligation to confide in his friend.

'What did you do?' Brunetti asked.

'I stood up and said I'd leave unless he told me what was wrong, and he said I was free to go, but that wasn't how friends were supposed to behave.'

Brunetti was struck by how young Duso sounded as he spoke, arguing about who was a best friend, then offended that his best friend was not playing by the rules.

Brunetti nodded. Time passed, but no matter how long Duso stared at his hands, they did not speak, nor did he. Finally Brunetti asked, 'What happened?'

'I went back and sat down again and just waited for him to talk.' He looked up at Brunetti then, who smiled his approval.

'Did he finally tell you?'

Duso nodded, but then changed the motion and shook his head. 'I thought he did, but now I don't know.'

Brunetti sat and waited.

Both men examined their hands, Brunetti's fingers now intermeshed, Duso kneading the knuckles of one hand with the fingers of the other. The door to the *riva* opened and closed: once, twice.

'He said that he was in trouble, bad trouble, and he didn't know what to do.' Before Brunetti could ask, Duso said, 'No, not because of the accident – well, sort of, but not really. I told you the truth about that. So did Marcello. I rang what I thought was the alarm button, and I thought they'd be there in a minute, so we got away as fast as we could. Marcello was terrified they'd call the police: if they stopped us, they'd find out whose boat it was.'

'If it's not the accident, what is it he's afraid of?' Brunetti insisted.

Duso pressed his hands so hard that Brunetti could hear the joints cracking. He looked at Brunetti, then looked away. 'I just told you,' Duso said shortly. 'He's afraid of his uncle and going back to work for him.'

'Did his uncle find out his boat was involved in the accident?'

Duso shook his head. 'I don't think so. When we got back to the Giudecca that night, Marcello moored it at the dock behind the office. It's his uncle's oldest boat – that's why he let Marcello use it – so there were already a lot of dents and scratches, but it's solid. There was no way anyone could tell the dent in the prow was new,' he said, his relief audible. As memory came back he said, 'There wasn't much blood, really. I worked fast.' He paused, remembering.

'That's when Marcello began to feel the pain.' Duso grew thoughtful and added, 'I think we were both so frightened we didn't notice much until then, when it looked like it was all over, and we were safe.' Perhaps it was that last word that stopped him short: for a long time Duso did no more than repeat the word: 'Safe'.

Now that Duso had begun talking, Brunetti knew it was necessary to keep him from stopping. Screwing his face up in confusion, Brunetti said, 'Since you were both safe, why is he afraid?'

Duso threw his hands up in the air. 'I don't know. Marcello loves his uncle because he took him in when his father died. Pietro has only the two daughters,' Duso said and closed his eyes. 'Maybe Marcello is some sort of substitute for the son he didn't have. I don't know.'

But still his nephew was not to be his heir, Brunetti thought. Of course, that didn't mean he loved Marcello any less, only that he had weighed his nephew in the balance and found him wanting.

Duso shook his head wildly. 'I don't know what to do. I don't know. All Marcello said was that his uncle had found out that we'd been questioned at the Questura.' Bracing his elbows on the table, Duso put his face in his hands and shook his head.

'Did he see his uncle?'

'No. His cousin who lives here came to visit him in the hospital, and she said her father was angry with Marcello because he'd talked to the police, really angry. Her father's worried it could get him into trouble.'

'Who?' Brunetti asked, 'Marcello or his uncle?'

Duso at first seemed confused by the question, but closed his eyes as if listening again to what his friend had told him. 'His uncle,' he said, surprised to hear himself say it.

A long pause radiated from that and lasted until Brunetti asked, 'Do you know the uncle?'

Duso's manner changed. He pushed his chair back from the table, as though wanting to establish a greater distance between Brunetti and himself. His face moved, but he said nothing. Brunetti thought he was trying to find the right way to answer the question.

Finally Duso said, 'I met him once.'

'When?' Brunetti asked.

'Ten years ago.'

'And not since then?'

'No.'

'If I might speak as a father,' Brunetti said with an easy smile, 'that sounds very strange.'

Duso's voice was nervous as he asked, 'Why?'

'Because my son has a lot of friends. I don't know all of them, but I know his closest friend very well: he's even come on vacation with us a few times.'

Duso stared across at Brunetti, as though assembling a new way of examining human relationships. 'How long have they been friends?'

'Since they began school. They sat in the same row then, and they still sit near one another at university,' Brunetti said, as if ignorant of any other way for best friends to sit during the same class.

Duso looked down at his hands again, then pushed his chair even farther back to allow him to look at his shoes. Head still bowed, he asked, in a very low voice, 'They're only friends?'

Pieces of the puzzle slipped into place in Brunetti's mind and he said, 'They're both heterosexual, if that's what you mean.' Then, after a pause, Brunetti added, 'Not that I see it would make any difference.'

'To you?' Duso asked.

'To me. To Raffi. To Giorgio,' he said and watched Duso try to contain his surprise. 'They love one another. Well, they're friends, so they should, don't you think?'

Duso opened his mouth to speak, but no words emerged. Finally he managed to ask, 'And if it was more?' unable to say what that 'more' would be but leaving no doubt about what he meant, 'you wouldn't mind?'

Brunetti thought about it for a moment, never having questioned his son's preference but thinking of the other possibility now. 'No, I wouldn't mind. Yet,' he began and saw Duso grow suddenly more alert. 'Yet I'd worry that it might complicate his life or make it difficult.' He gave himself time to follow this idea, then finished by saying, 'But not as difficult and painful as it would be if he pretended to be heterosexual and wasted his life with that.' The thought ran along with itself until Brunetti said, with finality, 'That would cause me limitless pain.'

'I see,' Duso said. 'Thank you.'

'Could this be the reason Marcello's frightened?' Brunetti asked.

'Maybe,' Duso answered. He glanced at Brunetti and added, 'Everyone's afraid of Pietro.'

'Are you?'

'Why do you think I haven't seen him for ten years?' Duso asked and gave a smile that transformed his face, the sort of easy smile a person gives when slipping off a pair of too-tight shoes. 'He doesn't believe Marcello and I are just friends. Like brothers.'

He looked at Brunetti, who said, 'You're both lucky to have that bond.'

'You think it's a good thing?' Duso asked, his voice as neutral as he could make it.

'One of the best things that can happen, I'd say,' was Brunetti's response. Seeing that Duso had trouble masking his relief at hearing this, Brunetti risked saying, 'His uncle's afraid you'll … influence him?'

Duso nodded, then smiled and said, 'That's why we go to Santa Margherita, so people can see us picking up girls and maybe go and tell his uncle.'

Brunetti laughed. 'That's very clever of you.'

'It was Marcello's idea. His uncle didn't believe him when he said we went out looking for girls, so then we'd go to Campo Santa Margherita on the weekends, and sometimes his cousin would see us there, with girls.'

'What did you do?'

'Excuse me, I don't understand.'

'With the girls.'

'Oh, we'd have a drink with them and talk, and then Marcello would ask them if they'd like to go out into the *laguna* for a ride. He always left the boat on the other side of the bridge. So we'd go there with the girls, and the word got around about it, and lots of people thought we were picking them up – you know – but all we did was go out into the *laguna*. Sometimes we'd go out to Vignole and have the grilled chicken at that place there.'

'And then?' Brunetti asked.

'Then we'd take the girls home. Marcello always took them to the *riva* nearest where they lived or where their hotel was.'

154

'Nothing else?'

'No, but the next day Marcello made sure to brag about it at work, without ever giving any details: he'd just boast about it and say how easy it was to pick up girls if you have a boat.' Duso smiled and again grew handsome.

Brunetti remained quiet, aware that they'd arrived at the point in this conversation where Duso would have to reveal more, especially about why Marcello was so afraid.

Neither spoke for a long time, Brunetti determined to make that time grow longer by not speaking. He sat calmly, trying to imagine what it must be like for Vio to be trapped between his uncle and his friend.

Duso leaned forward and said, 'His uncle's been violent with him in the past.'

Brunetti nodded but said nothing.

'Once he was making a delivery in one of the small boats – I think it was going to Caputo. It was electrical stuff: microwave ovens and blenders, and small things like that. While he was taking the first load to the shop – just down the *calle* by the Ponte delle Paste – someone must have jumped down into the boat and stolen a carton of *telefonini*: the little Nokia ones, before everyone got an iPhone. This was years ago, when people still used them.'

'What happened?'

'Marcello told me he called his uncle.'

'Not the police?' Brunetti asked.

Duso shook his head. 'He said his uncle told him never – but NEVER – to call the police.'

Brunetti let that pass without comment.

'So he called his uncle and told him what had happened.'

'And the uncle?'

'He told him to get back to the office.'

'And?'

'And that's what Marcello did. He got the papers signed for the delivery and went back to the Giudecca, just the way his uncle told him to do.' Duso's voice staggered through the last words, stopped for a moment, and then went on. 'When he got there, he tied up the boat and started up the ladder. His uncle was waiting for him at the top.'

Duso's breath had tightened as he spoke. 'He told me … he told me that, when he got near the top, his uncle stamped on his hand and then put his foot against his forehead and kicked him off the ladder, into the boat.' Duso stopped here and looked at Brunetti, who remained silent.

After a few breaths Duso continued, speaking very quickly. 'Two of the men who work there saw what happened.'

'They didn't try to stop him?'

Surprised, Duso said, 'He's their boss.'

'I see,' Brunetti said, then asked, 'What happened?'

'As soon as Pietro was gone, one of them climbed down the ladder and helped Marcello up to the dock. Two of his fingers were broken: he'd twisted around and broken his fall with his hands. But they had to take him to the hospital.'

'What did he do?' Brunetti asked.

'What could he do? After he got back from the hospital – he lives with his uncle – he said he apologized to him for leaving the boat unguarded for so long.'

'And?'

'His uncle said the price of the *telefonini* would come out of his salary, and he was to be at work the next day.'

Brunetti was at a loss for what to say about this. Duso waited a bit, and when Brunetti still said nothing, added, 'That was the end of it.'

'And now?'

'He told me he's afraid to go back to his uncle's place when he gets out of the hospital.'

'Could he stay with you?' Brunetti asked.

Duso froze. His hands fell into his lap. Brunetti had the feeling that, had Duso been able to do it, he would have got up and left the room, but he seemed incapable of motion.

'He'd kill me,' Duso said. Hearing himself, he raised his hand halfway to his lips in the hope of stuffing those three short words back into his mouth.

Ignoring what Duso said, Brunetti asked, 'Then could he stay with some other friend? Or leave the city for a while?'

Duso shook his head. 'It's impossible. Where could he work? All he knows is boats.'

'Will his uncle calm down if they don't see each other for a while?' Brunetti asked.

This time Duso shrugged. 'Marcello says he never knows what his uncle will do. It could be that he'll need him for a job and tell him to come back to work. God knows.'

Well, Brunetti thought but did not say, he's a Giudecchino, after all.

Both men sat silent for a long time, Brunetti bereft of ideas or suggestions to give Duso. 'How much longer will they keep him in the hospital?' Brunetti finally asked.

'Why do you want to know?'

'I want to talk to his uncle, and after what you say about him, I'd like Marcello to be in a safe place when I do.'

18

After Duso left, Brunetti began to consider how best to go about questioning Vio's uncle. He could present himself unexpectedly at the office of the transport company and ask to speak to Signor Borgato, or he could arrive with the full panoply of the law: visit not announced, police launch with an armed officer as well as the pilot, demands in place of suggestions. And certainly more trouble for Marcello.

Brunetti had always loathed, above all, bullies: he despised their arrogance, their contempt for people weaker than they, and their calm assurance that they were to have more of everything for the asking or taking. To oppose them was to provoke them, and to provoke them was to lose. To provoke Borgato was perhaps to endanger his nephew, Marcello.

He found the homepage of Borgato Trasporti and dialled the number. A man's voice answered neutrally with the name of the company.

'Good afternoon, Signore. This is Ingegnere Francesco Pivato from the office of *Mobilità e Trasporti*. I'd like to speak to Signor Borgato if he's available.'

After what seemed a long time, the man said, 'This is Borgato.'

'Ah, then good day, Signor Borgato,' Brunetti said warmly, switching to Veneziano. 'I'd like to speak to you about a problem that concerns you.'

After a moment's silence, the voice asked, 'What's this about?'

Brunetti allowed himself a nervous laugh and said, 'I'm not all that sure, Signor Borgato.'

'What's that supposed to mean?' Borgato demanded in a belligerent voice.

'I think this is something that the Polizia Municipale should be dealing with, and not us,' Brunetti said, doing his best to sound prissy. 'It has to do with the registration of a boat that belongs to you but that seems to have the same licence number as a boat registered to someone in Chioggia.'

Again, a long time passed before Borgato responded. 'That's impossible,' he said roughly, then, perhaps remembering who he was talking to, he changed tone and asked, 'What do you want from me?'

'That's the question I asked when I spoke to our Director, Signor Borgato,' Brunetti said, trying to sound exasperated. 'He said it should be evident. But it's not, so you're the person I have to ask.'

'Afraid of your boss, are you?' Borgato jabbed at him.

Brunetti decided that Ingegnere Pivato was probably accustomed to listening to provocation and so said, 'I'm merely trying to close our file on this matter, Signore. It's been dragging on for months.' Brunetti was careful to speak with the beginning of tight-lipped annoyance. 'I thought we could do that more quickly if I spoke to you directly.' He waited a moment before continuing, 'Or we'll have no choice but to pass it on to a higher authority.'

Borgato considered that for a moment but came back with the sarcasm of the strong. 'And just how do we do that?'

'One way is to have you come to our office, Signore, and —'

'That's not going to happen,' Borgato interrupted, as Brunetti had thought he would. 'You can come out here if you want to see me,' he added, again conforming to Brunetti's expectations. To refuse to speak to a patent weakling would be to lose the chance to play with him, push him around a little, show the bureaucrats who was in control.

Brunetti allowed a muffled 'ah' to escape. He grabbed some papers that were on his desk and riffled loudly through them, then said, 'I could come after lunch, Signor Borgato. About three?' he inquired, being careful to sound uncertain.

'I'm a busy man. Come at four,' Borgato said and put down the phone.

Brunetti had promised Paola he would be home for lunch, so home he went. Both of his children were there, something that happened with lesser frequency as their school lives and the demands of friendship took up more and more of their time. He noted the birth of their friendships, as the names of classmates were introduced at the table, their qualities described or praised, their opinions introduced, always at first with enthusiasm, later with thought, sometimes with scepticism. He learned of the family lives of some of these children, for to him and to Paola they were still children. Most of the families were unexceptional as the parents lived out their middle-class lives: going to the office, travelling, acquiring.

He sometimes wondered what his children said of him and Paola to their friends. To be a policeman, regardless of rank and however unusual, was not to be a professional, not the way a doctor or a lawyer was. Paola's full professorship, however, let her fit effortlessly into the ranks of the acceptable and respected. The social position of her parents, Brunetti understood, gave her an added footstool from which to view the world around her: she hardly needed university degrees to be well regarded.

When he tuned back to the conversation, he heard Chiara say, 'I was on the bus from Mestre last week, and two boys started to shout at an old man. No reason; they just chose him and started saying he was useless and ought to do them a favour and die.'

'How old was he?' Paola asked, unable to moderate her surprise.

'I don't know,' Chiara said. 'It's hard to say how old old people are.' She thought about it for a moment and said, 'Maybe sixty.'

Brunetti and Paola glanced at one another but said nothing.

'What happened?' Raffi asked between bites of pasta.

'He ignored them. He was reading a magazine.'

'And so?'

'The bus was pulling into Piazzale Roma, so we all knew the ride was almost over. I guess they did, too,' she said reflectively. 'Just as the bus got to the stop and the doors opened, one of them grabbed the magazine from his hands and tossed it in his face. Then they both ran out of the bus. Laughing.'

'What did the man do?' Brunetti asked.

'I think he was too surprised to do anything. He just sat there. But then another boy picked up the magazine and handed it back to him. Then, looking at him directly, Chiara asked, 'Can't the police do anything about it?'

Brunetti set his fork down. 'We'd have to be there, or someone would have to take a photo or film it, and the person they bother would have to make a complaint. And we'd have to identify the person who did it.' He pulled his lips together and raised his eyebrows. 'There isn't much chance of catching them.'

'They'll only get worse,' Raffi broke in to say.

'I agree,' added Paola.

'I agree, too,' Brunetti said. 'But until we have evidence or the names of the boys ...' he paused and looked at Chiara, who nodded, '...doing it, it's not likely that we can stop them.'

'Thank God it's not America,' Chiara said. 'And everyone has guns. It would be Far West every day.'

Brunetti, who read crime statistics and knew this was true, chose to say nothing.

As his appointment with Borgato was not until four, Brunetti found himself with too little time to go back to the Questura. So he took his copy of Tacitus into the living room and extended himself on the sofa to read of the death of Agrippina, one of the passages he remembered from his student days.

The index directed him to Chapter Fourteen, where he read with returning horror Tacitus's description of Nero's slapstick plan to drown his own mother: the boat fell apart, but did not fall on her. She swam to the shore, leaving her maid thrashing in the water to be killed in her place. So completely did the plan fail that the Emperor had no choice but to send three assassins to put an end to her.

Brunetti remembered then that there had been some sort of prophecy, and after a few paragraphs found it. 'She consulted the Chaldeans and they prophesized that Nero would surely reign, and would surely kill his mother. To which Agrippina replied, 'Let him kill me, so long as he will reign.' Brunetti closed his eyes to think about this.

When he woke, he glanced at his watch and, seeing the time, hurried to their bedroom and found a badly scuffed pair of light brown shoes that he no longer liked but had failed to throw away. With them, he wore a grey suit that had seen better days and should have had narrower lapels. Before putting on the suit, he removed his shirt and clenched it in his hands to wrinkle it lightly and then put it on again. Next he chose a particularly unattractive green tie. In the back of the closet in the storeroom behind the kitchen he found an old trench coat he'd bought as a student and never had the will to throw away, even after he'd brushed against a greasy door hinge and left a stain on the left pocket that had refused to disappear. He found a briefcase he'd carried at university, leather dried and peeling, and put it under his arm.

Paola looked up from the papers she was grading when he came into her study to say goodbye. She removed her reading glasses and studied his appearance. 'Carnevale doesn't start until February, Guido,' she said, then added, in a sweeter voice, 'How clever of you to go as Hercule Poirot.'

Standing in the doorway, Brunetti ran his hands down the sides of the trench coat and turned a full circle. 'I was trying for something closer to Miss Marple,' he said.

'Tell me it's necessary for you to go out of this house looking like that,' she said, 'or I'll try to stop you.'

'I have to interview someone who thinks I'm a weakling and make him show me how superior he is.'

She replaced her glasses, said, 'Then you go with my blessing,' and returned her attention to the papers.

To avoid embarrassment, Brunetti had asked Foa to pick him up at the end of the *calle* beside the house: he was waiting when Brunetti arrived. Foa gave Brunetti a long look and reached out a hand to help him jump on board. The pilot said nothing, and Brunetti went down the steps into the cabin.

Foa cut through Rio San Trovaso and emerged into the Giudecca Canal. He pulled up at the Palanca stop to allow Brunetti to step up on to the *embarcadero*. 'Would you like me to come back for you, Commissario?' he asked. Before Brunetti could refuse, Foa said, 'I'm not on duty this afternoon, so I can take this boat and dock it at the Questura and come back in my own.' Again, anticipating Brunetti's response, he said, 'It's much smaller and doesn't have a cabin.' Seeing Brunetti's reluctance, the pilot said, 'I'll be back in forty-five minutes,' revved up the engine, and started back in the direction of the Questura.

Brunetti walked along the *riva* and turned into the *calle* that would take him to Borgato's place of work. A middle-aged woman with a round face sat at a desk in a small office to the right of the main door and looked up when he came in. Brunetti wondered if this could have been the woman who met Marcello Vio in Campo Santa Margherita.

'Good afternoon, Signora. I have an appointment with Signor Borgato,' he said in Veneziano. He pushed up the worn cuff of his left sleeve and looked at his watch. 'At four,' he said and bent his wrist as though he were going to show the watch to her. Instead, he set the briefcase beside him on the floor, careful to knock it over, then stooped to pick it up. It dangled from his right hand.

'He's out back, helping the men unload a boat. If you go out there,' she said, waving towards a door behind her and to the left, 'maybe you can talk to him.'

Brunetti nodded, then spoke his thanks and started towards the door. He found himself in a large, cement-floored passage with padlocked wooden doors on both sides. It led towards the back of the building and, presumably, a canal.

Brunetti counted three doors on either side, placed about four metres apart: the distance suggested separate storage rooms of considerable size.

As Brunetti had expected, the corridor led out on to a landing dock that ran along the back of the entire building. A transport boat was tied up beside it, both sides of its prow bearing the wounds of many years of service: the strip of metal meant to protect the top of the sides was battered and dented in many places, the wooden sides scratched and streaked with the paint of other boats.

A crane anchored to the dock was just then raising a large wardrobe, secured by straps and bands, from the wooden boards that created the deck of the boat. Slowly, wrapped and cradled, it floated up and over the dock, where two men waited for it, one in a flannel shirt and an older man in a dark blue sweater. The one wearing the shirt turned the wooden wardrobe effortlessly until its feet were aligned correctly to fit on to a loading platform sticking out from a small cargo fork-lift. The man waved his arm, and the wardrobe stepped four-footed on to the platform. He freed the straps and bands, while the man in the sweater climbed behind the wheel of the the fork-lift, moved it backwards, turned, and came at full speed towards Brunetti.

Hurriedly Brunetti stepped aside, careful to raise his hands in fear, his briefcase waving on a level with his head. The man standing down in the boat laughed so hard at the sight of him that he had to bend over and prop his hands on his knees.

Brunetti lowered the hand holding the briefcase and hurried back into the corridor and back to the secretary, who looked up from some papers when he came in. 'Is Signor Borgato wearing a dark blue sweater?' he asked, hoping that he was.

'Sì, Signore,' she said.

'Is there some place I can wait for him?' Brunetti asked nervously.

'He doesn't let anyone into his office unless he's there,' she said. Then, pointing to a straight-backed chair on the other side of the room, she added, 'You could wait for him there.'

Brunetti thanked her and went over to the chair. He set his briefcase beside it, took off his trench coat and draped it over the back, sat, and pulled up his briefcase. He opened it and removed some papers.

It was fifteen minutes before Borgato appeared, indeed the man in the blue sweater who had aimed the fork loader at Brunetti.

'Pivato?' he asked as Brunetti stood.

Brunetti put the papers in his briefcase, tried unsuccessfully to close it, grabbed up his trench coat, and stepped over to

Borgato. Seeing Brunetti embroiled in coat and briefcase, Borgato extended his hand, which forced Brunetti to switch the briefcase to his left hand in order to shake Borgato's. None of his bones were broken by Borgato's handshake, but Brunetti made no attempt to muffle his groan.

Saying nothing, Borgato turned to the door on his left and opened it. 'No calls, Gloria,' he called back over his shoulder.

He closed the door after Brunetti and went to stand in front of his desk, leaning against it and facing Brunetti. He had the thickened nose of a drinker and the even thicker body of a man who had done hard physical work all his life. His eyes were a pale blue, striking in his sun-darkened face. Brunetti looked around and, seeing a chair, draped his coat over the back and stood his briefcase on the seat.

'What's this all about?' Borgato asked in a not very friendly voice. He walked around his desk and sat.

Brunetti opened the briefcase, searched for a few moments, and pulled out two papers. He walked to the desk, leaned over it, and passed the first paper to Borgato. 'This is the registration of your boat,' he said.

Borgato took it and glanced at it. He read out a series of letters and numbers and said, 'That's my topo. It's registered to me, under this number' – he slapped the back of his fingers against the paper for emphasis – 'for seven years.' He thrust the paper back towards Brunetti, who took it and handed another paper to Borgato, one that Signorina Elettra had managed to falsify that morning. This one stated that there existed another boat of the same type and size, with the same registration number and licence plate number as Borgato's boat. The only difference was the owner's name.

'What is this shit?' Borgato demanded, then jumped from his seat and tossed the paper in Brunetti's direction.

'I'm not sure that word is justified, Signor Borgato,' Brunetti said in his most pedantic tone as he picked up the paper.

'It's justified if I've got a copy of the registration in my files.' Then, the idea suddenly occurring to him, he turned to Brunetti and demanded, 'Have you spoken to this Chiogiotto?' he asked, reading out the name as though it were an insult: 'Samuele Tantucci.'

'Who?' Brunetti asked, looking at the other man with a perplexity sure to push him closer to the edge of his patience.

Borgato turned, grabbed the second paper from Brunetti's hand and shook it under his nose. 'This one, you idiot, this Chiogiotto who has the same number. Have you even bothered to look at these papers? Have you spoken to him?'

Brunetti took the paper from Borgato and spent some time trying to remove the wrinkles the other man's hand had made. When that was done, he returned to his chair and slipped both papers carefully back into his briefcase. He looked at Borgato and said, 'I came here to try to do you a favour, Signore, not to be abused by you. If you don't want my help to settle this matter now, then you can wait until the process goes a little bit further, and then, when the Guardia Costiera comes to ask the same questions, you might be sorry you didn't pay attention when you had the chance.' He took his trench coat and folded it carefully over his arm, took a firm grasp on the handle of his briefcase, and turned to the door.

He'd taken three steps when Borgato said, 'Wait a minute.'

Brunetti took another step and reached for the handle of the door.

'Please, Signore,' Borgato said in an entirely different voice, all anger, all arrogance, gone.

Brunetti stopped. He turned back to him and asked, 'Are you going to be reasonable?'

'Yes,' Borgato said. He walked to Brunetti's chair and pulled it over to his desk. With something resembling a smile, he waved Brunetti towards it. 'Have a seat and let's go over this again.' He tried to make his voice friendly, but it was clear this did not come easily to him.

Brunetti sat on the edge, trench coat over one arm, briefcase in his lap. Borgato went behind his desk and sat, looking at Brunetti.

'What is it you want to know?' Borgato asked.

'Do you know this man in Chioggia – Samuele Tantucci?'

'No.' Borgato almost shouted the word but quickly got himself under control and repeated it in a lower voice. 'No.'

Brunetti set his briefcase on the floor and said, 'I see no reason why you can't be told this. A boat with this number has been seen off the coast, at night, and reported to the Guardia Costiera.'

'Who did that?' Borgato snapped.

'I'm not at liberty to say, Signore,' Brunetti answered in his most officious voice. 'All we were told is that your transport boat, this one,' he said, leaning down to tap at the side of the briefcase where the information was, 'was seen off the coast at night two months ago, and because it was not a fishing boat, it was reported to the Guardia Costiera.'

'Fucking fishermen, can't mind their own business,' Borgato said angrily.

Brunetti allowed himself to nod. 'The Guardia seems to be of the same mind and doesn't want to be bothered about it, so they asked us to check on the licence plate duplication and let them know what's going on. That way,' Brunetti said with a softening of his voice, as though he were asking a colleague to understand and help him avoid spending more time on a bureaucratic tangle, 'we can settle this and close the file.' Then, speaking to himself, Brunetti muttered, 'As if we don't have enough to do.'

Borgato put his hands flat on his desk and held that position for a few seconds, then looked across at Brunetti and said, 'Well, you can tell the Guardia that my boat was out at night because we had the motor overhauled at a place in Caorle, and when we got there in the afternoon to bring the boat back, it wasn't ready, and we didn't get it until after eleven – the fucking workers refused to miss their dinner – so we had to sit around in fucking Caorle until they ate and got back to work on the motors.'

'Caorle?' Brunetti asked. 'Can't people fix it here?'

'The specialist for these motors is the company in Caorle: that's where we bought them.'

'Caorle?' Brunetti repeated, making no attempt to disguise his astonishment. 'That must take hours.'

As though it had just occurred to him, Borgato asked, 'What time did this person say he saw the boat?'

Brunetti reached for his briefcase but pulled his hand back slowly. 'I didn't bring those reports with me. Do you remember when you started back?'

'No,' Borgato said. 'Midnight? No later than that.'

Brunetti pulled a pen from his jacket pocket and hunted until he found a piece of paper. 'Do you remember what day that was?' he asked.

Borgato closed his eyes in thought and said, 'I think it was during the second week of August, maybe the tenth because that's when Lazio was playing, and we missed the game.' Then, trying to make a joke, he added, 'We didn't stop to go fishing, that's for sure.'

Brunetti gave a small laugh and wrote something on the back of the slip of paper – the receipt he'd received for a coffee in a bar the last time he'd worn the jacket – then stuffed it carelessly back in his pocket.

'There's just one more thing,' he said, getting to his feet. 'Could you show me the original registration?'

'Of course,' said a suddenly affable Borgato. He went and stood in front of a shelf filled with thick file holders of different colours. After a moment, he pulled down a white one and set it on his desk.

He paged through it until he found what he wanted, turned the book to show the page to Brunetti and said, 'Here it is.'

Brunetti opened the briefcase and pulled out one of the papers and compared it with the one in the folder, saying, 'Very good.' He nodded and put the paper back, then asked Borgato, 'May I take a photo?'

'Of course,' Borgato offered with a rather dramatic wave of his hand.

Brunetti took out his phone and, remaining true to his role, fumbled with it a bit before turning on the camera. He took a photo of the page, moved the lens back about ten centimetres and took another one.

'Good,' he said. 'A colleague of mine is seeing Signor Tantucci today, so all we have to do is send the photos he takes, and these photos to the licence office and let them sort it out.' He considered what he'd just said and added, 'That should be the end of it for you, Signor Borgato.'

The other man smiled for the first time. It didn't help his appearance much. He came around and stood next to Brunetti for a moment before accompanying him to the door. He opened it, gave a handshake that was less a proof of virility than the other had been, and closed the door.

As he walked across the small office, Brunetti said, 'Thanks for your help, Signora.'

'Will you be coming back?'

'Oh, no, not at all, thank heaven,' Brunetti said, a bureaucrat pleased at having so easily settled what might have become a problem.

She smiled, and Brunetti left the office to go and meet Foa, who was waiting for him in his *sandalo*, sitting on one of the cross-planks with the *Gazzetta dello Sport* open on his lap. Brunetti knew the boat, slow and patient.

Brunetti stepped aboard, sat opposite Foa, and pulled his trench coat over his legs. The pilot wore jeans, a heavy sweater, and a blue windbreaker. 'Where would you like to go, sir?'

'Back to my home, Foa. I don't think I want to go back to the Questura looking like this.'

'I assumed that, sir,' he said, revved the engine, and launched them back towards the Giudecca Canal.

19

At home, Brunetti changed into jeans and a sweater. He packed the shoes, the suit, and the briefcase into one of the free shopping bags the city provided for paper garbage and set it by the door. Tomorrow morning, he could pass by the church of Santi Apostoli and leave the bag at the door to the used clothing shop the parish ran there.

He ambled to the kitchen, in search of he didn't know what. It was just after six, so dinner was still a few hours away. He took the nutcracker from a kitchen drawer and selected a few walnuts from a bowl on the counter. After eating them, he needed something to drink, and what better than the Masetto Nero he had put to rest on its side a few nights ago? He opened it and poured himself a glass, left the bottle on the counter to drink with dinner, then went back to Paola's study to reflect upon his meeting with Vio's uncle.

It was not Brunetti's habit to take notes when he interviewed people or questioned suspects. He let time pass after speaking to them and waited for something to present itself as the gravest concern of the person he'd spoken to. Borgato had been irritated by the mistake with the licence, but he had not been worried. His entire demeanour had changed, however, when Brunetti had mentioned the possibility of a visit from the Guardia Costiera. He had suddenly become accommodating, had even said 'please'.

Borgato had hastily told the implausible story of maintenance that could be performed only in Caorle, hours away, and claimed that the work could not be done by anyone in Venice. Brunetti, even though his experience with boats was limited, could find three mechanics in an hour capable of fixing anything attached to a boat; Vianello could probably find ten. Or fix the motor himself. Only a fool like Pivato would believe the story.

Borgato had said that his trip to Caorle had taken place on or about the tenth: that he had offered it suggested that it was not true. Most liars didn't go far from the truth, so it was likely to be one of the days before or after the tenth. Why had Borgato been in the sea between Caorle and Venice around that time?

He took a sip of the wine, enjoying the taste as it rolled around on his tongue. Ordinarily, having already spoken to him, Brunetti would call Capitano Alaimo and see what he knew about strange or unusual incidents in the Adriatic two months before. His trust in Griffoni's instincts, however, made it impossible for him to call the Capitano: if her radar had detected something amiss, Brunetti would trust in that. It left him, however, with no reliable source working for the Guardia Costiera.

He took another sip of wine, kicked off his shoes, and put his feet on the low table in front of the sofa. He needed what Paola would call an Ancient Mariner, with stories to tell. He paused there and surprised himself by realizing Paola was wrong. He needed someone who knew about the Guardia Costiera as it was now, who the good guys were, who the bad.

He went back to his jacket and retrieved his *telefonino*, found Capitano Nieddu's number and dialled it.

After a few rings, her cello voice was on the line. 'Nieddu.'

'It's Guido Brunetti,' he said, giving his last name as well as his first, as seemed proper.

'Ah, I'm glad you called, Guido,' she said with something that sounded like relief.

'Why is that?'

'We agreed to share anything we learned. I've heard something you might be interested in.' Her uncertainty was audible as she paused, as if to reflect on her own choice of words.

'Was it in a pencilled note from someone in your crew?' he asked, showing that he remembered that detail from their conversation.

'No, it's something I was told by someone I spoke to, two days ago.' After a moment, she added, 'A prostitute. Nigerian.' After a considerable pause, Nieddu added, 'I know her.'

Brunetti considered that for some time, then asked, 'Did you believe her?'

'I'm not entirely sure. Sometimes what she says is … hard to understand.' Her difficulty in finishing that sentence kept Brunetti from responding.

Nieddu said, 'That's why I didn't call.' She said nothing further for a while, then added, 'She was in a bad state. She told me things.'

'Is she in custody?'

'No. You know how it is. We bring them in and then let them go.'

Brunetti resisted the temptation to comment and waited silently.

'I thought of calling you yesterday,' she said, 'but things happened and I didn't. I'm glad you called. Really.'

'Can you talk, or can I come out there?' he asked, only then realizing that what he heard in the background sounded like street noise, not the quiet of an office.

'I'm in the city,' she began and then laughed and added, 'See what happens to people who live or work on the Giudecca? Venice becomes "the city."'

'Where are you?'

'In the bio supermarket in Calle della Regina.'

'Can we talk?'

'No, not on the phone, not here. It's long, and it's sort of complicated.'

'Do you know Caffè del Doge?' he asked.

'The one on this side of the bridge?'

'Yes,' Brunetti said and got slowly to his feet. 'I'll be there in ten minutes.' He waited for her reply.

It was some time in coming. 'All right.'

'Good,' he said and broke the connection.

She was there when he arrived, sitting in the booth at the far right corner of the caffè, usually reserved for regular patrons, who came to find that day's *Gazzettino*. Although she sat facing the door, Brunetti almost didn't recognize her, for she was not in uniform and had pulled back her hair. And was prettier for both reasons.

She half stood and raised her hand a bit as he came in, as if to prove to the two young women behind the bar that she really had been waiting for someone. Brunetti glanced around and saw that most tables were occupied, and at least four people stood at the bar. He walked quickly over to her and put out his hand.

After they shook hands, Nieddu surprised him by moving in front of him to take the chair opposite where she had been, putting her back to the entrance.

Her face was flushed, perhaps from the heat of the crowded room. She sat and smiled at him, repeating, 'I'm glad you called.' She shifted on the padded chair, moved back in it, then forward. 'I think I needed to talk to someone, but I couldn't think of anyone.'

'Your commander?' Brunetti suggested.

She shook her head without answering. 'I'm still not sure she was telling me the truth. Maybe all I need to do is listen to myself telling someone else and see if it sounds believable.' Her grimace showed how absurd this sounded, even to herself.

The waitress came and asked what they'd like. Nieddu asked for a Spritz with Aperol, and Brunetti decided to stay with red wine.

'Did you arrest her?' Brunetti asked when the waitress was gone. When she offered a shrug as an answer, Brunetti asked, 'What happened?'

She sighed and shifted around again, then grew quiet. 'It's one of those territorial things. The municipal police refuse to patrol Parco San Giuliano, so we had to answer the complaint: a woman was taking her children for a walk and saw what was going on, so she called us. Her pimp – not the woman with the kids – I mean this prostitute's pimp, thought he could put them in the park to work – there were four of them, and when they were all brought in, I got to question her because I know her.'

It took Brunetti a moment to sort all of this out, but soon he understood the plot.

'How do you know her?' he asked.

She lowered her head to hide her expression. 'We go to the same church.'

'I beg your pardon.'

'She started coming to Mass about two months ago; in Mestre, where I live. Her behaviour was strange, and no one would sit next to her, so I did.' She looked across at him and said, voice swooping into a higher range, 'For the love of God, it's a church and we're all Catholics going to Mass together, and they won't sit beside her. Or give her their hand when it's time to do that.' Then she added, not bothering to hide her disgust, 'Peace be with you.'

The waitress brought them their drinks. Ignoring hers, Nieddu said, 'So we started to talk, well, to the degree that we could understand one another; we were sort of friends after a few weeks, just by sitting together. And giving the sign of peace.' Then she said, 'Her name is Blessing.' She picked up her Spritz and took a sip, then another. She set it down. 'After a month or so, she told me what she did for a living. I suppose she thought I'd be shocked or not want to sit with her any more.'

Nieddu looked at him, smiled, and went on. 'So I told her what I did for a living and, believe me, I had the same fear.'

'And?' Brunetti asked.

'She laughed. She laughed so hard I had to hit her on the back to try to help her stop coughing.' Another sip, head lowered to hide her smile. The waitress brought a dish of potato chips. Nieddu took one and nibbled at it as though she were a rabbit with a piece of carrot. 'After we had that conversation, about our jobs, we both agreed – but it was a silent agreement – not to discuss them. Fine with me. The only time they let her be alone is on Sunday morning, when she can go to church. That's where we talk.'

'Does she speak more Italian now?' Brunetti asked.

Nieddu nodded. 'Well, sort of: it's got better in the months we've known one another. She understands what I say.' As if adding the bitter punch line of an old joke, Nieddu added, 'As well as she can understand anything.'

Reacting to her tone as much as her words, Brunetti asked, 'What do you mean?'

Nieddu used her drink as a prop: she picked it up slowly, took a very small sip, and placed it carefully back on the table. Brunetti waited. Finally she asked, 'You've heard the saying, "Driven out of her mind," haven't you?'

177

'Yes.'

'That's what's happened to her. I think. That is, too much happened to her, and she's … well, some people would say she's mad.'

'Would you?' Brunetti asked.

Her answer took a long time in coming. 'If I didn't know her, probably. Sometimes she talks to herself or talks to people who aren't there. Sometimes she says strange things.'

'And when she talks to you?' Brunetti thought to ask.

'Usually, no. She's not mad, not in the least.' Nieddu paused for a moment and then added, almost reluctantly, 'Confused, maybe, and sometimes difficult to follow, but that's usually because of language. Once I figure out what she's using a word to mean, I understand. And I'd never say she's mad, at least not then.'

Brunetti saw that Nieddu needed to be encouraged to speak and asked, 'What has she told you?'

Nieddu sighed and continued. 'Usual story: her mother was a teacher in Benin City. Making about fifty dollars a month. When she was killed,' she continued, not pausing to explain this, 'there were four children and no money. So Blessing's aunt spoke to an agent, and Blessing signed the contract, did the juju ceremony and vowed to pay off the debt for her transport to Europe after she got there.' She reached idly for another chip but pulled her hand back and continued. 'They know who her family is and where they live, so if she ever tries to escape, they'll go and burn their house down, probably kill them, too.'

Nieddu shrugged and took a chip and ate it. 'She says she's eighteen.' The way she said it, Brunetti suspected Nieddu didn't believe it.

'After she signed the contract, they told her how much to pay the agent and the usual story about the job she'd have as an *au pair* in Milan: live with the family, take care of their two children, one day off a week.' Her voice grew angrier with each false promise. 'And now, a year later, she's one of the girls who work the beach at Bibione during the summer.'

'Um hum,' Brunetti muttered.

There was a long wait before she started speaking again. 'You've heard it before, Guido,'

'We've all heard it, Laura.'

Nieddu nodded and ate another potato chip. 'She told me she traveled by minibus, packed in with ten or twelve other girls. For days. They never knew where they were, and they were treated badly. So by the third day they all knew what the truth was.' Nieddu paused and lifted her drink. Instead of drinking, she rolled it back and forth between her palms and finally set it down on the table, untasted.

'They got to a beach – she has no idea where it was – men took them out and put them on a big boat. They were pushed down a metal staircase and locked in a room with about twenty other girls. She said there were big boxes in the room, so they were probably with the cargo.

'She doesn't know how long they were there, but she could hear the motors, and the boat rocked, so they knew they were moving. The lights were on all the time, but no one had a watch: no one had anything except the clothes they wore. Some of them were sick; she was, too. Then the boat stopped, and the men came down and pushed them up the steps and outside on to the deck, then down a ladder to a smaller boat.' Nieddu stopped and took a deep breath, as though she, too, were being forced on to that boat. 'She told me all of the girls were handcuffed in pairs when they got into the other boat.'

Brunetti had not heard this before.

Nieddu looked across at him, pulled her lips together nervously, and said, 'She told me it was a golden boat.'

'What?'

'She said the boat was made out of gold,' Nieddu repeated. Seeing Brunetti's response, Nieddu added, 'I told you. Sometimes she says strange things.'

'Did you ask her about that?' Brunetti asked.

'No,' Nieddu replied. 'She believed it, so I didn't insist. I needed to hear the rest of her story.' Nieddu folded her hands on the table and stared at them for almost a minute, then returned her gaze to Brunetti. 'Sorry, Guido,' she said. 'I got carried away. There are only so many of these stories I can stand to hear.'

Again, he made his noise. He, too, had heard too many of them.

'Blessing said that after this boat – the golden one – had sailed for some time – she didn't know how long – she could see lights in the direction they were heading and thought it must be the land, when a big boat started to approach from farther out at sea. It stopped and turned a searchlight on them: they must have spotted them because there was a full moon that night, and no clouds. Blessing said the men in their boat – there were four of them, two were white and two were Nigerians who spoke Edo – ordered them all to lie on the bottom. There was water and it stank. And the men put tarpaulins over them and told them not to move. She heard the other boat getting closer and closer.' Nieddu drew a very deep breath; her voice tightened.

'She heard the engines of the other boat grow louder, and then two of the men pulled back the tarpaulins and started throwing the women over the side.'

Something inside Brunetti froze and he had to tell himself to breathe.

'Blessing knew how to swim, but the other girl didn't. She said there were girls all around her, in the water, screaming. Then one of the white men was in the water, too, pulling at the girls like he wanted to get them back close to the boat. Blessing grabbed a rope that was hanging over the side of the boat and wrapped her arm around it. Another girl was at the end of her other arm, but she couldn't let go of the rope to try to help her. No one was screaming any more: the other pairs of girls were gone, and the one she was handcuffed to was quiet: Blessing said she floated. She held on to the rope. The men in the boat grabbed the man and hauled him up; they shouted at him.

'In the meantime, the big boat passed them and kept going. She doesn't know why. It went away, and then she heard the Nigerian men in the boat laughing and saying these weren't real mermaids because they couldn't swim.'

Nieddu stopped here and brought her drink to her lips but set it down without drinking. She pushed the glass away from her.

Brunetti picked up his napkin, folded it into a small square, and abandoned it on the table.

'After a while,' Nieddu went on, 'the men started the motor again. That's when they noticed the dead girl floating in the water. And then they saw Blessing, hanging on to the rope. So they dragged her into the boat and unlocked the handcuff and threw the other girl back in the water. And they made jokes about one mermaid being better than none. She just lay on the bottom of the boat, and I suppose it didn't matter to them that she could understand them.' There was another long pause, but Brunetti, numbed by what he had heard, was looking at the soccer shirt hanging on the wall and trying to imagine why it would be there and what was the significance of Number 10?

'Then they took her ashore. She was the only one, and they pushed her into a van.'

Does that mean, Brunetti asked himself, that she was lucky? She's a madwoman turning tricks on a beach or at the side of the road: is that better than being dead? 'I'm sorry you had to hear this,' Brunetti said.

'And Blessing?' she shot back.

'My God, she exceeds all pity,' Brunetti said. For long moments, speech was impossible.

'By the time we finished talking,' Nieddu continued, voice emotionless, 'everyone had gone home. My colleagues had questioned the other girls, but not really, and let them go. So I told Blessing she could leave, too.' Nieddu started to say something else, paused, and pretended to cough.

'What is it?' Brunetti asked.

'I gave her one of those cheap Nokia *telefonini* you can get for twenty Euros. My number's programmed into it, so she can call me if she needs help.' She tried a tentative smile and added, 'I put twenty Euros of pre-pay in it.' She shook her head, as if at her own foolishness, then added: 'The number is registered to a cheese store in Cremona. So she can say she found it if she has to. Or toss it away.'

'Very clever.'

Nieddu said, 'She doesn't need more risk in her life.'

'A rock would cry,' Brunetti said before he thought. He reached over and touched her arm lightly.

She nodded. 'Once they were people, and now they're merchandise.'

'Except they kill them now,' Brunetti said.

Nieddu stared across the small table at him, apparently at a loss what to say. He watched as she started to say something but then pause and edit it. Finally she said, 'Dante has lots of circles, but it's still all Hell.'

Brunetti made no comment. He looked at his watch and saw that it was close to eight. He took some coins from his pocket and put them on the table.

He got to his feet. Without understanding why it was important to know, but knowing that it was important, he asked, 'Is there someone you'll go home to?'

She looked up at him, incapable of hiding her surprise, and then she smiled, incapable of hiding that, too.

'Yes,' she said getting to her feet. 'How kind of you to ask.'

'I'm sorry for ...' he began but let his voice trail off. He waved a hand over the table, as if the glasses were representative of the women they had talked about. One glass had somehow shifted dangerously close to the edge of the table and was in danger of falling off.

He reached down and slid it towards a safe place near the centre of the table.

'If only it were that easy,' Nieddu said, patted his upper arm a few times, and left without saying goodbye. It was only when he was walking home that he remembered he had forgotten to ask her opinion of Capitano Alaimo.

20

Dinner, which Paola and Chiara were just putting on the table when he got home, failed to lift Brunetti's spirits. There was pumpkin soup, which he loved, and then grilled branzino, but even this historically magic combination did not work its spell, and he sat, listening to what was being said but not engaging in the conversation.

Chiara was complaining about a new rule the school was trying to impose upon the students: from the beginning of the following week, they were to leave their *telefonini* in a set of lockers – each student was to be allotted one and given the key – during class time. They were free to use the phones during the lunch break, but *telefonini* were prohibited from classrooms, nor were they to be used during the rest of the school day.

Chiara was, expectedly, indignant and spoke of her 'right' to remain in touch with the world during the day and insisted that she was old enough to know how to moderate her use of time. 'We're being treated as if we were slaves,' she said in the tone of righteous indignation common to those whose luxuries are questioned or compromised.

Brunetti set his fork on his plate, careful to do it quietly. 'I beg your pardon?' was all he said.

She looked across at her father, her rhetoric impeded by his calm voice. 'For what?' she asked, puzzled.

'You said you were being treated like slaves,' Brunetti said.

'That's right,' she told him. Then, ignoring the warning his dispassionate tone had given, she added, 'It's true: they're treating us like slaves.'

'Slaves?' Brunetti repeated.

'Slaves,' Chiara confirmed with the same certainty that sprang from Foxe's *Book of Martyrs*.

'In what way?' Brunetti asked, reaching for his glass.

'It's what I was just saying, Papà. They're telling us we can't use our phones while we're at school.'

This was already an exaggeration of what she had first said, Brunetti reflected, but he did not point this out to his daughter.

He took a sip of wine, set the glass down on the table, and shifted it from side to side. Both Paola and Raffi had grown silent and joined Chiara in looking at him. He glanced up at his daughter. 'I'm not sure I understand the comparison,' he said in a soft voice.

'But I told you, Papà,' Chiara said. 'They won't let us use our phones during school.'

Brunetti smiled and said, 'I understand that, Angel. It's the comparison I don't understand.'

'What's not to understand?' she asked. 'We're being stopped from doing what we want to do.'

He held the stem and twirled the wine around to the right, then to the left. He took a very small sip and nodded, although it was not clear if he was nodding in approval of the wine or of what Chiara had said. Finally he asked, 'And that's a definition of slavery?'

He kept his eyes from acknowledging the presence of Raffi and Paola, silent as owls. Nor did he look directly at Chiara; she, nevertheless, responded to something hidden in his voice by setting her fork on her plate and giving him her complete attention.

'Papà,' she said and smiled. 'You're setting up one of your traps, aren't you?' She put her elbows on the table and her chin in her hands as she looked across at him. 'Next you're going to ask for a definition of slavery, and I'm not going to be able to give you an adequate one, and every time I try, you're going to point out holes as big as melons in what I say.'

She sat up straighter and pushed out her left arm to support the barrel of an invisible rifle, her right arm pulling back so she could put her finger on the trigger. She took aim at something in the air above Brunetti's head, pulled the trigger and gave an energetic 'BAM' before her arm jerked up and back with the power of the recoil.

She turned quickly to her right side, raised the gun higher and shouted, 'There's another one. A Bad Definition!' She sighted along the barrel as the second Bad Definition floated towards the table. Another 'BAM,' another falling victim, this one noisy when she set down the rifle and slammed her hand on the table to make the sound of the falling Bad Definition.

Brunetti watched in silence, shocked only as parents can be by legitimate protest from their children. He lowered his head to the table, pressed his right cheek against the tablecloth, and muttered, in English, 'How sharper than a serpent's tooth...' but before he could say more, Chiara, joined by Paola and Raffi, united in finishing the line for him ...'is it to have a thankless child.'

Order, or something resembling it, was restored by the arrival of dessert.

The next morning, Brunetti arrived at the Questura punctually at nine. Although he had no information to give Patta, he thought it would be politic to go to his office and seek his advice about the case. It was always easier to take charge of Patta when he believed he was in charge. When he entered Signorina Elettra's office, Brunetti found her behind a copy of *Il Sole 24 Ore,* which she had long maintained was the only newspaper worth reading. He had no idea why she would read the financial newspaper, for she had never given evidence of an interest in the accumulation of wealth, although she did seem familiar with the major national and international companies and spoke well or ill, but always knowledgeably, of the various officials and officers of those companies as they followed one another into and out of the courtrooms – seldom the prisons – of the Northeast.

'Good morning, Signorina,' he said. 'Is the Vice-Questore in his office?'

'Ah,' she began, using the tone she reserved to announce Vice-Questore Patta's absence from the Questura. 'I'm afraid Dottor Patta won't be in until tomorrow afternoon.' Brunetti stood in front of her desk, smiling to show that no explanation was necessary.

She folded the newspaper closed and set it aside before asking, 'Is there some way I might be of help?'

Brunetti did not hesitate to take advantage of the situation. 'Commissario Griffoni and I spoke to a Capitano Alaimo at the Guardia Costiera two days ago,' he began, pleased to see Signorina Elettra drag a notebook towards her. 'I'd like you to have a look.'

'At?' she asked, looking up, already curious.

'Anything you can find,' he began, 'that might be interesting to us. All I know is that he's Neapolitan.'

From long experience, Brunetti knew that Signorina Elettra viewed a piece of information much in the way a shark viewed a leg dangling from a surfboard.

'I'll start with his performance record, then,' she said. She was not crouched on one knee, palms resting on the surface of the track, but the faster rhythm of her speech seemed to suggest to Brunetti that he hasten from her office.

Before he did, however, she informed him that she had received a call from the hospital in Mestre, requesting that the commissario in charge of the investigation of the accident in the *laguna* involving the two young American women give them a call. Signorina Elettra told Brunetti that she had taken the liberty of assuring the person who called that Commissario Brunetti would certainly call as soon as he could. He nodded his thanks.

In the corridor, he dialled Griffoni's number and, when she answered, asked, 'Coffee?'

When Griffoni came into the bar, she stopped at the counter and gave her order to Bamba, the Senegalese immigrant who had pretty much taken over the work of Sergio, the proprietor, then came back to slip into the booth opposite Brunetti.

Before he could bring her up to date, Bamba came to the table and set a coffee in front of Brunetti and a pot of hot water in front of Griffoni. 'We don't have any verbena, Dottoressa, so I brought you these,' he said, placing a saucer with four or five tea bags of different varieties in front of her. He nodded and went back to his place behind the counter.

'No coffee?' Brunetti asked, tearing open the envelope and pouring in the sugar.

Hand poised over the saucer, Griffoni said, 'If I had any more, I'd take wing and fly back to my office: wouldn't even have to use the stairs.'

'The window's too small,' Brunetti said. 'You'd never fit in.'

'I hadn't thought of that,' she said, dropping one of the bags into the hot water. Then she asked, 'What did you learn yesterday?'

He told her about his conversations with Borgato and his nephew, she laughing with delight as he described his costume and mouse-like behaviour. Then he told her what he had learned from Duso, but she surprised him by asking no questions. Further, she seemed impatient for him to finish.

He stopped speaking and asked, 'What is it you want to tell me?'

She smiled. 'Am I that obvious?'

Brunetti nodded, as if to give right of precedence to a person who arrived at a narrow *calle* just as he did.

'I had a look for Borgato, to find out where he was during those years he was gone,' she said, struggling to sound calm.

'And?' Brunetti encouraged her.

'He never changed his residence, was always registered at his address here,' she said. 'So I began thinking of the traces I might leave if I were living somewhere and not resident there.'

'And what did you come up with?' Brunetti asked, happy to help her towards her revelation.

'Something a Venetian would never think of,' she answered.

'Do I get three guesses?'

'It wouldn't help, Guido, believe me.'

'Why?'

'Because Venetians don't drive, and more importantly, because you don't drive too fast or go through STOP signs or get into automobile accidents.'

Brunetti's face was blank for a moment and then lit up with a smile.

'While we feckless Neapolitans do all of those things,' she went on. 'And more, so I'd naturally think of them,' she said, lifting Brunetti's spirit with her casual joke about the customs of Neapolitans.

'You found him? Oh, wonderful. Where?'

'Castel Volturno,' she said, then added, though it hardly needed saying, 'home of the Nigerian Mafia.'

'Tell me.'

'He was in an accident – ran into the back of a car that was stopped at a red light – fourteen years ago. Then he was stopped for running a red light in Villa Literno, about ten kilometres from Castel Volturno. That was twelve years ago, and then for speeding on a state highway near Cancello, ten kilometres away. That was ten and a half years ago. Since then, there's been nothing, and he never had any real trouble with the police.'

'That's a sign,' Brunetti interrupted to say.

Griffoni nodded. 'Are you thinking what I'm thinking?' she asked.

'I am if you're thinking he's involved with the Nigerians, in which case the police would leave him alone.'

'Who else could he have worked for?' Griffoni asked. 'They're the only employers in that area,' she said, then added, 'and the only work is crime.'

Neither of them spoke for some time, until Griffoni tired of the silence and asked, 'What do we do?'

'Nothing,' Brunetti said immediately. 'I think we assume he's involved with them and continue to learn whatever else we can about him.'

After a long time, Griffoni said, 'I've never known you to say there's nothing we can do.'

It troubled Brunetti to hear it put like that, but that made it no less true. He'd read and heard – every police officer in the country had – about the Nigerian mafia for years: impenetrable, vicious, omnipresent in the area around Castel Volturno. A colleague of Brunetti's had spent a year there and then taken early retirement rather than endure a second. He refused to speak of the experience, save to say that the city was in 'another country'.

'The only thing we can do for the moment is learn as much as we can about him,' he said. 'We need more than the fact that he lived in Castel Volturno: he's not a criminal because he lived there. Until we find a link ...' he began and decided to repeat himself, 'there's nothing we can do.'

Brunetti knew Griffoni well enough to read her frustration and anger simply by looking at her hands, which were clenched tightly in her lap.

'I'm still interested in the accident with the Americans. It was Borgato's boat,' he said.

Silence fell between them until Brunetti said, 'I called the hospital.'

That surprised her into asking, 'And?'

'I spoke to one of the doctors, who didn't seem to know much. He passed me to a nurse, who said she thought the girl was awake.'

Griffoni failed to restrain her surprise and said, 'I hope they know what's going on and this isn't some sort of mix-up.'

'What do you mean?'

She picked up her cup, looked at it as though surprised to see it in her hand, and set it back in the saucer. 'When I called them yesterday morning, I was told she was still unconscious.'

'Then she might have woken up,' Brunetti said, although well he knew the danger of putting trust in the information a hospital released on the phone.

'What will you do?' Griffoni asked.

'I'll go and at least talk to her father,' Brunetti said. 'When did you last actually see her?'

'Two days ago, on my way home; she was unconscious then, too. The nurse told me she was being given painkillers, and that might be the cause.' It did not sound as though Griffoni believed what she had been told.

'How long were you there?' Brunetti asked.

'An hour, perhaps less.' Seeing Brunetti's surprise at this, she said, 'Her father was there, and I told him to go down to the cafeteria and have something to eat while I sat with her.'

She poured more tea into her cup and took a sip. A few drops of colourless tea had fallen on the table. Griffoni stuck her finger into them and drew them into circles, wiped her fingers on her napkin, then said, 'The assistant surgeon was on duty, but he couldn't tell me much. He said the only thing to do was wait and see what happens, that she'll wake up when she's ready.'

'What's that supposed to mean?' Brunetti asked.

Looking across at him, Griffoni said, 'It means they don't have any idea of what's going on.' She lifted her cup to her lips, sipped, and put it down again.

'He told me they did what they could for her nose,' she said.

'Meaning?'

Griffoni ran the first fingers of her right hand across her eyebrow. 'He told me the cut above the eye was easy and will be pretty much invisible in six months. They taped it closed.'

She looked out the window at the people passing on the *riva*. 'Then he told me that they moved her nose back in place and taped it. They can't operate until she's conscious again.' She spoke hurriedly, not wanting to linger over this.

Brunetti continued to look at Griffoni's eyebrow, recalling the photo he had seen of the girl's face. Unconscious of his gaze, she raised her hand and placed it over both eyes, as though the gesture would ward off imagination. Keeping it there, she continued. 'It's all they could do, at least for the moment.' She uncovered her eyes and looked at him with a face wiped clean of all emotion, then said, 'Later I found myself thinking it was like having an archaeologist tell you how he repaired a Greek vase.' Griffoni paused, then added, 'God, surgeons are strange.' She looked down at the table and shook her head, as if unable to believe what the doctor had said.

She looked up at Brunetti and took him prisoner with the power of her gaze. 'I couldn't believe it when he kept talking about it. We were at the nurses' station – it was after her father came back and I was leaving – and he wanted to draw me a picture to make it clear just what they'd done.'

'Does he have an idea of how she'll look?'

'I asked,' Griffoni answered. 'He told me there might be a small difference in the arch in the middle of the eyebrow, but taping the wound was something they did often, and it would be covered by her eyebrow, anyway. He said the nose was different and might not look the same. But then he smiled and said that she could have it repaired surgically in a year or so, and she'll look like she did before the accident.'

She lifted the teapot and tilted it over her cup, but it was empty. She set it down and pushed out of the booth. 'Let's go back,' she said to Brunetti, then she went over to the counter and exchanged a few words with Bamba while paying their bill. Unlike his employer, Sergio, the Senegalese barman rang up the correct sum and gave the receipt to Griffoni: Sergio was more likely to take the cash, say thank you, and not bother giving a receipt, the older man being of a mind that any member of the Guardia di Finanza lurking outside would hesitate to stop and question a police officer about whether he'd been given the slip of paper that proved he had paid the bill and thus the tax on it.

Brunetti stopped and asked Bamba how his wife and daughter were and was informed that his daughter Pauline had the best marks in her class in mathematics and geography, and his wife went in three mornings a week to clean the homes of two old people in their building.

'Good, that you're all busy,' Brunetti said.

Griffoni added, 'And good that you're all here.'

Bamba smiled at her and made as if to touch her arm, but stopped and set his hand on the counter. 'Thank you, Dottoressa,' he said, giving her a look Brunetti had never seen in Bamba's eyes.

He had no idea what strings Griffoni had managed to pull with her friends in Rome, but the immigration office, after sitting for some years on Bamba's application for permission to have his wife and daughter join him, had granted the request within two months of the conversation a weeping Bamba had had with Griffoni the day after his last appointment with the immigration office.

Brunetti had once asked her what she'd done to hurry things along, and she had categorically denied having interfered in what she called, 'the slow grinding down of hope,' a phrase she often used to describe the function of the bureaucracy of the Ministry of the Interior charged with processing requests for immigration. They were silent on their way back to the Questura.

21

When he approached the Ospedale dell'Angelo, Brunetti was struck by its resemblance to a cruise ship becalmed in a soccer field. From a distance, a glass wall appeared: six, seven floors high, seeming to slant backwards as they rose. The ends had an unsettling resemblance to the prows of the massive ships that once plied the waters in front of San Marco, occasionally crashing into the *riva* or coming close enough to fill the front page of the *Gazzettino* for days.

Brunetti approached the shape with a certain timidity, as though, as soon as he stepped aboard, it would break free of its moorings and set off, giving in to some atavistic desire to slide itself into the *laguna* and, like the frog in the fairy tale, be transformed by the kiss of the water back into its true, princely self.

He freed himself from these fantasies and went to the Information desk, where a young man at a computer quickly found Signorina Watson's name, gave him the floor and room number, and told him the elevators were to his left.

Brunetti hardly needed to be told, for he saw signs and arrows pointing to the different clinics and wards. It would be, he realized, difficult to become lost; how different from the old, comfortable, confusing Ospedale Civile in the city, with buildings spread out in no apparent pattern and many signs contradictory or confusing. Instead of the many-pillared cloister with its dozing cats, Ospedale dell'Angelo had pathways threading through what appeared to be a rainforest and an almost palpable cleanliness about everything that met the eye.

He arrived quickly at the third floor and, after showing his warrant card to the nurse at the desk, asked where he would find Mr. Watson and his daughter. He followed her directions to the room. The door was open, so he stopped there and looked inside. Two beds, the near one empty, a man sitting on the opposite side of the other bed. He might have been Brunetti's age, but he had gained more weight and lost more hair getting there. His bulk put the chair at possible risk of collapse: he was deeply intent on the phone he held in his hand, fingers tapping out a message. What was it? 'Come and save my daughter'?

Brunetti's glance moved to the small figure lying under the blankets. In the centre of the face, a white plastic triangle was taped over her nose. Another tape ran the length of her left eyebrow: one perpendicular strip of tape secured it under the plastic covering, another anchored it to her forehead. Her eyes were closed, her mouth open. The skin above and below her left eye was almost black, radiating out to a circle of yellow, and some swelling remained. Her lips were open and pink.

A transparent plastic bag hung suspended from a metal rack, and from it, a pale liquid ran to a needle taped to her arm. A second bag hung below the other; the tube disappeared under the covers.

As if he'd been tapped on the shoulder, the man on the other side of the bed looked up and towards Brunetti. He blinked and dropped his phone, leaned forward in his chair, his hands on the arms, and pushed himself to his feet, hands raised, ready to confront whatever danger Brunetti might represent.

'Scusi, Signore,' Brunetti began. 'Sono qua per ...' hoping to calm the other man by explaining why he was there.

The man took two slow steps towards him and stopped. 'Who are you. A doctor?' he asked in English.

Brunetti answered in the same language 'No, I'm not a doctor, Mr Watson,' he said, realizing it would be best to tell him immediately who he was. 'I'm Commissario Guido Brunetti, from the police. I've come to visit your daughter.'

The man's expression changed from curiosity to something harder.

'Why are you here?' the American asked, coming one step closer. 'What do you want?'

The words would have been aggressive had he not sounded so curious.

'To see if there's been any improvement in her condition, sir.'

The man glanced towards his daughter, as if he hoped to catch her listening to their conversation, but she was not. In a voice he forced to sound calm, Watson said, 'You can see. There's none.' His voice choked off the last word.

'I'm sorry,' Brunetti said, conscious of how useless it sounded.

Before Brunetti could say anything more, the other man stepped back to where he had been sitting, bent and picked up his phone, and put it in his pocket. He came around the bottom of the bed to Brunetti and held out his hand. 'Alex Watson,' he said. His grip was firm but quick, the sort of handshake Americans often gave: eager to establish friendship but reluctant to give any indication they wanted it to continue. He had reddish blond hair that had begun to whiten with age and very pale blue eyes that reminded Brunetti of a Border Collie's, although the man had none of that animal's restrained nervousness.

Brunetti took Watson's hand and repeated his name, leaving off the title.

Watson looked at his daughter and closed his eyes for a long time, then turned to Brunetti and said, 'Perhaps we could talk in the corridor. I don't want to disturb her.'

With a brief nod, Brunetti turned and went into the corridor. Two white-jacketed women stood a few doors down, talking in soft voices.

'Have the doctors told you what's going on?' Brunetti asked.

'They say now that she's in a coma. When they called me to tell me about the accident, they said only that she was unconscious.' He remained silent for a long time and then said, 'Now it's a coma.'

Brunetti nodded and made a noise, which Watson must have interpreted as a request to continue. 'They say it sometimes happens with head injuries. Brain injuries, that is.' Brunetti heard how difficult it was for Watson to speak the words the doctors had actually used.

Watson walked over to one of the windows that looked out on a parking lot. He braced his hands against the windowsill and lowered his head for a moment, then pushed himself upright. 'I spoke to one of the doctors through a translator.'

'What did the doctor say?'

'Something about a piece of bone – I think he said it a was really a fragment. But he didn't tell me how big it is, or I didn't understand.' Before Brunetti could ask Watson if he remembered the Italian so he might translate, Watson said, 'It's not the translator's fault. I'm having a hard time remembering what people tell me. When I talk to my wife, I try to repeat what the doctors tell me. She does speak Italian, but she can't be here.'

Brunetti's expression must have revealed his surprise, for Watson said, 'She's in the middle of chemotherapy, in Washington, and she can't be in a hospital, any hospital, because her immune system is … it's not working very well.'

Brunetti nodded to acknowledge hearing this and, after a pause, asked, 'Is that all they've told you, Signor Watson?'

'They said the only thing they can do is wait and see what happens.' Brunetti noticed motion and glanced down to see Watson's hands, clenching and unclenching repeatedly.

'I've been told that she and Ms Petersen are friends at university,' Brunetti said, trying to re-establish the normality of their conversation.

Watson opened his mouth in surprise. 'Yes. They live in the same dormitory.'

'So you don't know her well?'

'No,' Watson answered, shaking his head several times, as if he'd forgotten it was moving. 'She stayed with us in Rome last year.' His face softened and he added, 'She's got a lot more sense than some of the girls who went to high school with Lucy.' In evidence, he offered, 'She helped my wife with the cooking. Made Lucy help keep their room clean while they were staying with us.' Then, voice wavering, Watson added, speaking as though it were a declaration of love, 'Lucy's never been the neatest girl in the world.'

Before Watson could spin entirely out of control, Brunetti said, 'Neither is my daughter,' and smiled.

The truce of shared parenthood descended, and both remained silent for some time.

Deciding to make a clean break with their preliminary talk, Brunetti asked, 'Did JoJo tell you what happened that night?'

Watson turned his back to the window and half sat on the sill as though suddenly in need of support. After a moment, he nodded and went on. 'They were in a piazza with a lot of other kids, and they met two young men, Italians, who asked them if they'd like a drink.

'When they went into a bar, JoJo had a gingerino, and Lucy had a Coke. Then the boys both had apple juice and they all started to laugh about that.' Watson paused here, and a smile removed a decade from his face. He stopped, and Brunetti saw him cast his attention towards the door to his daughter's room.

Brunetti let a good deal of time pass and then asked, 'Did she tell you about the accident?'

Watson nodded. 'She said it took her some time to remember, but then it started coming back.' Brunetti said nothing, and Watson went on. 'The fact these guys didn't drink reassured them both, so they accepted their invitation to go out in their boat. Everything was fine until they were out in the open water, when the one at the motor kept going faster and faster until JoJo asked him to slow down. But he didn't understand. Though I don't know how much there is to understand, really, if a girl starts shouting at you while you're speeding in a boat.' Brunetti heard the tight breath of anger slipping back into Watson's voice but said nothing.

'She said she asked the other guy to tell him to slow down, but he just shrugged.'

'What else did she say?'

'She grabbed his arm and tried to pull him away from the motor, but it was impossible. She stood up to move back to where Lucy was sitting, and that's when they hit something and she fell over.

'When she sat up – she doesn't know how much time had passed, Lucy was still lying on her stomach and the other one – not the driver – was kneeling next to her, talking to her.' Watson kept nodding his head, as though that would force him to remember what he'd been told.

'JoJo said her arm started to hurt then, really hurt. No one spoke except the guy who was trying to talk to Lucy.' He stopped and bit at his lip, as though he had to punish himself for saying her name.

'The other guy started the motor, and they began moving again; it seemed very slow to JoJo, but she said she wasn't sure because her arm hurt so much and she was cold. She said a lot of water had splashed into the boat when they stopped.'

'Does she remember being taken to the hospital?' Brunetti asked.

'No. She said she might have fainted from the pain because the boat kept hitting waves and she and Lucy were knocked around in the bottom of the boat.' He paused here and added, 'She thinks her mind kept going in and out: things were real, and then they weren't. At one point, she thinks she heard one of them say, "He'll kill me. He'll kill me," but she isn't sure because of the pain and the fear.' Watson stopped.

'Nothing else?' Brunetti asked softly.

'She woke up in the hospital, but Lucy wasn't there. After a while, the policewoman came, and things began to make sense.'

Then, as if his senses had suddenly been restored, Watson asked, 'Who took them there?'

'The men who were in the boat,' Brunetti told him, since it would soon be common knowledge.

'Who are they?'

Brunetti took it upon himself to answer, 'What they seemed to be, sir: two young men, both Venetians, who had ...'

'I know that,' Watson said shortly. 'JoJo told me. But you know who they are?'

'Yes,' Brunetti answered. 'I've spoken to both of them.'

'Without telling anyone?' he asked, moving towards anger. Brunetti saw that all signs of amiability had disappeared. 'What did they tell you?' Watson demanded, seeming to grow larger as he spoke.

'I'm afraid I'm not at liberty to tell you that, sir, not while the investigation is still in progress.' Brunetti spoke calmly, in what he tried to make sound like a friendly voice.

'So they took them to the hospital? And then what did they do?'

Brunetti realized there was no use in lying to him. 'They left, sir. One of them was badly injured himself.'

'I don't care about him,' Watson shot back. He was silent for a moment, and then anger drove him to repeat Brunetti's words. '"They left them." Just dumped them there and left...' Watson began, his anger now unleashed, 'and left them there like they were ... .' Watson stopped and looked around the corridor, as though the words he wanted were hiding from him. But then he found it, and it burst from him, '... like trash.' He raised his hands in fists but did no more than bring them down at his sides.

'Did you ask them about drugs? About alcohol?' Watson demanded.

Brunetti shook his head.

'You didn't ask them?' Watson all but shouted.

'I'm sorry, sir. We did question them, but I'm not at liberty to discuss this with anyone who isn't involved in the investigation.'

The man nodded, but Brunetti saw the tightening of his jaw as he fought back words. Brunetti wondered how well he'd succeed in controlling himself if it had been Chiara on that boat, Chiara in the bed in the room opposite them, and suddenly he felt admiration for Watson's powers of restraint.

The man looked at Brunetti and then at the door to the room. He nodded a few more times, then said, 'I think I need to get back.' He turned away from Brunetti and went into the room, closing the door quietly behind him.

22

Because it was almost five when Brunetti left the hospital, he decided to go home directly but to do so on the tram, which he had never ridden. *Il Gazzettino* had, for years, kept him informed of the tram's many malfunctions, derailments, and crashes as well as the frequent breakdowns of no known origins. But he had never taken it, and he wanted to, so he looked at the schedule of the buses going to the centre of Mestre, where he assumed he could connect to the tram, and took the 32H to Piazzale Cialdine, where the Number One tram stopped on its way between the cities.

'Is this for the tram that goes to Piazzale Roma?' he asked an elderly woman who stood at the stop, a COIN shopping bag in her hand. Ah, how his mother had aspired to being able to shop in COIN, but she had succeeded only in looking in the windows. The woman smiled, moving her wrinkles closer together, then said, 'It should.'

That too, was a statement his mother had favoured: his father should be home at eight, the plumber should come that afternoon, there should be enough money for his school books.

'*Dovrebbe*,' he repeated, and the woman smiled and shrugged. 'I just missed one, so at least we know they're running,' she said, generously allowing him to be a part of her certainty.

No sooner had she said that than a Number One tram slid into the stop on the other side of the street: people got off, people got on. Brunetti recalled a story his mother had told him of the only trip she ever made to what she always referred to as 'Italy', meaning to anywhere else in Italy, aside from Mestre, where she'd been twice. She'd gone to a cousin's wedding, more than fifty years before, had taken a train for the only time in her life, had ridden on a tram, and had met the '*Torinesi*,' those members of her family who had emigrated to Torino to work in the Fiat factory and who had, in the doing – at least according to his mother – grown rich, rich enough to have earned the name, '*Torinesi*,' which word was always used in reference to them and was, for her, a synonym for 'rich'. And he had married one, Brunetti reflected, and now had two children his own mother would consider '*Torinesi*'.

He felt a hand on his arm and turned suddenly towards it. The old woman moved back half a step and said, 'It's here, *signore*.'

The woman's hand had pulled him back to Piazzale Cialdine and to the tram, which stood, doors open, in front of them. He smiled and thanked her, took her arm and helped her step up into the tram. She lowered herself into an aisle seat while Brunetti thanked her again and moved to the front, the better to see the traffic that came towards them. Ahead of them, he could see the single rail on which the tram ran, amazed that this could be possible.

They glided: every acceleration and deceleration a fluid change of speed. They slipped past the motionless lines of cars and on to Il Ponte della Libertà. To the right stretched the horror of Marghera, smokestacks stretching out endlessly; then the shipyard and the half-finished carapace of yet another cruise ship: how perverse, that they were built here – how even more perverse that they were still built anywhere – so close to the city they savaged with their every passage in and out.

It seemed to Brunetti that they slipped into Piazzale Roma and slid to a stop. He moved back and helped the woman to step down and wished her a pleasant evening. She patted his arm but said nothing.

All Gaul was divided into three parts, the first of which were those who commuted out of the city to work on the mainland; the second were those who commuted the other way for the same reason; and the third were people like Brunetti, who lived and worked in the city and who did not ordinarily take the tram. Walking towards the bridge that would take him into Santa Croce, he felt as if he had exchanged his routine with one of the Venetians working out on the mainland and was only now back on familiar ground.

As he walked along the Canale del Gaffaro, Brunetti was struck to see so few people on the street, but then he remembered the *acqua alta*. The moon was not full, there had been no rain in the north, nor strong wind behind the tide coming in from the Adriatic, yet two days ago the water had risen relentlessly to the knees of the people who walked in Piazza San Marco. Within minutes, those photos made the orbit of the planet, and within a few more, the cancellation of hotel and B&B reservations had flown back to the city to fall upon the already-bowed heads of the owners of those rejected empty rooms.

Brunetti was of two minds: he felt a residual sympathy for the people who would lose income, but most of those earning the income were doing so at his cost and the cost of the other residents: rents impossible for normal people, fast food on offer where once normal people could buy what they needed, masks, and blah blah blah. Brunetti had recently vowed no longer to enter into this discussion nor comment on tourism or cruise ships because there was no longer anything to say, add, proclaim, or hope. Like *acqua alta*, tourism came when it wanted, could be stopped by nothing, and would gradually destroy the city.

He pulled out his phone and hunted through the numbers he had filed under Vio's name, stopped at Filiberto Duso's and pressed his number.

At the second ring, Duso answered, '*Sì?*'

'Signor Duso,' Brunetti said in a friendly voice. 'It's Commissario Brunetti.'

'Good evening, Commissario,' the young man answered.

Brunetti remained silent, a tactic he used with people inexperienced in the methods of the police.

After what seemed like a long time, Duso said, 'What is it you'd like, Commissario?'

'I've just got back to the city and wondered if you'd have time to talk to me again,' he said, hoping to sound jovial.

'Where are you?'

Brunetti gave a laugh and said, 'Since I'm asking the favour, Signor Duso, I'll gladly come to wherever's convenient for you.'

'I'm at home,' Duso said.

'Ah, near to Nico's,' Brunetti enthused. 'Perhaps we could meet there for a coffee. What I have to say will take only a minute.'

'Can't we do it on the phone, then?' Duso inquired.

'I'd rather talk face to face, if you don't mind,' Brunetti answered.

After a long hesitation, which Brunetti imagined the other man spent trying to find a way to worm his way out of this, Duso said, unable to disguise his reluctance, 'All right, then. How long will it take for you to get there?'

'Ten minutes,' Brunetti answered, already quickening his pace.

*

Duso was standing in front of Nico's gelateria, gazing down at the ice cream displayed in the metal containers behind the glass case in front of the bar. As he came down the bridge, Brunetti slowed to watch the young man. It was obvious that he had no interest whatsoever in the ice cream. Quite the opposite: he shifted restlessly from foot to foot, as though only force of will kept him anchored there.

Duso turned to his right and looked in the direction of the Gesuati church, one of the two directions from which Brunetti could arrive. He stuffed his hands in his pockets, then ran one hand through his hair and turned around to look in the direction of San Basilio.

When he saw Brunetti, he started walking towards him. As they got closer, Duso remembered to smile, almost remembered how to do it.

The two men stopped and shook hands. Duso's nervousness conveyed itself to his hand: first he grasped Brunetti's too tightly, then he dropped it as though his own hand had been burned by the contact.

The younger man turned back towards the bar and went inside, preventing Brunetti from suggesting they sit at a table on the terrace, where there was still a slice of sunlight. Duso stood at the bar and waited for Brunetti to join him. When he did, Duso turned to the barman and ordered a coffee.

Brunetti nodded to the barman.

The coffees came almost immediately, and both of them added sugar and stirred. Duso took a small sip of his, replaced the cup in his saucer, and opened another packet of sugar. He held it above and spilled some in, stirred it around, and drank the coffee.

From beside him, Brunetti saw the young man's left eyebrow rise. Duso slid his cup and saucer away with a delicate push of his forefinger, as though to suggest the coffee had offended him by being too strong. Then he turned to face Brunetti, waiting for him to speak.

Brunetti decided to tell the truth. 'I told you I went to see Borgato.' Duso nodded. 'From what I saw, I'd say it's dangerous for Marcello to be around him.'

Duso considered this for a long time and finally could do no better than ask, 'Even though he's his uncle?'

Brunetti took another sip of his coffee and set the cup down. He said nothing.

'Didn't you hear me, Commissario?' Duso finally asked.

Brunetti turned to Duso. 'Yes, I did. But we both know that means nothing.'

'It means they're part of the same family,' Duso said defensively, trying to sound offended.

'And this is Italy, the home of the united family, where everyone lives only to be of service to his relatives,' Brunetti said roughly. To relieve the tension, he asked the barman for two glasses of water and remained silent until they came. He drank half of his and set the glass down on the counter, then pushed the other closer to Duso.

Brunetti watched the younger man drink down the water as though it were an August day and he'd not had anything to drink for hours. He had not protested about Brunetti's remarks on families.

'Your friends call you Berto, don't they?' Brunetti surprised them both by asking.

Duso was so startled by the question that it took him some time before he could nod, then smile. 'I couldn't pronounce my name – my own name – until I was four, but by then everyone called me "Berto" so it was too late.' He gave Brunetti another lopsided smile and shrugged.

'Good,' Brunetti said, patting Duso on the shoulder. 'It's much easier to talk to a Berto than to a Filiberto.'

The smile slid back as Duso said, 'It's a lot easier to be called Berto, too. Believe me.'

'I do,' Brunetti said and extended his hand. 'Guido,' he said, and Duso responded with both his hand and 'Berto.'

Brunetti was surprised at the realization that he had not calculated this last scene in an attempt to end Duso's reticence. Young enough to be his son, Duso had not hidden his love for Marcello from him and given him a clearer sense of the tangled wires connecting Marcello to his uncle.

'Will you tell me more?' Brunetti asked.

'Yes,' Duso replied. Then, looking around, he added, 'But not here. Let's walk down to San Basilio.' He pushed himself away from the bar and went out to the broad *riva*. Brunetti followed after putting a few coins on the counter.

The day was cool; it had rained in the night, the air was still fresh, and the view across to the Giudecca was radiantly clear. Fewer cruise ships were coming now, but still there were two in port. Someone had mentioned it at the Questura that day, adding, 'I'd hoped they'd all been killed off,' only quickly to hold up his hands at the shocked faces around him to add, 'I meant the ships. I meant the ships, not those poor devils on them.'

Duso set off slowly, and Brunetti adjusted his pace to his. At the bottom of the bridge, Brunetti decided not to wait for the other man to begin and so asked, 'Has Marcello ever talked about having to work at night?'

'For his uncle, you mean?' Duso asked.

Recognizing Duso's question for what it was, an attempt to delay – if he was lucky, postpone – further questions, Brunetti said, 'Yes,' and immediately repeated the question, 'Has he ever talked about it?' Duso kept walking at the same slow pace, unlike some people who tried to walk faster to escape questions. And the need to answer them.

After a few steps, Duso said, 'Yes. Once.' No sooner had he said that than he added, 'At least that's what I think he was talking about.'

'When?' Brunetti asked.

Duso stopped walking and turned to look at the houses on the other side of the canal. Brunetti paused beside him, silent.

'About two months ago.' He waited for a moment and said, surprised not to have thought of it until then, 'It was the night of Ferragosto, so the city was quiet: everyone was away on vacation. Marcello called me at four in the morning and told me he was outside my apartment and asked if he could come up.' Before Brunetti could ask, Duso said, 'He didn't want the other people who live in my building to hear the bell and wonder what was going on.'

Duso gave a sigh, as would a person who suddenly realized just how very tired he was, and went on. 'I went downstairs in my bare feet and let him in. He was wet. Not just wet. Soaked.' Duso turned and started to walk again; Brunetti moved up to his side as they continued.

'He came in and stood there, dripping on the floor. If he moved, his shoes squished. When we got up to my apartment, I bent down and took his shoes off, then his socks. He was shaking so much I told him to go and take a shower to get warm. But he went over and sat on my sofa and asked – like he was a guest in my house – if he could have something hot to drink. I knew he loved hot chocolate, so I asked him if that's what he wanted.' As Duso had spoken, his steps had slowed even more, weighed down by memory.

He stopped but continued looking ahead, down towards San Basilio and, beyond that, the offices of the port, and beyond them, the docks for the cruise ships. 'I left him there and went into the kitchen to make the hot chocolate. It took a couple of minutes, and when I came back with it, he was lying on the sofa, crying. Like a little kid, sobbing like his heart was broken. And shivering.

'I went and got a blanket. It was still very hot, and I don't have air conditioning, but he was shivering like it was winter. I helped him get his clothes off and wrapped him in the blanket and made him sit up. I asked him what was wrong, and he tried to make a joke. It was terrible: he showed me his watch. It was one I gave him for his birthday, but it wasn't waterproof, and he showed it to me and said he was crying because he ruined the watch in the water. And then he started to cry again, harder, and all I could think of to do was give him the hot chocolate, but he drank it too fast and burned his mouth, so I took it back and blew on it until it was cool enough for him to drink.' Duso looked at his feet and saw that one of his shoes was untied. He knelt and tied it, and Brunetti saw that he double knotted it, the way his mother-in-law had taught his own children to tie theirs.

Duso stood but remained still. 'I sat down beside him and asked him to tell me what was wrong. All he did was shake his head and keep drinking the chocolate. He'd take a sip and shake his head and take another sip and shake his head again. When it was gone, he held the cup like he didn't know what do with it, so I took it and put it on the floor.'

Duso looked down at the pavement, as if he needed to see where the cup was so he wouldn't knock it over. 'He was still sort of crying, sort of hiccuping and wiping his eyes and nose on the blanket.

'I asked him again to tell me what was wrong, but the only thing he said was, "We killed them. We killed them." And then he started to cry again.'

Duso resumed walking, Brunetti at his side. They passed the pizzeria where he and Paola often went with the kids, the restaurant, the post office, and were almost at the end of the *riva*. Duso stopped in front of the almost invisible entrance to the supermarket.

Brunetti noticed the African refugee who always stood there start towards them and waved him away with a quick motion of his hand. The man, sensing something he didn't understand, moved back to his place to the right of the doorway.

After a long time, Duso said, 'That's all that happened. Marcello fell asleep sitting up. I pushed him over and pulled a pillow under his head, got him another blanket. And I went back to my room and lay awake, thinking about Marcello and how much I love him.' He gave an enormous shrug and let out a sigh.

'I guess I fell asleep. When I woke up, he was gone. He'd left the blankets on the sofa. His shoes were by the door, he'd taken a pair of mine; they're a size bigger, so he could wear them. And he'd taken an old sweater I've had forever.'

'When did you see him again?'

'Oh, about a week later. We went out for pizza with some friends,' he said, pointing back towards OKE. 'We could sit outside in the evening.'

'Did he ever say anything about it?'

Duso shook the idea away with a sudden motion of his head.

'Never?' Brunetti prodded

Duso refused to answer.

'Did he change in any way?'

'Not that anyone else would notice.'

'But you did?'

Duso nodded.

'How?'

'He didn't talk as much as he used to, and he didn't seem to have as much fun with the things we did.'

Brunetti wondered what else might have happened that night in Duso's apartment, but then he remembered the way Duso had spoken of the love he had for his friend, and he cast away the idea, ashamed of his curiosity.

Before Brunetti could say anything, Duso smiled and reached out to touch his arm. The younger man let some time pass and then said, 'That's all.' He turned and started back in the direction from which he had come. Brunetti went in the other direction, turned right, and started for home.

Brunetti dawdled on the way, wanting to have time to think through his meeting with Duso. Poor boy, he thought, to be in love with his best friend. Especially with – what was it people used to say when he was younger? – 'A love that dared not speak its name'?

In recent years, Brunetti had come to wish that some sorts of love would decide to speak their names a bit less loudly. Did people not realize how tiresome so much of this conversation was to anyone who thought the sexual behaviour of other people was not a matter to discuss or judge?

Brunetti could barely imagine what ideas about sex Pietro Borgato carried around in his head, but he was sure there was no room for a man who loved another man, especially if that man was Pietro Borgato's nephew. Brunetti had felt the radiant violence in the man: his own performance as a weakling had certainly allowed Borgato to surge on unhindered by any fear of opposition or concern that he might be revealing too much of himself. It was only the mention of the involvement of the Guardia Costiera that had tamed his ascending anger and turned him into the semblance of a reasonable man.

When an inattentive Brunetti found himself in Campo San Barnaba, he decided not to stop to see if his parents-in-law were home. He wanted to continue walking, have time to consider a possible link between the story Nieddu had told him of the women tossed overboard and Marcello Vio's desperate visit to his friend's home.

Brunetti's phone rang, and he saw Griffoni's name.

'*Sì?*' he answered.

'Alaimo's clean,' she said with no introduction.

'What?'

'I called some people at home.'

'In Naples?'

'It's home when I need it to be,' she said. 'Yes, Naples.' Then, sounding curious and not offended, she asked, 'Why do you need to know?'

'I don't need to know, Claudia. I just like to know how these family things work.'

'How did you know it was family?'

'I figured they'd be the ones you trusted most, or at least the first ones you'd call.'

She laughed. Then she said, 'I have a cousin who's a Carabiniere. Maggiore. He works at the Port, so he knows a lot of things.'

'And he knew Alaimo?'

'No, he knew his father, who was also a carabiniere. He was having a coffee in a bar, years ago – Alaimo was still a kid – when a man walked in, pulled out a pistol and shot him in the head. Twice. The man was gone from the bar even before Alaimo's father hit the ground.'

Brunetti waited for her to say more.

'Years later, a *pentito* gave the police the name of the murderer, but he'd already been killed.' Brunetti was struck by the casual way she said this, as though Mafia wars were a part of everyday life. Perhaps the Mafia attack on her own father, years ago, allowed her to sound casual about such things.

Brunetti said nothing, and she continued, 'Alaimo, the one who was murdered, had three sons, all kids then: one's already a colonel in the Carabinieri; the second is a magistrate; and the third is the one we met.'

She went silent again, prompting Brunetti to ask, 'And?'

'And they're religious, all three of them, about what they do.' Before Brunetti could ask how she knew this, Griffoni said, 'I asked around, and so did other people for me. Believe me, he's clean.'

'As to his being religious, there's still the fake aunt at San Gregorio Armeno, isn't there?' he asked, not that he doubted what she'd told him but simply to clarify things fully.

'She's his aunt. Well, sort of an aunt. It's very Neapolitan.'

'Meaning?'

'His uncle married a woman from Manila, and it's *her* aunt who's the Abbadessa.' She paused a moment, as one does before the punchline of a joke. 'Crocifissa?'

'Abbadessa Crocifissa?' Brunetti asked, taking another poke.

'Yes.'

'I see,' Brunetti responded. 'So we can trust him?'

'If what I've heard from my friends and my family is true, we can trust him absolutely.'

'When do we do that?'

There was a brief hesitation before Griffoni said, 'We have an appointment with him at eleven on Monday morning.'

'Good,' Brunetti responded. 'Let's meet at nine, at the Questura. Then Foa can take us there.'

'Aye, aye, Signore,' she said in English and then was gone.

23

On Monday morning, a message from Signorina Elettra was waiting for Brunetti when he opened his email. It confirmed, giving specific dates and actions, what Griffoni's friends and family had stated: Alaimo was clean.

Brunetti told Griffoni about this when she came down to his office and then told her about his conversation with Mr Watson. When Griffoni asked how the young woman was, Brunetti could do no more than raise his hand and let it fall to his knee, repeating what his mother had always said in times of uncertainty: "We are all in God's hands."

Griffoni let a long time pass and then sat up and all but shook herself free of the effect of Brunetti's last remarks.

'I confessed,' she said.

'What do you mean? To whom?'

'To Alaimo,' she said, at first avoiding Brunetti's eyes. 'About his aunt. And my conclusion.'

'Ah,' Brunetti let escape him. 'How did he react?'

'He was ...' she began. 'He was gracious.'

Brunetti forbore saying something to the effect that his years in the North might well have accustomed Alaimo to being treated with suspicion and merely nodded to show he had heard her.

They spent some time, now that they viewed Alaimo in the light reflected from Griffoni's relatives, in thinking of how they could involve him in their investigation of Borgato. It took them little time to decide to tell Alaimo what they knew and then try to persuade him to help them learn more.

Griffoni agreed with Brunetti that they needed to connect the murder of the Nigerian women – of which there was no evidence, no date, no location, no information save the wandering talk of an African prostitute who was probably mad – with Vio's desperate night-time visit to his friend. Once that was done, they would have a witness who was not mad. Nor dead.

'Alaimo will know if women are being brought in this way,' Griffoni said. 'Up here, I mean. It's common enough in the South.'

Brunetti found no adequate response and got to his feet to start down to Foa and the launch.

Twenty minutes later, Foa glided them to a stop in front of the Capitaneria; a young man in a white uniform came out of the front door and walked across the *riva* on time to catch the mooring rope Foa tossed him. Some sort of nautical sign must have passed between them because he made no attempt to moor the boat, simply hauled on it, keeping the boat close to the *riva* while the two passengers disembarked.

He passed the rope back to Foa and saluted the two commissari, then led them back to the building and opened the door to let them enter.

They were quickly at Alaimo's office, where he got to his feet as they were ushered in and came around his desk towards them. His smile was warmer, if anything, than last time. Alaimo went first to Griffoni and shook her hand, saying, 'Ah, Claudia, if only I'd known when you came the first time. Think of the time we could have saved.'

'Ignazio,' she answered, 'caution's a habit it's hard to lose.'

'Especially when one is dealing with a Neapolitan,' he said and released her hand.

She laughed at that and, turning to Brunetti said, 'Guido, this is Ignazio, who, as it turns out – at least when he's in Naples – plays tennis with my cousin's husband.'

Brunetti was amazed: was this, in Naples, the basis upon which friendships were formed and trust given? He permitted himself a tiny, faintly inquisitive, 'Ah.'

'And who was stationed here . . .' she went on.

Alaimo raised a monitory hand at this point and said, 'That's not important, Claudia.'

She turned to Alaimo and asked, 'May I say anything?'

Alaimo ignored her question, stepped forward and took Brunetti's hand. They moved automatically to the places they had taken the last time they were in the room.

When they were seated, Alaimo took the initiative of host and began, 'I was equally . . . hesitant the other day.' He turned to Brunetti and smiled. 'I knew your name, Guido, and your reputation, but Claudia had never worked on anything that involved us, so all I knew of her was what she showed me that day.' He let them consider that for a moment and then went on. 'The very convincing portrait she painted of a person – once I mentioned my sainted aunt, that is, and raised her suspicions – whom I would not, in my wildest dreams, think of trusting.'

Brunetti, sitting opposite Griffoni, saw the blush that crept across her cheeks. Having always believed her beyond shame and capable of anything, Brunetti was surprised to see it there. And relieved.

Alaimo must have seen it, too, for he turned to her and put up a hand in a calming gesture. 'If you thought I was lying to encourage your trust, Claudia, you were wise to be cautious.'

He paused, smiled, hesitated a bit longer and then said, 'I behaved the same way and for the same reason. Your mention of Vio and Duso, and then so casually of Vio's uncle, sounded like a fishing expedition to me.'

'Was I that obvious?' Griffoni asked.

The question seemed to embarrass the Captain. 'Only when it became obvious that I'd said something to alarm you: I had no idea what or how. The more you talked, the more you were a person I didn't want to be involved with.' Another pause. Another smile. 'You set off loud alarms by naming Vio and his uncle.'

Alaimo suddenly tossed both hands in the air. He looked at Brunetti, then at Griffoni, and then went on, speaking in an entirely different voice: no more playfulness, no more jokes, flirtatiousness dismissed. 'I've been paying attention to them for a long time. That's why when Claudia behaved as she did, I sent you away promising to ask around. I didn't want the police to alarm them by showing interest in them.'

It seemed that Alaimo had finished, but he added, his voice a bit warmer, 'It's a good thing I'd heard about you, Guido, because it was enough to make me call a few friends in Naples and ask about ...' he turned to Griffoni, smiling, 'you.'

'I passed the test, I hope.'

'It was decided when I spoke to Enrico.'

Griffoni raised an inquisitive eyebrow, and Alaimo nodded and smiled. 'Enrico Luliano,' he said.

Griffoni froze. She started to speak but failed to produce any sound. Brunetti asked, sounding as casual and uninterested as he could, 'Who's he? The name sounds faintly familiar to me.'

Alaimo removed his glance from Griffoni and looked at Brunetti. 'A magistrate. A very good one.'

Griffoni suddenly shifted around, crossed her legs the other way, and said, her voice sounding perhaps a bit too steady to Brunetti, 'With two bodyguards and three different apartments where to choose to sleep, at random.'

'Doesn't sound like a very attractive life,' Brunetti said, trying to make it sound ironic but failing.

'Shall we talk about the immediate situation?' Griffoni asked briskly.

Alaimo nodded, got up, went over to his desk, and came back with a few manila folders.

He sat down and handed one to each of them, opened his own. 'These are all the same,' he said as they opened theirs. 'As you look through them, I'll add prejudicial and unverifiable information to what's written here.'

And that, for the next quarter of an hour, is exactly what he did. The first entries in Pietro Borgato's file listed his arrests and convictions during the years before he disappeared from Venice. Alaimo remarked only that his pattern was fairly common to young men of a certain class on the Giudecca forty years before: jobs taken and lost, fights that put someone in the hospital, theft, drugs, a withdrawn accusation of rape.

And then he was gone, and the missing years remained missing.

The next two pages began with his return to Venice a decade ago and documented the creation and expansion of his transport business and his own growing wealth in the years after his return. Alaimo added, 'We don't know where he got the money he brought with him when he came back, but he used it to buy his apartment, the warehouse and dock, and two small boats.' He turned a page. 'As you can see, he opened the transport business immediately after he got back.'

'And in those early years?' Brunetti asked.

Alaimo looked up from the last sheet of paper, where Borgato's assets were listed, and added, 'We didn't begin to pay close attention to him until recently, when he managed to buy two more boats, very large ones, and three more properties in the city. Where'd the money come from?'

As if Brunetti had not spoken, Alaimo said, 'About six months ago, a friend of mine in the Guardia di Finanza called me about him, and when I asked why he wanted to know, he said they were preparing an investigation of his finances. His business was growing, but so were his expenses, and still he could buy more and bigger boats.' Alaimo smiled. 'My friend said they were curious about this.'

Alaimo lowered the papers to his lap and looked aside at Brunetti. 'It took me a long time, days, to convince them not to approach him, but to leave him to us.'

'Why was that?' Griffoni asked.

'Because we'd charge him with human trafficking, not tax evasion.'

So there it was, finally named, Brunetti thought: human trafficking. The merchandise originated, as it had centuries before, in the poorest parts of the world: Africa, Asia, South America – places on the borders of these continents. And the traffic still went back to the colonizers, to where the bodies would be put to use or work, doing what wealthier people could still afford to pay other people to do for them: grow and harvest their food, care for their old and their young, warm their beds and submit to their desires, produce their necessities and their treats.

Or, as in the past, he mused, they could simply be sold and thus become the de facto property of whoever was willing to pay the price and run the risk of possession. They could become household staff, field hands, sex toys, perhaps even organ donors, each step stripping off successive layers of humanity from both their persons and from the souls – if Brunetti could permit himself the use of this word – of their owners.

When Brunetti's attention returned to Alaimo, the other man was saying, 'Once I convinced them that they could charge him after we arrested him, we came to an agreement.'

'But for how long?' Griffoni asked.

Alaimo bowed his head, as though he were somehow responsible for the delay. 'We needed enough evidence to persuade a magistrate to authorize us to go ahead, but we had to be careful about getting that information.'

And choosing the right magistrate, Brunetti thought but instead asked, 'Not to alarm him?'

'You're Venetian, so you know how it is: you touch the web there,' Alaimo said, pointing his finger at a spot in front of his left shoulder and then extending his arm off to the right and pointing to another equally invisible spot. 'And it trembles here. Especially – if I might add – on the Giudecca.'

Brunetti nodded, then asked, 'What have you learned?'

Alaimo said nothing for a long time, but neither Brunetti nor Griffoni broke the silence: they sat and waited for Alaimo to continue. Finally he did. He tossed the papers in his hand on to the table between them, made steeples of his fingers and tapped their tips together a few times, then said, 'This is going to sound like science fiction.'

The two commissari remained silent, motionless.

Alaimo continued. 'One of our men fishes a lot, and since he's got relatives in Chioggia, he goes over there to do it. He's told us for years that he's found a place where two currents meet, both bringing lots of fish. But he won't tell us where it is, whether it's out in the sea or in the *laguna*. There are some Chioggiotti who know the place, he says, and over the years they've become friends. Or at least they share the place, and no one tells anyone else about it.'

Brunetti began to wonder where this tale would lead and when it would end: sailors' stories had a habit of following currents and not straight lines. And it certainly didn't sound like any science fiction he'd ever heard.

'Anyway, one of the guys who fishes there is a boat-maker,' Alaimo continued. 'He was talking one day about a way he's invented to let boats escape being seen by radar: it was something about long copper panels that can be raised above a boat to cover it: like a teepee, but horizontal.' Seeing their confusion, he went to the bookshelf behind his desk and brought back a toy model of a boat, obviously handmade, and lovingly.

Alaimo put it down on the table and pulled two letters, still in their envelopes, from a pile on his desk. He set them, long-side down, on either side of the model, then tilted them until the tops met above the boat. And there it was, a horizontal teepee.

Alaimo went on, pointing as he spoke. 'This man told him that if radar came from the side, as from another ship, the rays would slide up the copper.' He approached the side of the boat with an outstretched finger, then, a few centimetres before touching it, his finger went up and away from the panel and continued into the air beyond it.

'See?' he asked them, 'the radar beams are deviated and keep going into the sky, showing nothing, so, it's as if the boat weren't there. If it's dark, there's no need for the patrol boat to give itself away by using a searchlight because the radar hasn't detected anything in the water.'

He disassembled his radar shield and moved the model boat closer to the centre of the table.

'Tell us more,' Brunetti said.

'If the mother boat stays outside the twelve-mile limit, in international waters, we can't touch it. What we think happens is that the smaller boats – and they'd have these copper panels – go out to the bigger boat. A ship, really. And they pick up the women.'

He paused and then added, bitterly, 'The cargo. There's probably more than one boat going out to get them, and they can each make a few runs every night.'

He waited for questions, but none came.

'Where do they take them?' Brunetti asked.

'We don't know. We've gone out at night and found the big ships, but we don't have the manpower to stay out there with them all the time, and they have every right to be there. Because we can't board them, we don't know what's on them.'

'What do you do?'

'We come back to port and go home and go to bed.'

'What could change that?' Griffoni asked.

'Ah,' Alaimo let out on a prolonged sigh. 'We need to know when and where the transfer will be made, and we need to know where they plan to land.'

'And have people in place, waiting for them?' Griffoni asked.

'Se Dio vuole,' Alaimo said.

Griffoni made a noise, half gasp and half laugh. 'If God wills,' she said. 'Every woman in my family says that. About the olive harvest, about the time a train will arrive, about whether someone will get well, or a baby be born healthy.' She thought about this for a moment and added, 'And now, you say it about whether we'll manage to arrest these men.'

'That's why I'm interested in him.'

'Borgato?' Brunetti asked.

'No, Marcello Vio,' Alaimo said and gave a smile that frightened Brunetti.' 'He's the weak link.'

24

After hearing that, Brunetti spoke at length to Alaimo, with Griffoni attentive to what he said. It took time and some repeating to recount what Duso had told him about the upsetting night-time visit from his best friend. After that, to explain Vio's tortured state, Brunetti repeated Captain Nieddu's account of the African women who had been thrown from the boat and his conjecture that Vio had been aboard the boat that carried Blessing to shore.

Alaimo's expression did not change as he listened to these stories, although his face grew discernibly paler. As Brunetti continued, Alaimo shifted himself backwards in his chair, as if in response to his body's instinct to distance itself from what was being said.

After finishing, Brunetti backtracked to provide the detail of the *telefonino* Nieddu said she gave to the woman.

'Do you have any idea how many phones she might have given away?'

'No. None,' he said, but then he remembered how the telling of the story had shaken her, and he added, 'Probably a lot.'

Silence fell again. Brunetti thought about what a strange people we are: often judged to be superficial, emotional, and self-involved, sometimes untrustworthy, usually polite. And yet, in those horrid days, still recent in memory, doomed always to be there, how many doctors and nurses had died; how many others had, knowing this, returned from retirement to go into the hospitals and themselves be gathered up into the numbers of the uncountable dead? Nieddu's gesture came of the same mysterious, irresistible urge to make things better for other people. For a relative, for a stranger: the urge to make things better was in our marrow. He lowered his head and rubbed at his face with both hands as if suddenly tired of all this talk, talk, talk.

Turning to Alaimo, Griffoni asked, as though eager to get back to what she thought important, 'What use do you want to make of the weak link?'

The Captain gave her a grateful look. 'If he's back on the Giudecca, he's probably gone back to work with his uncle.'

'But he's got a broken rib,' Griffoni objected.

'He's from the Giudecca,' Alaimo said in response.

'Oh, stop it, Ignazio,' she snapped. 'All this crap about the Giudecchini being real men makes me sick. Every man a Rambo who can leap over buildings, when in reality the only men you see there are some old geezers playing Scopa in the bars and talking about how the government should be run, and all we need is a strong leader to tell the people what to do.'

Alaimo smiled at her and nodded. 'But the old geezers don't live in fear, and I'm afraid Borgato's nephew does: and I think many of his neighbours, as well.'

'What else have you heard?' Brunetti asked.

From the speed with which Alaimo answered, it was evident that he had been waiting for the question. 'Borgato's boats go out at night – not his transport boats, but the passenger boats – those two Mira 37's he's got, with the big engines. Stripped down, they could run rings around his transport boats and carry tons of contraband.' Then, more soberly, he added, 'Tons of anything.'

He looked at Griffoni and said, 'You keep telling me not to talk about the Giudecca, but everyone knows everyone there. And people know his boats are going out, but if we were foolish enough to ask about it, they'd tell us they don't know anything. The best they might say is that he's probably going fishing.' His voice was tight with disgust he proved incapable of disguising.

'No one would mention the two motors with at least 250 horse-power: I can't even calculate how many more times stronger that is than a motor on a boat that transports mineral water or boxes of detergent to the supermarkets. He could move ...' he went on, growing more outraged as he spoke, ' ... this building, for God's sake, if someone put it on a big enough raft.'

He looked directly at Brunetti, aiming the next remark at him. 'And he's managed over the years to persuade every one of his neighbours to sell him their docking places along the *riva* where he has his warehouse.'

'That's impossible,' Brunetti shot back before he thought about it. 'No one ever sells their docking place. They've been in families for generations.'

Alaimo held up his empty hands, as though he were trying to show his ignorance of this reality. 'It took him three years to persuade them all.'

'How many were there?' Brunetti asked.

'Six.'

'That's impossible,' Brunetti repeated.

This time Alaimo smiled as he continued. 'That's what every Venetian I've told about it says. It's impossible. But still it's true.'

'Didn't anyone complain?'

'If they did, they probably would have complained to you, not to us. We deal with problems at sea; you're supposed to take care of problems on land.'

'So he's got the whole canal?' Brunetti asked.

'Almost.'

'Who held out?'

'No one,' Alaimo said. 'There's another space, but it's part of a contested estate.'

'On the Giudecca?' Griffoni asked, then put her hand over her mouth, looked at Brunetti, and said, 'Excuse me, Guido.' She paused; Brunetti saw her scuttle around for a way to explain her casual assumption that no one on the Giudecca could have an estate worth enough to contest. In the end, she didn't bother, and he decided to act as though he found that a reasonable opinion for her to have and let it pass.

'All right,' Brunetti said. 'We agree he's a bad guy and,' he paused for a moment before inserting the next word, 'probably mixed up in human trafficking.' He folded his hands together and stuck them between his knees, leaned forward and continued, 'But we don't have anything tangible: no evidence, no credible witnesses, no one who can give us specific information about where he does it.' He sat up and pulled his hands apart.

'The money?' Griffoni surprised them both by asking.

'What?' Alaimo asked.

'He must sell these women.' Her voice was harsh, brittle. 'Girls. Who buys them, and how do they pay him? And if it's not cash, how does he explain its arrival?'

'It could go to another country,' Alaimo suggested.

She nodded. 'Fair enough. But it's no use to him there.' She considered her own words for a moment and then said, 'It doesn't matter where it goes, does it?' Before either of them could speak, she went on. 'He can't put it in the bank. He can't buy more boats or property because, if he continues to spend more than he earns, sooner or later the Guardia di Finanza will see the red flags and take a closer look at him.'

'Then what does he do with it?' Alaimo asked.

Griffoni held her hands up protectively in front of herself and said, 'I have no idea.' Then, with a smile, added, 'What to do with too much money is not a problem I anticipate having, so I've never given it much thought.'

'Why don't we?' Brunetti asked.

'What?' Alaimo asked.

'Give it some thought,' Brunetti answered.

'I think we can be sure he's not spending it to take care of widows and orphans,' Griffoni said coldly.

'He's divorced,' Alaimo added. 'And he doesn't seem to have a companion.'

'Of which sex?' Griffoni asked.

Brunetti turned to her suddenly. 'That's a strange thing to say.'

'I suppose it is,' she conceded, 'but he sounds like a very strange man.'

'Why?' Alaimo asked.

'Because he's a homophobe, for one thing,' she said, turning to Brunetti. 'You told me what Duso said.' Then she added, 'Imagine what he thinks of Duso's friendship with his nephew.'

'He could just as easily be spending it on drugs,' Alaimo interrupted, but they could hear that he didn't really believe this.

Brunetti's memory flashed back to something Paola had read to him early in their marriage, decades ago. He no longer remembered why she was reading the book: had she been teaching the American novel that year? She'd read him a scene in which a man secretly watched a woman lying on a bed in the building opposite. She had a secret hoard of gold coins, and as he watched, she pulled the coins close to and on to her naked body. With a start, he remembered the erotic rush he'd felt as Paola, golden-haired and lying on the sofa, read him the scene.

'Would you accept women as a reason?' Alaimo turned to Brunetti and asked, as though he believed their united male vote would settle the matter. Brunetti failed to speak; Alaimo shrugged.

'Maybe it's money,' Brunetti said, surprising them.

'What?' Alaimo asked, as if reluctant to abandon a sexual motive for Borgato's actions.

'Just that. Greed. Money. Maybe he simply wants it, more and more of it.' Brunetti considered the idea as though one of the others had offered it. 'There are people like that. I've known one or two. It's the motive for everything they do.'

As if speaking from far away or through a bad connection, Griffoni asked lazily, 'Does it matter?' When neither of the men answered, she said, 'Really?' Still neither man spoke, so she said, 'It doesn't matter why he does this; it matters only that he does it, and our main concern is that he can be caught while doing it.'

She looked back and forth between them, waiting for one of them to say something, and when they did not, she spoke into their radiating silence, 'Which brings us back to the weak link.'

Somehow, Griffoni had become the master of the hunt: the two men pulled their chairs closer to the table and they began to plan just how to bring Pietro Borgato down.

25

They spent endless time in discussion about the best way to make use of Marcello Vio. Lunchtime came and passed; finally, alerted by hunger, Alaimo sent out for a tray of sandwiches and drinks. One of them suggested that they stop while they were eating and talk about something else, but they failed to find that something else and were soon back at finding a way to persuade Marcello to … here, the discussion fell apart because Griffoni used the word 'betray', and the two men said the word was too strong.

'Would you prefer "deceive", she asked them. Or, "mislead"?' When neither of them answered, she added, 'Or, "Give him over to the police"?'

This time, Alaimo chose to go to the door and ask one of the men sitting outside to bring three coffees. When he came back and sat down, he looked at her and said, grudgingly, 'All right. "Betray".'

Brunetti gave no indication of his approval of her having won the point and remained dispassionate, saying, 'He's got to tell us when and where.'

'For which part of it?' Griffoni asked.

'Transferring the women from the bigger ship to Borgato's or where Borgato lands them?'

'Since there's nothing we can do legally when they're in international waters,' Alaimo said, 'all we need is to know where the transfer will happen; then we track him until he lands on Italian territory.'

Alaimo went to his bookshelf and came back with a book of nautical charts. He paged through it for a moment, found what he sought, and placed it, open, on his desk. The others came to stand on either side of him while he ran his forefinger down the open expanse of the Adriatic and stopped at a certain point, tapped there, then moved his finger due west and up and down the coastline. 'My guess is that it would have to be along here somewhere,' he said. He slid his finger back across the water to the first point. 'The ship would have to be here, twelve miles off the coast.'

He pointed to the names of some of the places on the coast. 'These aren't easy places to land a small boat; well, most of them aren't.'

'Why?' Griffoni asked.

'The water's too shallow. A boat like the ones he has would run aground a few hundred metres from the beach at most of them. Well, depending on the tide. So they'd have to force the women to walk through the water, maybe even carry them.'

He leaned closer to the map to read the names of the locations. 'My guess is that they'd want a place like this,' he said, pointing to Duna Verde. He slid his finger farther north and stopped at Spiaggia di Levante. 'This is a possibility, but storms sometimes change the shape of the sandbanks.'

Alaimo turned the map to make it even easier to read and finally tapped a few times at Cortellazzo. 'That would be the best place,' he said, 'but it's dangerous.' Before they could ask, he explained. 'The Piave enters the *laguna* there, and all it's done for thousands of years is cut new channels and then wash them away. Even my best men wouldn't try to get up that channel at night.'

'If they knew the tide patterns?' Brunetti asked. 'Remember, Borgato's spent most of his life on the water.'

Alaimo considered this, nodded, picked up the book and left the room. Griffoni got up and went over to the windows to look across at the Giudecca; Brunetti sat and waited, surprised by how little he really knew about the waters around Venice.

Within minutes, Alaimo was back. 'One of my men grew up there. Yes, it's possible. If you're from there and know the tides.' Griffoni walked back to her chair, but neither she nor Brunetti spoke.

Finally, Griffoni asked, 'How do we get there?'

Brunetti's voice was low when he said, 'Before thinking about that, we should be sure Marcello Vio will cooperate.'

'So here we are, back at the starting point,' Alaimo said. He went to the door and pulled it open, called out that someone should come in and take the plates and cups away. No one spoke while a cadet cleared the table, and neither Brunetti nor Griffoni protested when Alaimo told the cadet to bring three more coffees.

'It all depends on him,' Alaimo said after they'd drunk their second coffees. Then, explaining the situation at the Capitaneria, he added, 'I haven't got the resources to patrol that area every night, and I haven't got the legal right to board a ship in international waters.'

Brunetti raised his hands in a gesture of near-resignation. 'So it has to be Marcello.' The other two nodded, however reluctantly, and Brunetti went on. 'If his behaviour at Duso's place was his reaction to what he saw, and did, that night, then there's a chance he'll agree to talk about it.'

'Talking's not enough,' Griffoni observed coldly. Then, as if in opposition to her own remark, she began again, saying, 'If he's really the *"bravo ragazzo"* everyone says he is … ' but she failed to finish the sentence.

Alaimo interrupted to do it for her. 'Then he'll tell us.'

'He won't do it,' Brunetti said, seeing it clearly now. 'He's too afraid of his uncle. That's why he was so slow going to the hospital. Two girls lying on the bottom of the boat, blood on them, and he didn't speed.' He raised his voice and concluded, 'Think what would have happened if the police had stopped him for speeding and found the two girls.' Before either could respond, he added, 'Once he got them out of the boat, he went home as fast as he could because if he'd been stopped, he would have been fined for speeding, if at all.'

He glanced at Griffoni and saw from her expression that she agreed with him. And Alaimo, when Brunetti looked at him, was nodding.

'Stalemate?' Alaimo asked.

Brunetti shook his head and said only, 'Duso.'

'His friend?' Alaimo asked.

Brunetti nodded.

'What's he got to do with this?'

'Marcello went to Duso's the night of Ferragosto and told him what he'd done. "We killed them. We killed them." There was a full moon that night, so it would have been easy to see the Nigerian women in the water. Drowning.'

He watched as both of them reached for their phones. 'There was a full moon the night of Ferragosto,' he said. 'We had dinner on the terrace, and we didn't need candles.'

Griffoni raised a hand, as if to signal that it was her turn to talk. 'The Nigerian woman said she saw a white man in the water, didn't she?'

Brunetti nodded.

234

'That must have been Marcello, then,' she said.

After the three of them had sat silent for some time, Alaimo asked Brunetti, 'Do you have a suggestion?'

Brunetti nodded again. 'It's probably a bad one, but it's the only one I can think of.'

Neither spoke.

'I need to speak to Duso again,' Brunetti began. 'And I need to persuade him to give Marcello some sort of tracking device.' He looked at Alaimo and said, 'You know what I mean: something that we can...'

Alaimo began to smile and finished the sentence for Brunetti: 'Follow.'

A pause spread from them and filled the room, suddenly allowing them to hear boats passing in the Canale. Griffoni turned to her left and looked out the window. She gasped, slapping her hand across her mouth and shifting her weight forward as if in preparation to flee the room.

Both men turned and saw the enormous white wall passing the window on its slow imperial passage toward the terminal on the far side of San Basilio.

It was perhaps twenty metres from them, but its enormity made it seem far closer. They sat, like Hansel and Gretel and a friendly host, and watched the *Witch of Destruction* slip silently past them, allowing them ample time to view the side of her passing body. And then, as her tailless back-end passed in front of them, they saw the dark trail she left above and behind, sure to be cancelled by the next creature to pass or by a puff of benevolent breeze. The true price of her passing would be obliterated by the magic incantation of the forces that commanded the *Witch* and that transformed her horror into beauty and made her a princess to be desired by all.

Alaimo looked away first, perhaps because this was a spectacle granted to him every day, and he had grown numb.

Finally, Alaimo said, 'We use a tracking device that fits in a watch.'

Seeing their curiosity, he said, 'We've had people who load cargo take them off and stick them into stolen cars that were on ships sailing to Africa; one ended up behind a refrigerator in the galley of another ship; another one was on the wrist of one of the officers. So long as the transmitter functions, it can be traced by satellites to within ten metres of where it is.'

'What happens if someone finds it?' Griffoni asked.

Alaimo smiled, as though he'd expected the question, and said. 'Because it's nothing special – a plain metal watch that might have cost thirty Euros – they give it to one of their kids or take it home and leave it in a drawer and forget about it, or maybe they wear it. If they're wearing it, they can just change the battery when it stops, and it will tell the time again.'

'And getting it on one of Borgato's boats?' Brunetti asked.

'Why not on to his nephew?' Griffoni asked.

The men looked at her in surprise.

'Not likely,' said Alaimo.

Brunetti said nothing but considered the possibility. He turned his attention to the view of the Giudecca across the water. Duso lived on this side, somewhere near Nico's.

Marcello, he kept thinking, might have told Duso even more about what happened on the boat and – if he had been the man who went into the sea – his vain effort to save … to save one of them? All of them? His soul?

If it had been Marcello, his leap into the water had failed to save the woman or the women, and there would be no changing that. With Duso's help, Brunetti could offer him another chance.

Duso met Brunetti on the terrace in front of Nico's. The hour had not yet been changed, so there was still daylight at six, and the weather had blessed them and remained warm even after the sun had disappeared behind the distant Euganean Hills. Few other people sat on the terrace: eight, nine, but all were wearing only sweaters and jackets, taking advantage of the sun's lingering generosity.

Duso asked for a coffee and Brunetti for a Pinot Grigio.

While they waited for their drinks to come, they made the predictable comments about the shortening days, the weekend ahead, when the hour would be moved back and the arrival of winter given no more resistance. After that, they simply sat and gazed off towards the west as the light gradually dimmed itself.

'Have you seen Marcello?' Brunetti finally asked.

Duso nodded.

'When?'

'Last night. He met me after his first day back at work, and we had a drink together.'

'How did he seem?'

Duso stared suspiciously at Brunetti for some time and finally asked, 'Why are you interested?'

Brunetti saw no reason not to tell him the truth. 'Because I have a son who's a few years younger than he and you are.' Brunetti was interrupted by the arrival of the waiter, who set their drinks in front of them, added small bowls with peanuts and chips, and went to another table to take the order.

'What does that change?' Duso asked, sounding curious, not aggressive. He sipped at his coffee, which Brunetti noticed he drank without sugar this time.

Brunetti tasted his wine. They knew him here, so the wine was good. 'I suppose it makes me protective.'

'Of the ones who are like your son?'

'No. It would be a lie to say that. But of some of them.'

'Which ones?'

Brunetti had never thought about this. It was an instinctive and impulsive response he had to some people, especially the

237

young, even some of the ones he arrested. Perhaps he felt protective of the ones who reminded him of his own younger self. He set his glass on the table and grabbed a few peanuts. He put them, one by one, into his mouth while he thought about what to say.

After he'd swallowed them all and had another sip of wine, he said, 'I feel it for the ones who find themselves in trouble and don't realize that they're good. In the ethical sense.' Brunetti said, not liking the pedantic sound of it when he heard himself say it. As if to alter his remark in some small way, he added, 'While other people don't believe they are.'

'Are you talking about the people you arrest?'

'No. Well, perhaps some of them,' Brunetti answered, reaching for more peanuts.

Duso pulled the dish of potato chips towards him and started eating. 'So you think Marcello's good?' he asked, keeping his eyes on the chips.

'He took the girls to the hospital, didn't he?'

Duso's hand froze halfway towards the bowl, and he gave Brunetti a look of open surprise. 'What else *could* we do?'

Brunetti was struck by the spontaneity of Duso's response. It was not a real question but a response provoked by shock. What else, indeed?

Brunetti thought he'd push him a bit farther and see the true direction of his feelings. Speaking with dispassion, he said, 'You could have taken them back to where you met them. No one would have seen you, not at that hour. Just put them on the *riva* by the bridge and go home.'

The crumbled pieces of potato chip fell on to the wooden deck beneath their feet. Within seconds, the lurking sparrows were upon them, feasting, hopping on Brunetti's feet in their greed.

It didn't take Duso very long to work it out. When he did, he said, 'That was some sort of test, wasn't it?' He spoke with shock he tried to present as contempt. 'Of my "ethical sense", as you call it.' He grabbed at the napkins the waiter had left on the table and wiped at the grease and crumbs on his hand, then crumpled the napkins and tossed them on to the table. But, Brunetti observed, he did not get up and walk away.

'Which you passed,' he told Duso in a far softer voice.

'So what?' Duso asked aggressively.

Brunetti ignored the tone and answered the question: 'So I believe you're a judge of Marcello's ...' Brunetti sat back in his chair and folded his arms. He looked down towards the church of the Redentore, built in thanks for the ending of the plague, almost five hundred years ago. That wasn't done any more, making a change in the city, pledging something new. They just went back to business.

'Excuse me, Commissario,' he heard Duso say. 'Are you all right? Would you like a glass of water?'

He opened his eyes and looked at the young man. Why do people always ask if someone needs a glass of water? Maybe it's because it's what's done in the movies.

'No, thank you,' Brunetti said. 'It's kind of you to ask. I was just thinking and I'm afraid I was distracted by my thoughts.'

'About what?' Duso inquired, his former resentment evaporated.

'About the way people find it hard to change. Even when they know they should do something, or not do something, they do the wrong thing and make things worse.'

From Duso's expression, Brunetti saw that his answer had surprised him.

'You weren't thinking about Marcello?'

Brunetti smiled. 'Maybe I was.'

'You think he has to change?'

'Don't you?' Brunetti asked but then immediately went on. 'Sorry, that's not an answer to your question, and I shouldn't have spoken like that. You're not a child.'

'Then what's your answer?'

Brunetti put his fingers around the stem of his glass, but it was empty. 'That he has to think about what he's doing,' Brunetti said. Then, to prove to Duso that he was speaking openly, he added, 'What he's doing with his uncle.'

'I don't know what that is,' Duso said, loudly.

'You don't know the details: I believe that. But you know what it's doing to him, so you know he shouldn't be doing it. And you know it's bad, probably very bad.' He withheld himself from repeating what Vio had said about 'killing'.

Duso opened his mouth to speak, but Brunetti didn't stop. 'You were with him in the boat when he started towards the hospital with the girls. Going slowly. Paralysed by fear of his uncle. You both knew he should have been speeding because they were both hurt, and you didn't know how badly. What happens if the next time there's something worse and someone dies, or gets killed?'

'Why do you talk about a next time?' Duso asked, sounding uncomfortable.

'Because he's working for his uncle again, and that can lead only to trouble.'

'For Marcello?'

'For Marcello, yes, but for other people, as well.'

'What do you mean?' Duso tried to ask forcefully, but he couldn't carry it off and succeeded only in sounding nervous.

'Berto,' Brunetti began, using a different voice. 'You told me what he said to you the night he came to your place. "We killed them. We killed them," and you saw what doing that did to him.'

Speaking quickly, as if to get it all out as soon as he could, Duso said, 'He's never said anything else about it.'

Brunetti leaned forward in his chair to be closer to Duso but made no move to touch his arm. 'Berto,' he said again, 'he doesn't have to say anything else, does he?'

240

Duso put his locked hands between his knees and bent over them. He shook his head a few times but did not look at Brunetti.

'They killed people, Berto. Marcello and whoever was with his uncle killed people that night. They were out at sea, on one of his uncle's boats, and they killed people.'

'Marcello said ...' Duso began and stopped, unable to go on.

Brunetti waited, motionless.

Duso cleared his throat a few times and then continued, voice almost inaudible because his head was still lowered, 'He told me that.' He nodded in agreement with what he'd just said and kept on nodding a few times, like a wind-up toy until, eventually, just like a wind-up toy, he unwound and stopped moving.

'Did he tell you about the women?' Brunetti asked.

Duso froze, then shook his head. Brunetti suddenly noticed that the front of the boy's shirt, light blue, thick Oxford cloth, appeared to be spotted, though not from the coffee, for all the liquid had done was make the blue a bit darker, as is the way with that colour, especially when it is Oxford cloth.

Brunetti allowed a long time to pass. He heard footsteps, probably the waiter returning. Without looking around, he held up his arm and waved whoever it was away. The footsteps retreated.

Some boats passed. A seagull got into a fight with another one over something a person on the dock tossed into the water.

Brunetti watched the young man, then turned away out of some archaic sense of decency about what one could and could not watch. He looked at the hotel that had once been a flour mill and pasta factory until – rumour had it – a disaffected employee had stabbed the owner to death. The crime was unrecorded in the police files, but this seemed not to stop people from telling and repeating, and believing, the story.

He'd been there once after the transformation into a hotel, hadn't much liked the place, paid five Euros for a not particularly good coffee, and gone home.

'Commissario?' he heard Duso say and turned towards him again.

'You wandered off again,' Duso said. It must have been some time: the darker blue dots on his shirt had almost disappeared.

'You see,' Brunetti began, 'this is very difficult for me.' He turned a softened face to Duso and said, 'Because I don't want to do it, I delay and I try to think about something else.' He waved his arm at the spectacle that faced them from the other side of the Canal, still glorious even in the diminished light.

Duso's head turned to follow the sweep of Brunetti's arm down past the Zitelle, all the way to the docked boats of the Guardia di Finanza.

When he turned back, Brunetti was reaching into the pocket of his jacket.

'No, please, Commissario,' Duso said, putting his hand on Brunetti's arm to stop him. 'I'll pay for this.'

Later, Brunetti was to remember that.

26

The waiter had disappeared. Brunetti suddenly lost all patience with his own moral cowardice. And Duso's. The drowning girls, who had thrashed in Brunetti's imagination ever since Nieddu had told him about their deaths, seemed to encircle the table as he spoke. Duso sat silent, asking nothing, not questioning the truth of what he heard. He sat and stared across at the Giudecca as he listened. Finally Brunetti asked again, 'Did Marcello tell you about the women?'

Duso was slow in answering, but when he did, the young man said, 'He didn't tell me anything, only that people died, and they killed them.' He took a few deep breaths and added, 'Since then, he's been ... strange.' He looked at Brunetti, who nodded.

Duso opened his mouth to speak but failed to make any noise. A small boat with two young men in it skidded past them, heading towards the Zattere, seeming to hop from wave to wave, as if slamming down onto them was what it was meant to do.

When the noise was dulled, Brunetti reminded himself that his task was now to persuade Duso to – he did not mince words, at least not to himself – betray his best and oldest friend, who also happened to be the man he was in love with. And possibly a party to murder.

He asked, 'Would you help him if you could?'

Duso stared at him as if he thought Brunetti had lost his senses.

'Of course, I'd do anything.'

'Good.' How to say it? 'We need Marcello to do one thing.'

Raising his voice, Duso said, 'He won't do anything to hurt his uncle.'

'The uncle who kicks him down a ladder and involves him in human trafficking and murder?' Brunetti asked softly, almost hissing.

Duso tried to defend his friend. 'He took Marcello in when no one else would help. He gives him a salary that allows him to support his mother and their family. Marcello owes him everything.'

Brunetti threw up his hands and, before he thought, said, 'One of you is crazy.'

Duso put his own hands on the arms of his chair and started to push himself to his feet.

Without thinking, Brunetti reached out and spread his palm on Duso's chest. 'Sit down,' he ordered, and Duso sat. Brunetti grabbed his arm.

'He can owe him all he wants, but unless Marcello gets free of him, his uncle will corrupt him.' Before Duso could protest, Brunetti leaned closer and, voice tight with anger he forced himself to control, said, 'His uncle will have him go out on the boat another night, and they'll bring in more girls. Or kill them – it's all the same to Borgato. And sooner or later, Marcello will stop crying about it and then stop being able to cry about it.' Brunetti closed his eyes until he felt his own arm move and move again, and when he looked at it, he saw Duso using his free hand to try to loosen Brunetti's grip from his arm.

244

Brunetti pulled his hand away, waiting for his rage to lessen. He listened to his heart throb, propped his elbows on the table and lowered his head into his hands.

After some time, he recognized the sound of a vaporetto, arriving from the right. He raised his head and opened his eyes to look at the boat, white and slow and familiar, before allowing himself to look at Duso's empty chair.

Instead, he saw the young man sitting there, staring at him, waiting.

Brunetti asked, 'Will you help him?'

Duso nodded.

Brunetti took the box with the watch from his inner pocket and handed it to Duso. The younger man examined the box with little interest and placed it, unopened, on the table in front of Brunetti.

Into his silence, Brunetti said, 'Please open the box, Berto.'

Duso did as he was told and revealed a thin watch with a metal band. 'What's this?' he asked.

'It's a watch.' There was no sign of recognition on Duso's face.

Duso picked it up again. It was nothing special: metal, normal thickness, no snazzy diving meters, two hands. Brunetti told him, 'Inside is a transmitter. It gives a radio signal that can be followed from a great distance.'

'By whom?' Duso asked, eyes still on the watch.

'In this case, the Guardia Costiera. Some of their boats are equipped to do it.'

The sun had gone down, and the evening's chill was setting in. Duso shivered but showed no eagerness to leave. 'What do you want me to do?'

The dispassion with which Duso asked the question could have been simple curiosity as much as assent. 'Give the watch to Marcello,' Brunetti answered, then smiled and added, 'Tell him this one is waterproof.'

He watched as Duso thought it through, 'Then what?' he asked.

'Nothing. If he wears it, they'll be able to track him, and the boat.'

Duso shifted around in his chair, as if suddenly aware of the drop in temperature. 'If I give it to him, he'll wear it.' It was not a boast but a simple truth.

Suddenly, the younger man pulled his jacket tight over his chest and hugged himself with his arms. 'It's too cold here,' he said. 'Let's move.' He put the watch in the box and the box in the pocket of his jacket and got to his feet.

When the waiter brought the check, Duso slipped a bill under his saucer and stood. He started off in the direction of the *calle* where he lived.

Brunetti caught up with him and walked at the quick pace the younger man set. When they got to the place where Duso had turned off the last time, Brunetti slowed to a stop.

Duso faced him. His expression had tightened, and he seemed older than he had a few minutes before. 'One condition before I agree about the watch,' he said.

'What's that?' Brunetti asked, his suspicion audible. When Duso didn't speak, Brunetti insisted, 'What do you want?'

'When they go after him, I get to go with them.'

'I can't guarantee that,' Brunetti said, meaning it.

Duso reached into his pocket and took out the box. 'Then take this back,' he said, holding it out to Brunetti.

Automatically, Brunetti put his hands behind his back. 'I can't.'

'Then I won't.'

Brunetti stood frozen. He wasn't the one to decide this.

'Ask them,' Duso ordered.

There was no question about how serious he was. Brunetti stepped away, pulled out his phone and found Alaimo's number.

The Captain answered on the second ring. 'What is it?' he asked.

'He says he won't do it unless he can go with us when it happens.' Not until he heard himself say 'us' had Brunetti realized how fully he now felt himself involved in this.

There was a long silence before Alaimo asked, 'Is he serious?'

'Absolutely.'

The line went silent for some time, but then Alaimo said, 'Then tell him yes.'

'All right.'

Brunetti broke the connection and slipped the phone into his jacket pocket.

He took the two steps back to the now-shivering young man. 'He agreed.'

'Good,' Duso answered and put the watch in his pocket. Suddenly his face loosened and changed back to the face that had sat across from Brunetti at the table. He put out his hand, and Brunetti shook it.

'Thank you, Commissario,' Duso said, his politeness restored, as well. He turned to walk away but stopped before Brunetti could call to him. He came back and asked, 'What do I have to do?'

Slowly, thinking it through as he spoke, Brunetti said, 'You have to convince Marcello to tell you when he's going out with his uncle again.' Duso started to speak, but Brunetti held up his hand. 'He has to tell you when they're going out at night. And give him the watch. That way, they'll be able to trace Borgato's boat without getting close to it.'

Duso rubbed at his face with both hands, as if trying to wake himself from a dream that had become unpleasant. 'We message all the time, all day long,' Duso said. 'So he'll tell me when he's going.' Duso nodded a few times, then looked at Brunetti. 'He'll tell me.'

Keeping his voice normal, Brunetti said, 'Give me your number; I'll send you mine.' Duso recited the number while Brunetti entered it, then Brunetti sent his own number, which Duso locked into the memory of his phone.

'You promise to let me come?' Duso asked, placing his hand on Brunetti's arm.

'Yes,' Brunetti said.

'You swear?'

'By all that's holy,' Brunetti said, telling the truth.

By the time he got home, Brunetti was chilled straight through and found that the apartment was cold. The landlord had no legal obligation to turn the heat on in the building for another week and had chosen not to do so. A disgruntled Brunetti spent some time in the shower but realized he had been defeated by his children's beliefs about the environment and was no longer capable of enjoying a shower that lasted more than – he was sufficiently grumpy to think, 'than a heartbeat' but changed it to 'five minutes'.

Wrapped in a towel, he left a trail of damp footsteps back to the bedroom and pulled on a pair of brown woollen trousers and then, remembering he'd moved it to the back of the closet at the arrival of spring, a beige woollen shirt that Paola had given him for Christmas but that had always seemed too elegant to be worn and which, therefore, had spent almost a year by itself, unworn, abandoned and unadmired. His body still radiating the heat of the water, Brunetti pulled on a white T-shirt, then the woollen shirt. Soft first in his hands, it caressed his arms as he slid them into the sleeves and seemed almost to help him fit the buttons into the buttonholes. Leaving the top two unbuttoned, he found a patterned scarf, put it around his neck and tucked the ends inside the shirt.

He paused to look in the mirror, smiled at himself and said, in purest Veneziano, '*Son figo, son beo, son fotomodeo.*' He might be too old to have any right to think of himself as *'figo'*, and there would certainly be some dispute as to the *'beo'*, and he certainly never would be a fashion model, but he looked good and knew it.

There had been no noise from any other part of the apartment, but that did not exclude the possibility of Paola's presence, especially if she had given her soul over to reading. He sometimes told her that Attila could storm through the house and she'd not notice if she were reading. She had most recently disputed this by claiming that it would depend on the book.

Her door was open, so he went in. And found her on the sofa, with Henry James. She looked up at him and smiled. 'What a beautiful shirt that is,' she said.

'My wife gave it to me.'

'Did she?'

'Yes.'

'Good taste, I'd say.'

'Especially in men,' he answered, then said, 'Let me get something to drink. I want to talk to you.'

As he passed through the door, heading for the kitchen, he heard her call from behind, 'Bring two glasses, then.'

During the time it took him to tell Paola the story of Marcello Vio, his uncle, the two Americans in the boat, the women tossed into the sea, and Duso's reluctant agreement to help the police, Brunetti got up three times. Once he went into the bedroom and came back wearing a thick sweater over his woollen shirt; twice he got up to turn on lights in the room. When he finished, their wine was barely touched and Paola was visibly shaken by what he'd told her.

'How can you do this, Guido?' she asked, her face stricken. 'Day after day, learning about what people will do to one another.'

'What else can I do to earn a living?' he asked before he realized how perilous was the ice onto which this subject might lead them. If he was without work, his wife would support the family or, more unthinkable, his wife's family would. He realized how primitive this feeling was but, as a friend of his father had often said, he had only one head, so he had only one way to think about things. 'There's little I'm qualified for,' he said, dragging them both away from a consideration of economic realities.

'Law?' she asked, although she surely knew the answer.

'I'd have to pass the exams again, and that would be a nightmare.' Curious now, he wondered out loud, 'What else could I do?'

She smiled and suggested, 'Convert and become an Anglican, and then become a priest.' When he snorted at this, she said, 'People confide in you, Guido. They trust you.'

He shook the idea away with both his head and his hands.

'Then what?' she asked.

It took him some time to think of an answer, and the best, and truest, he could find was, 'I'd like to live in the country and work the land.'

His wife of many years, the true reader of his heart, looked at him in open-mouthed surprise and was, for one of the few times in their marriage, incapable of speech.

27

Things changed little regarding the case. Lucy Watson remained in the Ospedale dell'Angelo, her condition unchanged. JoJo Peterson, the Questura was informed by email, had moved forward the date on her ticket and had already returned to the United States. She would, of course, supply any information they required from her.

Marcello Vio was finally charged with leaving the scene of an accident, although the full legalities regarding the incident in the *laguna* were still unclear. His legal representative explained to the authorities that the city was responsible for maintaining the safety of its waterways, that his client had been in so serious a state of shock as a result of the accident that he could think of nothing but getting the girls and himself to a place of greater safety. He took them to the hospital out of his sense of responsibility for their well-being but was himself so traumatized by the accident and by his own unexamined injuries that he had perhaps acted rashly. But still his first thought had been their safety, and he had taken it upon himself to take them to the hospital, not called to report the accident and wait for help to arrive. The fact that he later returned to the hospital, specifically to the Pronto Soccorso, where he had last seen the girls, was presented as evidence of his concern for them and his desire to learn that they had received treatment.

As Brunetti read the lawyer's explanation, he paused to consider the skill with which both the presence of Filiberto Duso and Marcello Vio's abandonment of the girls had been swept under the carpet. His trip to the Emergency Room – which the document failed to mention had happened at the instigation of the Questura – was presented as proof of his sincere concern with their well-being.

Brunetti read the lawyer's explanation with growing interest in the way it flirted with the truth while avoiding it, but when he looked at the last page, he recognized the name of the lawyer. 'Oh, you old devil,' he said and laughed, as one would at the appointment of the former CEO of Exxon to the board of the WWF.

Well, Marcello Vio was in good hands if Manlio De Persio was handling his case. There were few tricks he did not know, few policemen who had not had a case evaporate when De Persio argued for the accused, and when his client lost, no lawyer in the Veneto was better at dragging the case through appeal after appeal to ever-higher courts until, quite often, it outlasted the statute of limitations and the case was dropped. It was rumoured that De Persio's friends referred to him as 'The Pharmacist,' for the number of 'Prescrizioni' he had won for his clients. Judicial time ran out, and the cases were dismissed.

De Persio was held in grudging admiration – a mixture of respect and envy – by his colleagues, although none succeeded in genuinely liking him.

Marcello Vio could never have afforded to pay him. The fact that his uncle must, therefore, be paying De Persio's bill suggested to Brunetti how important it was to him that his nephew not be convicted of a crime, especially not one involving a boat, and that attention not be drawn to the family. If Brunetti's assessment of Borgato's greed was correct, he was not likely to pay a bill for anyone, neither employee nor relative, unless it was in his own interests. He would pay only to keep himself – like his boats – off the radar of the authorities.

The other, equally interesting, information was supplied by Signorina Elettra, in the form of Pietro Borgato's financial records. He had a safe deposit box at a small private bank in Lugano, where he also had a savings account with something approaching three hundred thousand Euros, deposited in cash during the last five years. He also, nearer home, had another savings account at the San Salvador branch of Uni Credit that contained about nine thousand Euros. Beyond this, he had a business account used for running the transport company. So far as Signorina Elettra could discover, this account was handled primarily by his secretary, who had been with the company from the beginning.

Yes, Signorina Elettra had taken a close look at her: Elena Rocca, resident at Sacca Fisola, 53, married to a boat mechanic, two daughters and four granddaughters. She and her husband had a post office savings account in which there were two thousand and twelve Euros, set aside month by month during the last nine years, since the account was opened. To the best of her knowledge, Signorina Elettra reported that this was the total of Signora Rocca's wealth, aside from the apartment where she and her husband had lived for twenty-six years.

Brunetti looked up from the papers and stared out of his window. A safe deposit box and three hundred thousand Euros in Switzerland. Well, well, well, perhaps he was right that Borgato's guiding spirit was greed.

His thoughts turned to a story he'd heard, ages ago – no doubt apocryphal, as so many of the best stories probably were – about some legendary American millionaire, who lived in an era when a million dollars was a fortune. The story recounted that the man was asked if he knew what 'enough' meant.

After some thought, the man is said to have replied, 'Of course I know. It means a little bit more.'

There was nothing else in the report. Brunetti continued to study the view from his window which now consisted of clouds and patches of blue sky.

The days passed, and he did his job, always on the alert for a call from Duso. He phoned Alaimo to ask if his men had scouted the area near Cortellazzo for a possible landing place. The Captain told him that his men were familiarizing themselves with the areas on both sides of the Piave and said very carefully that they were leaving no traces of having been there. The rest of Brunetti's time was spent on paperwork.

Brunetti read the reports of his subordinates and sometimes asked them to come and explain things to him or to tell him anything they seemed reluctant to commit to writing in an official report. He decided whom to assign to particular investigations.

The only real change was reported by Lucy Watson's doctor, who called from the Ospedale dell'Angelo to tell Brunetti that the girl had regained consciousness. Brunetti could hear the man's delight as he explained that she'd woken up in the late morning and, seeing her father sitting beside her, tapping a message into his phone, had asked, 'What are you doing here, Daddy?'

The doctor explained that, though she recognized her father and could speak normally, her memory of recent events extended back only to the beginning of the boat ride with the Italians they'd met that Saturday night. She was confused to be in the hospital, by the explanation of her injuries, and by the presence of her father.

In response to Brunetti's questions, the doctor told him that Lucy's memory of these events would, or would not, return and that his colleagues from neurology were confident that there was no permanent damage.

Brunetti felt a surge of relief for the girl and her father and then for Vio, that his conscience would have less to bear. And then he returned to going through the motions of work while waiting for word from Duso.

He and Paola were at dinner with friends when his phone rang. With haste that might have seemed impolite, Brunetti pulled the phone from his pocket and, seeing Duso's name, excused himself and went to stand on the other side of the door to the living room.

'*Sì?*' he asked in a voice he was careful to keep calm.

'Marcello just called me,' Duso said.

Brunetti looked at his watch. It was already after eleven. 'What did he say?'

'Pietro called him and said they had a job.'

'Did he say anything else?'

'No, only that. Marcello's on his way to the boathouse now.'

Brunetti, hoping this call would come, had made a plan with Alaimo. 'Go down to the *riva* in front of your *calle*,' he told Duso. 'A boat from the Capitaneria will be there in a few minutes and take you to Piazzale Roma.' He heard a noise of assent from Duso. 'Wear a heavy jacket,' Brunetti said and hung up.

He dialled Alaimo's number and said, 'Duso just called. Tell your man he'll be on the *riva* near where he lives. He'll see him. I'm not at home. You can pick me up at the Santo Spirito stop in ten minutes.' They had discussed routes and times, so there was nothing more to say.

He hung up and dialled Griffoni's number. While he and Alaimo went by sea, she would travel with Duso and Nieddu, who was involved because the case concerned international crime. Alaimo had already sent a boat to go and pick up Griffoni – one that looked like a taxi that would avoid any possibility that Borgato should cross paths with a police launch at this hour – and take her to Piazzale Roma, where they'd meet Duso. Two unmarked cars and a small van would be waiting there to leave for Cortellazzo.

He pocketed his phone and went back to the room, an embarrassed smile on his face. Cool, calm, business as usual. He went over to his host, shaking his head in rueful resignation. Donato was an old friend, likely to believe whatever he said. 'Sorry, Donato. Work. They need me at an interview in Mestre,' he said easily, trying to achieve a tone of mild irritation mixed with resignation at the call of duty.

Paola, attuned to the sound of perfidy in his voice, put her napkin next to her plate and got to her feet. She walked around the table, saying goodnight to the other guests and kissing Donato and his wife on both cheeks before taking Brunetti's arm, saying, 'I'll go along with you at least to the vaporetto stop.' Her smile was quite as manufactured as his excuse, but it worked just as successfully on the people at the table.

When they were outside, Brunetti nodded to the vaporetto stop to the left. 'I'm being picked up there.'

'To go and arrest these people?' she asked.

'I hope.'

She shivered. The night had grown cold. 'You're wearing the wrong jacket,' she said and then laughed at the sound of it. 'I mean, it's too light, if you're going to be out on the water.' Over her coat she wore a dark green cashmere scarf, thick and long. She unwrapped it from her neck and wrapped it around his.

Brunetti reached up, intending to remove it and return it to her, but when it touched him with the lingering warmth of her body and the scent of her flesh, he pulled it tighter, tossing one end over his shoulder with quite a dashing gesture.

'Thanks,' he said, unable to think of any other way to express his emotion.

She took his hand. 'I'll wait with you until they come.'

There was the merest sliver of moon, but they both studied it as they walked to the *embarcadero*, hand in hand, like new lovers. Soon, from their right, came the sound of a motor. Quickly enough, a boat slid up to within a few centimetres of the dock. Brunetti kissed Paola goodbye and stepped on board. Three uniformed men moved around the deck; another stood at the wheel. As they pulled away, he picked up the end of the scarf that dangled in front of him and waved it at her. She raised an arm but did not wave. They watched one another until the boat turned towards the other side of the canal, and she was blocked from view.

Brunetti was just beginning to sense how cold the evening had become when Alaimo stepped up from the cabin and handed him a hooded camouflage jacket, which Brunetti was relieved to put on. He re-wrapped the scarf outside the jacket, its ends hanging in front of him.

The motor roared, destroying all possibility of conversation. Brunetti could not disguise his shock at the noise, which did violence to the night.

Alaimo leaned towards him and cupped both hands around Brunetti's ears. 'It has electric, too.'

Still stunned by the ongoing noise, Brunetti failed to understand the full meaning, although he heard each word.

The boat moved past San Giorgio, the sound of its engine bouncing back from the solidity of the basilica. One of the sailors went down into the cabin, leaving the others to the deck and the noise.

Brunetti tried to speak but failed even to hear himself. The pale light of the control panel allowed him to see the other men on deck, but the sound seemed to compromise his vision.

Alaimo placed his hand on the pilot's shoulder and leaned forward to say something to him. No sooner had he removed his hand than the boat slowed, greatly reducing the level of noise.

'Thanks for this,' Brunetti said, patting at the arm of Alaimo's jacket. It had rained during the day, and the humidity still clung to the air and to the night.

Alaimo nodded. 'The sea's always a few degrees colder, so it'll be worse once we get into the open water.' He looked to the left: they were just passing I Giardini. 'I thought I told you we might have to go out any time.'

'You did, but we were at dinner at a friend's place, and I forgot and just wore the jacket.'

Alaimo shrugged. 'Things always happen when they shouldn't, I suppose.'

Brunetti nodded, then asked, 'What did you say about electric?'

Alaimo smiled and said, 'The motors can be switched to electric.'

'It's much better now,' Brunetti told him. Indeed, the sound had diminished to a low throbbing growl, sounding far more powerful than the motor of any boat this size he'd ever been on.

'That's still the normal motor,' Alaimo explained. 'It can be switched to battery power.'

'And then what happens?'

'Then it's absolutely silent. You don't hear a thing. If it drove up beside you, you wouldn't hear it.'

'Is that possible?' Brunetti asked.

'It is for cars, isn't it?' Alaimo asked. Then he smiled and said, 'This system's sort of a prototype: it's bigger than what most boats use.'

'How does it work?' Brunetti asked, really curious.

'Down there,' Alaimo said, pointing to where the sailors had disappeared, 'and up in front, there are batteries.'

Brunetti looked to either side of the pilot and saw teak panels that looked like they could be slid open. He didn't know how to phrase his question, whether to ask about the number of the batteries or their size or their power, didn't know how that power was measured. He settled on asking, 'How fast can it go?'

Alaimo turned to the pilot. 'What do you think, Crema?'

Eyes still looking forward, the young sailor answered, 'I've gone as fast as fifty-five knots, Capitano.'

'And if I weren't here, and it was a friend asking you that question, what would you say?'

The young man smiled and bowed his head, then looked forward again and said, 'Well, sir, if you really weren't here, and I was alone, I'd say sixty, but really, only if I were alone in her.'

Brunetti saw Alaimo smile at the pilot's answer. 'That's faster than any of Borgato's boats,' the Captain said.

'Does he have the same system you have, and he can switch to electric, too?'

'Of course. Two of his boats have them, but he doesn't have the same number of batteries.' Before Brunetti could enquire about this, Alaimo said, 'He's got to leave room for his cargo, remember.'

'How do you know all that?' Brunetti asked.

Alaimo suddenly took an interest in something on the control panel and turned away from Brunetti to bend and look at it. Ah, thought Brunetti, the instinct to protect sources is universal. He tried to think of something to say and found it by asking, 'How much longer?'

'What do you think, Crema?' the Captain asked.

Before answering, the pilot bent towards an illuminated screen with a white circle, a steadily turning bar radiating from the centre. Like the ones Brunetti had seen in submarine movies, a blip of light flashed over the same point each time the bar passed over it. 'That's him,' the pilot said, tapping at the flash of light. 'Hour and a half, sir. Unless he really lets it rip: then maybe he could do it in a bit more than an hour.' Alaimo thanked the pilot, raised his shoulders at the growing chill, and said, 'Let's go down into the cabin. We still have time.'

The cabin, though not warm, was certainly warmer than it had been on deck. This had had its effect on the sailors, who were already asleep, leaning in the two back corners of the boat. A third, who must have been down there already, nodded when they came in but quickly adjusted his ear pods and returned his attention to his iPhone.

Brunetti and Alaimo sat facing one another on the padded side seats and leaned forward to talk above the sound of the motor, louder down here, closer to the engines. Alaimo explained that, of the many ships making their way north in the Adriatic, only two had slowed down in the evening and were now anchored for the night about forty kilometres north-east of Venice. If they sailed early, they would get to Trieste by late morning and could unload and reload cargo. One was a British-flagged oil tanker, and the other was a Maltese-flagged transport.

'If Vio told his friend that he's going out tonight, it's got to be to meet one of these two,' Alaimo said.

'What do we do?' Brunetti asked.

'We've got a fix on the transmitter that's on Vio's wrist, so we'll lag well behind them until they pick up the cargo from the larger ship. It will have radar, the big one, but we could easily be fishermen: we've already passed three of them.'

Surprised, Brunetti said, 'I didn't see them.'

'You don't know how to look for them,' Alaimo gave back simply. Brunetti didn't question this but did ask, 'What do we do when he approaches the ship?'

'We stay where we are and behave like a fishing boat: remain in one place for some time and then move to another.'

Suddenly there was a tapping at the door. Alaimo got to his feet, held up his palm to Brunetti, and went up on deck. After some time, Brunetti stood and went towards the door but stopped and went back and sat down again. The second time he got to his feet, the sailor looked up from his phone and shook his head, waving Brunetti back to his seat. He went and sat.

Ten minutes passed and then another ten, and then the motors slowed. In the silence, Brunetti heard footsteps coming down the steps and got to his feet. Alaimo pushed open the doors. 'It was the one with the Maltese flag,' he said. 'Borgato's boat stopped alongside it about fifteen minutes ago, but now it's cleared away and heading west, towards the coast.' He pulled out his phone and tapped in a message, quite a long one.

When he was finished, Alaimo said, 'I've told my squad that they're heading towards Cortellazzo. It's the best place for them to unload cargo.' Brunetti noted that he did not name that cargo.

'Are you sure?' Brunetti asked.

Alaimo surprised him by laughing.

'What's so funny?'

'We're sure, believe me,' Alaimo said, unable to suppress a smile. 'Last weekend, a colleague of mine and I took our sons and four of their friends, all of them dressed in their Boy Scout uniforms, and we went to where the river empties into the sea. We sailed up the river a bit, stopping at different spots and explaining to the kids the tidal patterns and the differences between the fish that swim in sweet water and salt.'

Seeing Brunetti's reaction, Alaimo went on. 'It was the only way I could think of for us to take a look at the possible landing places without calling attention to ourselves.' He smiled and shrugged, looking embarrassed, 'Just in case Borgato has friends who fish or live along there and might tell him about anyone showing interest in that patch of river.'

'How was it?'

'Cold. But the kids loved it and keep nagging me about when we can do it again.'

'Kids,' Brunetti said the word the same way parents sometimes spoke it: a combination of dismissal and adoration.

There was a sudden vibration as a message slid into Alaimo's phone. He bent over it and then looked up and said, 'The crew is there. They have to hide the cars and the van and then get to the place where we think they'll land.'

'Won't there be ... ?' Brunetti started to ask.

'People to meet them?' Alaimo asked.

'Yes.'

'That's why they'll leave the vehicles. They'll go downriver on foot.'

Only then did Brunetti think to ask, 'Who are they?'

'Commandos, from the Navy Special Forces. They've scouted the place, too. They're used to high risk night-time operations.'

Brunetti considered these words while thinking about what they were all going to be doing. They sounded bad when the person who said them had some experience of their reality. 'Risk for whom?' He asked.

It took Alaimo a while to find an answer, but even that couldn't take the menace out of it. 'Everyone.'

28

Brunetti leaned against the padded back of the seat and pulled the jacket closer around him, still not zipping it up. He found the pulsing of the engine, both the sound of it and the easy bobbing of the boat, comforting. His thoughts turned to the dinner he had left and the woman he had left at the boat stop. Although he had not thought the call would come that evening, he had still drunk only two glasses of wine and had turned down the offer of grappa. He wished now that he had had a coffee, even two, before getting on this boat, only to be comforted and rocked by ...

'Guido, Guido,' he heard someone call him, and he was immediately awake. And it was then that he remembered his gun. Safe in the metal box in their wardrobe, where he always kept it when it was in the house, the key equally safe on the key ring in his pocket. He looked to the right. The two sailors were still asleep, and the third was still engrossed in whatever he saw on his phone.

He looked at Alaimo, who was standing in the doorway. 'There's no question about it: they're heading for Cortellazzo.'

'How far are we from them?' Brunetti asked.

'About two kilometres,' Alaimo said in a normal voice.

Brunetti had no trouble hearing him. There was no hum, although the boat seemed still to be nodding its way through the waves. 'What's wrong?' he asked, nervous at the lack of noise.

'It's the electric motor,' Alaimo said.

'*Oddio*, what a difference.'

'Borgato's little more than a kilometre from the estuary.'

'Do we follow him?'

'We can. It depends on the squad.' Alaimo held up his phone as though he wanted it to speak to Brunetti. 'They've been in touch. They've found two empty vans parked close to the access road, and they can hear voices ahead of them.'

'How big is your squad?'

'Four, plus Claudia and Captain Nieddu.'

Immediately concerned by the mention of their names, Brunetti asked, 'These Navy guys are good?'

'These guys are good,' Alaimo confirmed and disappeared up the stairs.

Brunetti ran his hands across his face and scratched at his head, then got up and left the cabin. A cold wind hit him in the face and made his eyes water. He moved to the side of the boat and looked behind them: the black was absolute, punctuated only by tiny specks of light so small it was impossible to calculate their distance. The light from the control panel was so dim that it cast only the faintest glow of the bodies of the two men standing in front of it, Alaimo and the pilot.

Brunetti moved over to put himself between but slightly back from them. On the right side of the panel in front of the other men, equally spaced white rings radiated out from the centre. A bar of light swept round from sharp north to declining west, passing over and flicking at the same white blip of light.

264

Alaimo leaned down and pointed to the white dot. 'That's Borgato's boat,' he said softly.

In the same barely audible voice, Alaimo asked the pilot, 'What do you think, Crema?'

'I'd say about ten minutes until he enters the river, sir, then another ten or so to get up to where he's going.'

Alaimo nodded and pulled out his phone. He tapped in a message and kept his eyes on the screen until an answer slipped in. However soft the vibration, Brunetti still heard it, marvelling at the lack of any competing sound. Alaimo spent a moment pushing keys on his phone until he seemed satisfied. 'Turn off the sound on your phone,' he said, as though Brunetti were an enlisted man. Brunetti obeyed.

'You too, Crema,' Alaimo added.

'It's already off, sir,' the pilot said softly.

'I don't want even the sound of a message coming in,' Alaimo said. He put the phone in his pocket and asked the pilot, 'You think you can follow them?'

'If they're going to offload at the place you showed me on the map, sir, I can. But if he goes any farther, one of the sailors will have to lie on the front and keep testing the depth with an oar.'

That was in some movie, Brunetti thought but kept it to himself. He moved a bit to the side and leaned forward to look across the prow of the boat. He thought about himself lying there, perhaps anchoring himself to some bit of protruding metal, testing the depth of the water, as he had done as a young boy, out in the *laguna*.

The door behind them opened, and the sailor who had been playing with his iPhone came out to stand with them. 'We almost there, sir?' he whispered to Alaimo.

'Yes.'

The young man nodded and looked at the instrument panel. Turning away, he said, 'I'll wake the others up.'

'Good. Tell them we're getting very close to the landing place.'

'I'm going to switch on the night vision, sir,' the pilot said and flipped a switch on the panel. Brunetti raised his eyes to look ahead, but there was only darkness visible.

Alaimo tapped him on the arm and pointed to another instrument to the left of the radar. The screen showed the same approaching coast, the scene entirely composed of various shades of green on a black base. Brunetti made out trees on the right and left, even thin vines hanging from them. The centre was a dark path leading into farther darkness.

'Is that the river?' Brunetti asked.

'Yes,' Alaimo all but whispered.

'Do I follow them, sir?' the pilot asked.

'Wait,' Alaimo answered, and the boat slowed to a stop. He pulled out his phone. Careful to use the tips of his fingers, Alaimo pushed in the letters of a message and sent it off. Less than a minute passed before he felt the arrival of an answer.

'They've got men along the river. He's almost there.'

The pilot said nothing but shifted from foot to foot to demonstrate his impatience.

'Let's go, Crema,' Alaimo said, and an instant later the boat began to move forward.

Because he could see only darkness ahead, Brunetti kept his eyes on the screen, marvelling as their boat moved unerringly in the centre of the river. The water was dead still: the other boat had passed through long enough ago for the water to forget its passage.

Alaimo reached for his phone again. He sent a message, turned to Brunetti, and whispered, 'My men are in the trees behind the landing. Three men have come out onto the dock.' Then, after a moment's pause, he added, 'Two of them have rifles.'

Brunetti nodded. The boat continued, with serpentine silence, to make its slow way through the dark water.

Again, Alaimo glanced at his phone, then held it to show Brunetti, who read the message: 'Where are you?'

The Carabiniere pulled back his phone and answered. He leaned close to Crema and said, 'Speed up now if you can. I'd like to get there while they're still moored to the dock.'

Again, Brunetti felt but did not hear the increase of energy that quickened the speed of the boat. He kept his eyes on the green panel: looking ahead was no help. He had lost all sense of distance: how far were they from the green shapes in front of them? How close were they to the invisible banks of the river? And if this was a tidal river, how high were the embankments to left and right, and how easily could they get out of the water if they had to swim from the boat?

There was, he noticed now, the sound of nature; creatures rustled in the trees, birds made noises, other animals rustled on the ground. How mysterious and frightening nature was, so uninterested in what we did or what we were.

He and Alaimo heard the voice in the same instant: male, angry, authoritarian. 'No, over here.' There followed a shushing noise, then another one, and then silence. How far ahead was the speaker? There was still no sign on the screen.

And then there was. At first Brunetti thought it was ghosts, so pale, so ethereal did the figures seem. Some heads were wrapped in what could be burial dressings, their bodies draped to the ground; others had visible legs and arms; they gasped and groaned quietly and made spectral noises. Alaimo grabbed the pilot by the shoulder, and the boat slowed, then stopped without making a sound.

There was a heavy, thick noise, a flash of motion, and something large fell into the water. The man's voice said, '*Cazzo.*'

Another voice said, 'Pull them out, for God's sake. We have to deliver them alive.' Brunetti saw motion on what appeared to be a platform above the water; there was the sound of splashing and muffled screams. What could have been two green men lay on the dock and reached down to the water. Slowly, they pulled up a writhing creature with two heads and let it fall beside them. The screaming stopped.

Alaimo took a bullhorn from beside the steering wheel and switched it on. He tapped the pilot on his shoulder, and three searchlights on the prow of their boat flashed across the scene, illuminating the dock and the people on it, the boat moored to it, and the shore behind it. Everyone in the light froze: the two men with rifles, the third kneeling next to what looked like a pile of moving rags, and a large, tight circle of women, everyone shocked to paralyzed silence.

'Drop the rifles,' Alaimo's amplified voice commanded. The two men made no attempt to do so; one of them turned his body so that the rifle was pointing in the direction of the blinding lights.

From the tree-scattered land behind the dock, a man's voice barked, 'He told you to drop the rifles.' The one who had not moved bent down very slowly and placed his rifle on the ground near his feet. 'Now kick it away,' the voice from the land said, and the man obeyed. 'Arms over your head,' the voice added, and the man did that, as well. The two unarmed men raised their hands above their heads and stood motionless.

'I'm waiting,' the voice said, and the other man tossed his rifle onto the ground as though he were suddenly tired of holding it. 'Arms,' the voice shouted, and they went up in the air.

Alaimo called out, in English, 'Does one of you ladies speak English?' As though his voice had freed them from a spell, the women began to talk among themselves, to put their arms around one another. Some broke into sobs. Finally, from the centre of the group, a woman's voice said, 'I do, sir.'

Alaimo continued, speaking slowly. 'Tell your friends to move away from those men and go over onto the land behind you.'

The same woman's voice spoke for a moment in some other language, and then a woman in a long flowered skirt, pulling with her the woman to whom she was handcuffed, moved to the edge of the group, took the arm of another, and led them towards the promised land at the end of the dock.

The others followed slowly, bumping into one another in their eagerness to get away from the men.

Alaimo spoke into the bullhorn in a normal tone and said, 'Good, good, now walk towards the woods. There are people there who will help you.'

It was at this point that Nieddu, quickly followed by Griffoni, emerged from the trees and waved the women towards them. The women were apparently still too shocked to react quickly, but the group, their sobs audible to Brunetti, began to walk towards the two women, beacons of safety, especially Nieddu, in uniform, her service pistol in her hand, aimed at the two men on the dock.

Three men in military fatigues, carrying rifles, emerged from the trees and walked onto the dock. A fourth, weaponless, walked behind the two men standing with their arms in the air, lowered them, handcuffed their hands behind them, picked up their rifles, and led them from the dock.

That left the boat. It bobbled quietly beside the dock, moored, knots neatly tied. It looked, however, more like a giant Toblerone than a boat. From the side, Brunetti saw a row of copper panels that appeared to have been screwed into place, tilted up to meet another row tilting in from the other side. Just as Alaimo had explained to him, radar waves would slide up and over them, leaving the boat invisible. In this case, the panels also left invisible anyone who might be on board.

Alaimo called out, 'Anyone on the boat: come out, hands above your heads. It's over.'

Nothing. Time passed. 'You on the boat. Come out with your hands above your heads. It's over.'

After more waiting, Brunetti saw Alaimo raise the bullhorn again: apparently the man was patient enough to repeat the same message until the men on the boat grew tired of it and came out with their hands over their heads. But before Alaimo could give his orders again, the sounds of shouting came across the water.

They heard two voices, both male, then they heard crashing noises. Suddenly something banged against one of the panels; it broke loose at the top and fell backwards, dangling into the water.

Alaimo and Brunetti scrambled onto the dock. As he approached Borgato's boat, Brunetti thought for an instant that it was made of gold, like the boats painted in Egyptian tombs. There was more shouting, and then Marcello Vio appeared at the opening left by the fallen panel and put one leg over the gunwale, then stepped onto the dock. An animal noise erupted from behind him, and a hand grabbed at his shoulder. But Vio took the hand with both of his and thrust it away from him. There was a crash from the boat and then a roar; Vio stopped and turned back towards the noise but then suddenly screamed in pain and fell forward onto his knees, arms wrapped around his broken ribs.

From somewhere, from nowhere, a form flashed from between the trees and towards the dock. Duso. Brunetti had forgotten about Duso. He held up his hands and turned to shout at the armed men, 'Leave him alone. He's with us.'

Duso fell to his knees beside Marcello. He wrapped one arm around him and said, 'Come on, Marcello. You can't stay here.'

Everyone's attention was on the two young men, kneeling face to face. 'Berto,' Vio said. 'Berto, you're here.' He smiled and raised a hand to touch Duso's face.

So filled with emotion was the scene that everyone watched the two men. Except Griffoni, who had arrived at the edge of the dock and then stepped onto it, walking so calmly as to be invisible, her eyes not on the men but on the boat.

270

She was the first to see Pietro Borgato appear in the gap between the panels and the first to see the boathook in his hands. 'Watch out,' she shouted, and both kneeling men turned to look at her.

Borgato leaped from the boat onto the dock and walked quickly towards his nephew. Brunetti shouted, 'Borgato,' to distract him and started to run in his direction.

Before Brunetti could reach him, the man had reached the two figures kneeling between him and the rifle-carrying Carabinieri. He pulled back the boathook, raised his right foot and kicked his nephew out of the way. He stood in front of Duso and pulled the horizontal boathook to the right. 'You want to fuck my nephew, do you?' he shouted at the kneeling Duso, who was stiff with shock. 'Well, you get this, instead.' With no hesitation, he spread his feet and swung the wicked point and hook towards Duso's chest. Duso's shriek did nothing to stop Borgato from swinging full cycle until the hook caught on something, a bone, perhaps, and he was forced to pull it free.

Brunetti had reached him by then. Borgato turned and swung at him, but Brunetti was standing and was able to avoid the curve of the weapon's point. Borgato pulled it back and swung again, and this time it caught in the green cashmere scarf and remained entrapped in the cloth.

He let go of the hook and turned to Brunetti, who saw that froth was coming from the man's mouth.

'Liar. Liar,' he shouted at Brunetti and charged towards him. With the ease of a bullfighter, Brunetti stepped out of his way, and Borgato crashed into the wooden railing that ran along one side of the dock. Brunetti approached him and saw madness in his eyes. Borgato raised his arm and made a fist, as though he wanted to pound Brunetti into the ground.

Instead, Brunetti charged him, grabbed the raised arm at wrist and elbow, and brought it down with savage strength onto the handrail. He heard the bone break, felt the snap with his own hands. He stepped back and crashed into the chest of one of the soldiers.

'We'll take over now, sir,' the soldier said, and Brunetti turned away from him but not from what he had just done.

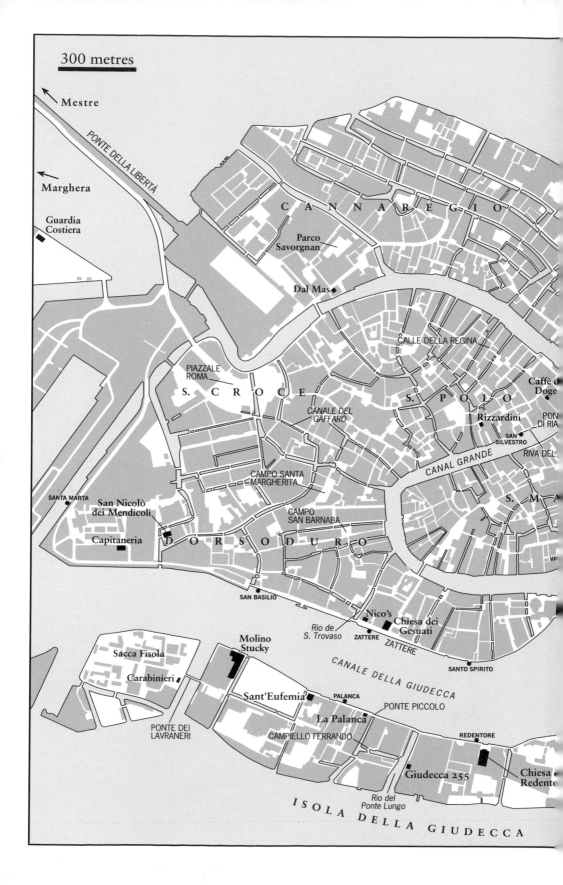